I0666082

CANNED TUNA

A Novel by
David Memmott

redbat
books

redbat books
2017

Printed in the United States of America

First Edition: October 3, 2017

Trade Paperback ISBN 978-0-9971549-8-6
Case Laminate Hardcover ISBN 978-0-9895924-4-4
E-book: ISBN 978-1-946970-98-5

Library of Congress Control Number: 2017950501

Published by
redbat books
2901 Gekeler Lane
La Grande, OR 97850
www.redbatbooks.com

Text set in Palatino and Trajan Pro

Cover Art: *West Battery* by David Memmott

Book design: Kristin Summers, redbat design | www.redbatdesign.com

PRAISE FOR DAVID MEMMOTT'S WRITING:

Praise for *LOST TRANSMISSIONS*, Poems

"David Memmott does as he has done over the last 40 years; he leads us from 'the edge of the American Dream' and all its contradictions, 'to the center of the world,' where generosity awaits our arrival."

—DAVID AXELROD, author of *What Next, Old Knife?*

Praise for *GIVING IT AWAY*, Poems

"There is harmony and wisdom imbedded here. And readers everywhere can savor the fruits of Memmott's located quest for the comedy, romance, tragedy, and irony of inner and outer life."

—GEORGE VENN, author of *Marking the Magic Circle*

"By turns prophetic, polemical, sensual, and humorous, these poems speak in stalwart witness to the outer and inner landscapes that he calls home."

—JOHN DANIEL, author of *The Far Corner: Northwestern Views on Land, Life and Literature*

"*Giving It Away* is infused with the generous and expansive spirit its title evokes."

—BARBARA DRAKE, author of *Bees in Wet Weather*

"David Memmott's fifth book of poetry is an engaging celebration of life in Eastern Oregon...and the many strong poems resonate with a lyric vitality."

—PETER SEARS, author of *The Brink*

Praise for *PRIMETIME*, A Postcyberpunk Novel

"A dizzying debut novel explores an extreme near-future that explodes into a post-cyberpunk extravaganza.... *PRIMETIME* is, inarguably and admirably, ambitious...and it will be interesting to see where the author goes from here."

—F. BRETT COX, scifi.com

Praise for *PRIMETIME* (cont.)

"...it's not easy to lift sci-fi to the level of literature, but Memmott has done it in brilliant fashion in *PRIMETIME*."

—DUFF BRENNA, *Perigee: A Publication for the Arts*

"What we've got to do is get books like *PRIMETIME* out there, and let those who appreciate them know they're out there."

—ERNEST HOGAN, author of *High Aztech*

About *SHADOW BONES*, Stories

"At his best, [Memmott] combines New Wave preoccupations with high style and unusual but effective storytelling devices."

—DOUGLAS SPANGLER, *The Bear Delux Magazine*

About *THE LARGER EARTH*, Cycle of Poems

"...beautifully written and a pleasure to interact with. A strange mix between David Bowie (The Man Who Fell to Earth) and Ted Mooney's *EASY TRAVEL TO OTHER PLANETS*. Great!"

—MARK AMERIKA, author of *The Kafka Chronicles*

"I admired the simultaneously autobiographical and visionary feel of the cycle."

—ANDREW JORON, author of *Science Fiction*

About *HOUSE ON FIRE*, Poems

"Here we find no versified SF stories; none of Memmott's poems depict generically typical SF situations. Instead, each poem weaves a language-pattern correspondent to a soul in crisis; here, intersecting and brilliantly colored planes of discourse slide past one another in a (speculatively conceived) carnival of existential doubt."

—IGNATZ MEES, *Science Fiction Eye*

*In memory of Pfc. Kenneth D. Phares, U.S. Marines,
killed in action during a mortar attack on
Dong Ha Marine Assault Base, Vietnam, May 18, 1967,
and for those men and women in and out of uniform
whose lives are forever changed by war.*

*We are all soldiers even if we didn't enlist. Whatever our
complicity in war, we cannot deny the music we share.*

Thank you for helping to build the peace.

Special thanks for the editorial advice of Greg "Bamboo" Johnson, and to Thomas E. Kennedy, Duff Brenna, and Lance Olsen for their comments and suggestions during the book's long gestation. To Randy Simmons, Misha and Mez, and Llawren Bird, thank you for your encouragement, and to Sue for her patience, under-standing, and unfailing belief that I might one day get this right. Thanks also to all the vets of various stripes I've known over the years. Thank you for your service.

Due to constraints of copyright law, in place of the many uncited lyrics, I have instead cited a veritable soundtrack of artists and titles you can search online and find full lyrics, access to tracks and music videos. Stream them liberally as you read this book.

References to "The Creation" by The Bards are based on research and the CD, "Resurrect: The Moses Lake Recordings," a 2002 release of the original 1968 unreleased recordings, produced by Curt Boetcher & Keith Olsen, available through Gear Fab Records, Orlando, FL.

These other realities are out there waiting to be illuminated by the searchlight of consciousness....

—FRED ALAN WOLFE, *The Eagle's Quest*

PART ONE

The only tribute you could really pay, and I can still pay,
is to remember.

—CLARK DOUGAN, "Memorial Day 1968," *Patriots: The Vietnam War Remembered from All Sides,* Christian G. Appy

1.

It was getting on to sunset. The jeep shimmied in and out of ruts. The downpour offered brief respite from the heat and humidity. Low beams bounced the jeep over potholes, its sharp beacons hacking through dwindling light.

Specialist 5 Nicolasa Bilbao performed small magic that sometimes made a difference in the war in Southeast Asia. No wonder Colonel Hedges, CO of the 4th Infantry's Officers Club in Pleiku, took notice.

Nico pulled a cable out of his cap for the Iron Horse's '62 Simca—a French car with cable-driven four-speed on the column, prone to snapping when cranked into reverse. The old Horse showed his gratitude by yanking Nico's skinhead from under the oil pan of a troop carrier and reassigning him to temporary duty at the officer's club.

The Colonel didn't so much need a mechanic as some initiative and ability to attain the unattainable. Nico was immediately assigned to a special project, The Splendors of Bangkok. He needed to learn who held what strings, and how and when to pull them to redirect resources from the officer's club to the Colonel's illegal nightclub in an old French café in town.

So in his latest sleight-of-hand, Nico made two young Vietnamese girls appear in his jeep after a brief road trip to the relocation camp of Kon Barr. He recruited Chu Len and Lu Bien as hostesses for The Splendors, which stepped up his game a bit. These two beauties promised to seal his reputation as a miracle worker.

Chu Len, the shy one in the backseat with lowered dark eyes, suppressed giggles and stole glances in the rear view. Beside him in the front seat was Lu Bien who boldly met his gaze, flashing a smile that burst in her mouth like a pop flare.

Nico's poor impression of John Wayne left the girls laughing at his antics. They couldn't understand a word of English, but he made them laugh. "It's better with the gestures," he assured them, trying to cock his shoulders like the Duke as the jeep jumped another pothole.

Lu Bien needed to tone it down. She came across as brash and Americanized. In the Iron Horse's lexicon for exotic splendors, this meant *contaminated*.

Kon Barr was two klicks north of the junction at Bridge 23 on Route 19, less than an hour from Camp Radcliffe. The road narrowed and corkscrewed through an uncharted obstacle course of mud holes and washouts in the thick jungle. The jeep jerked sideways then slipped back into ruts.

A medic named Rowdy Wight beat the bush for local girls after Nico asked for a scouting report and found Chu Len. It turned out Chu Len didn't come without Lu Bien. With Rowdy off circuit-riding, a French-Vietnamese Catholic interpreter named Tan Duy served as his proxy. Something in Tan Duy's character made Nico feel uneasy, but he didn't say anything because it might sound judgmental. Having no translator would limit Nico's bargaining power so he accepted his services. The elder's hooch seemed intimate and inviting so Nico flushed a chicken and took its spot on the floor. The interpreter nodded in unspoken complicity. His coolie hat and black pajamas had Nico checking for booby traps. He kept flashing on Tan Duy shaving punji sticks or burying landmines. They settled for a case of black market French cognac, a load of rations and a pallet of canned tuna the elder had developed a taste for. Nico radioed the Colonel, arrangements were made, and a First Team slick took to the air with the booty.

Both girls were young, maybe seventeen, shapely and clean, with bright teeth and supple breasts: exquisite flowers packaged into mail-order brides in high-necked traditional dress. Nico ignored the twisting in his gut during the ceremony, smiled through singing and chanting and smoking and drinking, following Tan Duy's histrionics, aping back meaningless vocalizations as villagers pumped his hand. There was a distinct possibility he was returning to The Splendors with one or maybe two wives.

In spite of repeated attempts to clarify his role, the girls beamed bounteous good health as the village chief embraced the American. His stained lips rolled back to expose a black smile, foul breath making Nico blink and gulp for air. Nico tried to ignore the low voltage of uncertainty that ran through his nerves when he wrapped the Colonel's surprise package in loose-fitting fatigues. Any moment might amp up into pure electric shock as his new charges hugged and kissed tearful parents, climbed into the jeep with him and stowed shoulder bags full of clothes they would never need.

After their departure, somewhere on Route 572 South, Nico reflected on Tan Duy's shifty eyes. They reminded him of Foghorn Leghorn. Nico couldn't decide whether his mistrust of the interpreter stemmed more from his being Vietnamese or French Catholic. Lack of eye contact was a common trait in the Vietnamese. The translator's true intent was not only hidden in his dark eyes but concealed like a weapon. A few too many shots of cognac in celebration dulled Nico's powers of discernment. By the time he left the village he couldn't read a stop sign.

One thing for sure. The girls were now his responsibility—at least until that freedom bird carried him home.

* * *

His plan was to double-back to Radcliffe once they reached Junction 19. Those in the First Airborne referred to Radcliffe as The Golf Course. The airstrip had been cleared by hand to avoid destroying the vegetation; so a Huey landing there didn't choke to death on red dust. Nico was never a helicopter mechanic. In the Motor Stable, he'd worked on enough halftracks, trucks and amphibious assault vehicles to know how enemy dust clogged up fuel lines and carburetors until their engines bled. The Golf Course was one of those things the Army got right, not like those M-16s left on the battlefield whenever a grunt could remove an AK-47 from the dead arms of the enemy.

The 100-mile journey from Qui Nhon on the coast to Pleiku in the Central Highlands inflicted the psychological stress of 300 miles for the 8th Transportation Group. The Golf Course lay in the middle of Ambush Alley with the steep Mang Yang Pass rising in the west and An Khe Pass in the east.

In a weak moment or two, Nico gave in to nostalgia. He missed the one-on-one interaction with a jeep engine or the straightforward physical feat of welding broken track onto amphibious assault vehicles. It was never mindless work, but work that occupied his mind. The maintenance of a machine was an unpretentious calling. Even thinking about engines provided a black and white escape from a world of dizzying gray, fading in the morning fog low on the mountains where the future had no horizon. An engine either started, or it didn't. It was because the battery was dead or wasn't.

Nico's dad told these Second World War stories to make the point that GIs were able to fix anything with wheels. That's how America won the war, he said, and Nico believed him. These Specialists in Vietnam couldn't whiteout a typo on a requisition form without messing up in triplicate. Instead of soldiers the Army had operators of equipment and machines they couldn't repair if their lives depended on it. American know-how didn't prevent an M-16 from jamming. Hueys came apart on a hard landing, broken rotors plowing up rice paddies.

Nico had never been in the bush before. The fog of war could descend over him at any given moment. His TDA with the old Horse had one commandment: *the end justifies the means*. So Nico learned to barter, scam, con and steal and sometimes go into the field for a little research. He had to know how much grease it took to get things going, which wrench to use on what nut. It was like taking apart and putting back together an engine. You needed an eye for detail. Too much pressure and some mechanisms broke down. His daily ration of degrees of gray made it impossible to tell black from white anymore.

When the Colonel first called Nico to his office, he was leaning back with feet on his desk, tossing back three fingers of scotch, striking a heroic pose even in recline. A square-jawed, gray-haired Korean War veteran and Georgia Bulldog, the old Horse cashed in R & R to do some personal research on Thai cabarets. Nico came on board with a sealed bargain of several manly shots of scotch and a private peek at the Colonel's illicit revue, curled yellow photos kept in a cigar box. Once the Tin Man oiled his jaws with enough liquor, the old Horse spread those photos out on his desk as backdrop as he pitched the scheme.

The enormity of the TDA intimidated Nico, but there was a challenge there that he couldn't shake from his mind. He worked overtime until he pieced together Vu Chi's little club into this hybrid between Thai cabaret and the properties room of *The King and I*.

Every king has somebody do his dirty work. The Colonel needed Nico. Who better to get their hands dirty than a mechanic?

He couldn't recruit Thai girls; he'd be trafficking. So the old Horse ordered Nico to dress up a line of carefully-screened young Vietnamese hostesses in traditional Thai clothing. War was no place for perfectionists, so you only needed to do enough to sell the dream. Nico and the Colonel sacrificed authenticity to complete the mission. Nico's MOS didn't include parting the Red Sea, but his tasks required disproportional feats of near-Biblical dimensions. He discovered capacities he never knew he had, better tricks than getting grease out from under his fingernails. The Colonel made him into someone he entrusted with the power to pull off a few miracles.

Magic depends on illusion. Nico helped make The Splendors of Bangkok a grand illusion. For the elite of the Central Highlands, the Colonel put up a rainbow bridge that arced out of a messy war into Valhalla and the soldiers came.

Nico preferred the most difficult challenge of materiel acquisition over lining up hostesses on stage to be skewered with ritual swords by a fake magician. He dickered for an ornate teakwood bar with elephants, cobras, even a Buddha-under-a-Bodhi-tree carved in relief. The owner of the local hotel nearly cried when they shook hands. The Colonel had investors who could afford a fair price. But finding girls? That was never a strong suit. Nico wasn't some headhunter on point. He didn't mind grease, but he didn't much like danger. Sure, some excitement was good, but he preferred a good routine. In the bush nobody had his back.

In the rear view, Chu Len's raven tresses cascaded over delicate white shoulders, her petite body wrapped in Siamese *panung*. She would stun any battle-weary warrior into handing over every red cent he earned in facing the enemy. If Colonel Jefferson Hedges wanted Suzy Wong in dragon lady dress, her white Indochinese thighs exposed to boys who hadn't seen such light for months on end, elegant legs of glazed porcelain catching their eyes, then that's what he had in Chu Len. Imagine the Colonel unwrapping these presents on Christmas morning in Athens, Georgia, 1938.

Girls in mini-skirts and t-shirts with too much makeup wouldn't cut it. No war-hardened suspected VC sympathizers or any of those easy-to-get girls were good enough. They were damaged goods. The Colonel was a patriot, not a pimp. When he said *fresh*, he meant virginal.

Heroes performed selfless acts. Maybe Nico wasn't a hero but he did make life in a war zone easier for somebody and that was service.

A twinge of guilt made him flinch at recruiting Chu Len and Lu Bien. When he presented them to the extinct warhorse, he patted them down with a smile and passed them onto customers, proud to be a patron of the fighting man while sporting one more erection in service to his country. Maybe Nico needed to give more thought to who he was serving.

Splendors of Bangkok was the Colonel's plan for bringing R & R closer to the field of battle. These girls, he reminded Nico, were *hostesses*. "Our boys deserve to be serviced by hostesses, not prostitutes." He sincerely believed this. He explained the honorable traditions of the Orient and how he abhorred the way Americans denigrated the feminine arts in a warrior society. Thai hostesses answered a traditional calling: to assuage the inner & outer wounds of the battle-weary. We should not dishonor that tradition.

Even Nico came to believe the old Horse wore shining armor and was somehow protecting these damsels in distress.

* * *

Not far from the junction, Nico fought to hold the jeep on the road. The sun had gone down. Their sphere of light bounced like a ball as the jungle darkened around them. Chu Len and Lu Bien chattered in Vietnamese. He wondered if they knew where he was taking them. Maybe they thought he was taking them to America. Maybe The Splendors would be their ticket there.

The Bilbaos knew something about escaping perdition. Nico's grandfather gave up his home in northern Spain to immigrate to America before the Spanish Civil War. He made his way west to Idaho and worked as a sheepherder in the Great Basin. He married into ownership of a sheep ranch. The shirt he wore on his back was the American Dream, woven from golden fleece and raw hope.

The muddy road followed a stream running red after rain. Nico's mind drifted to those summer days rafting the Boise River, basking in the sun, ogling girls in string bikinis. His reverie was broken by a sagging figure in the middle of the road. A wounded soldier. The soldier slumped toward the glare of headlights, shielding his eyes. The jeep skidded sideways, braking hard, and shuddering to a stop.

The panic in Lu Bien's eyes said it all. Nico pointed to the spot illuminated in front of the jeep. "He's wounded."

Lu Bien shrugged with curiosity.

The soldier slumped to his knees.

Nico killed the engine and the jeep lurched forward.

"Wounded," Nico repeated, hand to his head. "Hurt."

Lu Bien brought her cool hand to Nico's cheek. "Hurt?"

"Not me," he shouted, as if volume alone could overcome the language barrier, "HIM!"

He pointed toward the wounded soldier who wasn't there. A swath of green light burned in the jeep's headlamps. Nico blinked, repeatedly, shook his head and started up the engine. The jeep leaped forward and a sudden brightness blinded him.

* * *

Nico awoke on a low embankment, hearing a hissing from the mangled jeep that had come to rest upside down ten meters away. His uniform was caked in red mud and both his feet were at the end of a crooked trail from the smoking heap to the grassy spot where he lay. Diffuse green jungle washed into a red blur. He touched his head with trembling fingers and felt the warm blood. His fingers found the edge of a sticky glob of loose scalp. He must have dragged himself off the road.

Lu Bien lay in a shallow crater filling with blood, her back arched, arms thrown wide. The shrapnel ripped open her fatigues exposing red silk. Her face was turned toward him, lemur eyes staring. Black hair thick as hemp encircled her small breasts. Her head sagged on a long broken neck.

Afloat in a bubble of shock, Nico heard Chu Len's hoarse voice. He blinked, rolling onto his side. Her lower body was pinned under the twisted chassis. She called for her father in short bursts. "**CHA!** CHA! Cha."

Nico's feeble voice was drowned by the high-pitched scream of monkeys.

The jeep had struck a landmine.

A few feet away, the wounded soldier emerged from an eerie fog of rising steam. In the shadow of the helmet, the man's face was hidden but gray-blue eyes burned through like pilot lights. He wore a sleeveless t-shirt with no body armor. From Nico's vantage, the man looked quite tall. Large hands removed the helmet and he shook out curly blond hair that framed a smudged and sweating face. Heedless of his own glistening chest wound, the man kneeled in the waning light and checked Nico for injuries. His body odor was so strong it blocked the smell of burning rubber.

"Can you help her—please?"

The infantryman probed Nico's wounds. His black face melted into oily beads. He wiped his face on a strip of disintegrating t-shirt and lowered his ear to Nico's lips.

"Not me. Her."

A warm trickle cut through the mud caked on Nico's uniform. A dim memory of the soldier lifting him up by the armpits flickered through a semi-conscious state. The soldier had dragged him off the road. His memory was whistling an old tune, but Nico couldn't remember the title or the words, only the melody.

He heard the pulsating beaters of the Dustoff long before it was visible bobbing over trees with searchlight scanning. It set down in the road. Rotor wash sliced through fronds of palm trees, the instrument panel throbbed in a velvet glow.

Two shadows dismounted, fatigues rippling in the wash. Light broke around their silhouettes as they approached, faces grim. The men strapped Nico onto a stretcher and slid it onto the cargo deck. The chopper lifted off to a low hover, dipped its nose and zoomed up the road, pulling up suddenly and out over the trees. It made Nico's head swim. His eardrums felt like they'd explode as hot air rushed through the doorless cabin and reverberated inside his skull. He yanked at the restraints. Hugging his machine gun, the door gunner stared unblinking into twilight. The buried sun splintered into tracers. The tracers arced in a line of light over a suffused green sea. Nico watched the lightshow against darkening sky. Then came the sound: *tick tick tick*. The sound reminded him of locusts striking the windows of a train. It took forever in seconds before he realized it was live rounds.

Thick jungle scintillated in waves under him. He drifted in and out of consciousness, shivering with perspiration, mumbling incoherently. When the Huey landed, stretcher-bearers hustled in slow motion toward the open door, reaching in, pulling him out, carrying him over the tarmac. Nico looked down. His uniform was saturated with mud and blood.

Carried by waves of heat, he felt no pain. An eerie calmness settled over him. Faces in white masks floated above him as hands probed, snipped, prodded and stabbed. Morphine. Catheters. Blood infusions. Nasal oxygen. Shock blocks.

A weak voice he barely recognized as his own asked, "Am I gonna die?"

2.

The Columbia River rolled backward in the flood tide and surged under the cannery docks. At the stern of the *Alma May*, Milo peered into the water through shafts of refracted light. He leaned over the troller's bulwark, hacking the mist that settled into his lungs. The late morning sun lulled him into this strange quietude. His thoughts unfocused and scattered in reflections across the river mouth.

When he spotted the body rising, he wasn't surprised. It wasn't the first time. That was at the mooring basin. He'd mistaken the drowned man for a dead white sturgeon, floating belly-up in the bay. He felt his muscles tighten as if he was turning into a stiff. A human body, facedown, arms spread in a deadman float. It had unnerved him then as he conflated it with thoughts of his father, lost at sea.

So Milo Simonson accepted the drowned man as real when he filled up with darkness and sank. Now here it was again floating up, bloodless, stiff and cold as a block of ice.

A pilot boat bounded over wave crests over the bay to the channel to meet an inbound freighter. The boat's keel dropped into the trough with a *whump*, its wake rolling the drowned man in his dark sleep. Splinters of light were the only distinguishable features. The pale body tumbled forward, head-first diving into darkness.

Growing up in Astoria, Milo watched ships that came and went from the waterfront. He gained enough experience to judge nations by their merchant fleets: the Scandinavians in gleaming white freighters like luxury yachts compared to those rust-buckets deemed sea-worthy by the British or recommissioned Liberty ships from WWII. All the nations looked like last year's models compared to a Norwegian.

The pilot boat came about so bar and river pilots could exchange places—one stepping on, the other stepping off, riding a thin metal ladder near the waterline. The river pilot would steer the ship upriver to Portland. Milo admired men trusted at the wheel for their courage, confidence and experience. His girlfriend's father, Captain Seaver, was such a man, a man who knew the river.

"Wake up, Sunny. Comin' your way."

Milo grabbed the line. The young man of Finnish descent with blond crew cut and big mouth was his friend, Geo Kaartinen. Milo attached the hoist cable to the rope on the fish box packed with iced silver, hunched into a mustard yellow slicker plastered with fish scales. Geo swung the boom back to the dock. More stinking fish, he thought, pushing long bangs up under his cap. He was sick of fish; he was hungry for a steak.

"All yours!" Milo shouted, signaling to Geo. The winch whined. The cable tightened, jerking the wooden box into the air. Geo yanked back on the boom to swing it toward the dock when Milo heard the whiplash. Searing steel cracked around his ear. The fish box crashed, splintering on the deck.

He dove out of the way just in time. Frozen salmon skidded across the deck planks ramming his upper body with hard bullet noses where he landed against the bulwark.

"Sonofabitch!" he screamed, clutching his chest as if shot, his heart racing. The crash of the heavy box could have seriously injured him.

The leather-skinned owner of the *Alma May*, Eino Mattson, hurried from the dock to help Milo to his feet. Eino's hair was sun-bleached white in contrast to the ruddy good looks of an older man. Milo's mom thought so anyway. He sometimes bought her dinner at Davy Jones' Locker where she worked the late shift. The development left Milo indifferent. Eino was gruff and grim but he had a steady hand on the wheel. He was a fair man who paid decent wages to his hands and respected the sea he depended on.

Someone was applauding. Milo was stunned and wobbling but it wasn't that funny. The clapping echoed through shock-stilled air. Milo couldn't pinpoint the eruption of rudeness and nobody else seemed to be reacting, so blinked it away. All eyes were on him.

The glare of cold sun off clouds of steam billowing from the cooker room cast the offender into silhouette, standing just inside the open door, clapping. He was probably a puller. Those guys can be assholes sometimes after tedious hours of yanking racks of melting tuna over a hosed-down concrete floor. The heat'll make you light-headed.

The drowned man stepped into full daylight—still wet, white and slimy as a used condom—standing on the dock, still clapping.

On the dock, the heavy *thunk* of frozen tuna tossed into a bin sounded like church bells. Milo's face felt suddenly hot, but it wasn't because of anger. He touched his cheek and looked at his hand. He was bleeding.

3.

A calm but determined voice pulled Nico out of darkness. "Listen carefully," the voice said, "you need to wake now."

He blinked and bright sun streamed through the window into a whitewashed room. It was like drowning then waking, sore eyes adjusting to light splashing like waves over someone's head. Someone in bed next to him turned. Half his face oozed pink and black. One side was bald and wrinkled from burns, the other with wet blonde hair in long riotous strands. Gray-blue eyes of the wounded soldier fixed him on the road from Kon Barr. *My god*, Nico thought, *they put me in bed with a dead man! Don't they have enough beds? Don't they realize this poor bastard's gone?* The soldier sputtered finally, spraying the whitewashed wall with blood. Nico's throat burned as if he'd swallowed battery acid.

The light receded into a distant point and soon Nico sank back into darkness.

When he woke again, it was pitch black. His arms and legs were immobilized. He couldn't move. Wet cotton covered his nose and mouth as a team of doctors and nurses tried to suffocate him. They were holding him down in the bottom of a hole and burying him alive, the ground caving in, dirt filling empty cavities like nose and mouth. *Buried alive.* His thoughts were sluggish and his mouth was muffled. Words caught in his throat. He stared into the dark unknown, eyes unblinking, watching paralyzed as two white moons floated out of the black sky, descending like zeppelins on fire. The white moons dropped lower until they turned into the sweet round faces of Chu Len and Lu Bien. "Go home now?" Chu Len asked in English. "Please, go home?"

* * *

An angel fluted in Nico's ear, "As Tears Go By."

His eyes fluttered like swallows. The voice belonged to Coco Bird. But he remembered Coco Bird couldn't carry a tune. *"I must be dead!"* he thought. Coco Bird plumped up his pillows and gazed at him with eyes like bachelor buttons. Coco Bird leaned low over him. "Coco Bird," he murmured, "You came." Mere inches away her face. He reached to pull her lips down to his. Coco Bird turned into his high school nemesis, Jesse Walker. Jesse kissed him on the forehead and pinched off Nico's feeding tubes, pulled out a great big needle and rammed it into his arm.

"Did that wake you?" Jesse said. "Sorry."

Nico did wake and Jesse dissolved. The nurse's eyes were blueberries floating in cream and sugar, much softer than Jesse's. He yelled at her, "Where'd my angel go? What'd you do with Coco?"

This nurse was persistent as a horsefly, sticking him repeatedly with needles.

He tried to stay awake, but drifted into sleep. Each prick of a needle evaporated thoughts, slowing traffic in the confused circuitry of his brain. He tried to stay awake but drifted into sleep, the question of Chu Len and Lu Bien never quite formed on his tongue. He licked thick dry lips, took a long draw on a glass of water and convulsed to shake the maggots off his skin.

As she mopped his sweating brow with a sponge, the nurse quieted him. "It's okay. You'll be all right."

* * *

The nurse's name was Alyssa Parker. She cared for all of her patients, but Nico's not-well-knitted-to-reality brain interpreted the care as her having fallen in love with him. He was quite delusional. Nurse Parker did say he'd suffered a serious head wound, didn't she? Well, she would cut him some slack, wouldn't you think?

Parker never confirmed a dying soldier in his bed, but even if she did, she wouldn't have known the wounded soldier as he did. She did mention, however, that someone had been in the bed next to his. Maybe that's who he saw? She didn't say if he was dead or alive. Her only answers were more injections.

* * *

Nico got a little overstimulated during a bath. "At ease, Sarge," Parker said, then calmly whacked his willy with a tongue depressor. "At least you don't have to worry about *that* working." She gently applied a cool sponge to his forehead. "How's your head?"

His erection shriveled. He forced a grin. "Full of bees."

"Mosquitoes. Remember? You're in Vietnam." She laughed, tossing back her head, hair tangled from sweat.

Her laughter reminded Nico of wind chimes like the hollow metal tubes on the back porch of his parents' house in north Boise. The soft gong in a mild breeze next to the hummingbird feeder was Parker.

"How long was I under?" he asked.

"Three days."

"Wow." His surprise quickly turned comic. "I was hoping the war might be over."

"It is—for *you* at least." She sat him up and rolled a cart bedside with a cup of some brew.

"What's that?" he asked.

"Cocoa. You asked for cocoa."

"Coco's here?" He looked around, heart pounding. "I'm going home?"

"Any day now."

* * *

When Nico awakened, he heard shouting outside.

Parker was changing the dressing on his head wound, going about her routines efficiently and totally unruffled by the curses flying through his window.

"Why are they shouting?" he asked.

"Who?" Alyssa propped him up with pillows.

"Outside the window." He craned his neck. He didn't need to see them. He knew who they were.

Parker walked to the window, looked out, then drew the shade. "There's nobody out there."

"So why pull the shade?" he asked. "You saw him, didn't you?"

"Who?"

"Chu Len's father. He's the loud one. I recognize his voice. He's angry because I killed his daughter."

Concern darkened Parker's face. She shook her head. "No one's out there, Sarge."

There was no denying it. The voices were angry. One joined another until a mob of grieving villagers marched on the hospital with protest signs. *Murderer, go home.*

"I killed them both," he moaned.

The din of unforgiving disdain amplified like harmonics in Nico's head. The bed quaked with torment. He clasped hands over his ears. The curses of her ancestors pierced his ears like hot nails. Then they just stopped. The room was dark and silent but for the sound of ceiling fans.

* * *

The surgeon dropped by to check on Nico. He was a tall, fit major by the name of Wellington. Wellington had a gentle bedside manner, a genuine smile and sense of humor. It was Wellington's cool confident air that assured Nico no dying soldier ever lay in his bed. It was only a hallucination. Not at all unexpected under the circumstances. Nico wanted to believe him, but the vision had been too real. Hallucinations, Wellington pointed out, are super-real to the percipient.

Wellington's specialty was the body, not the mind, so he turned Nico over to the hospital's shrink. Captain Butkus clarified right off that he was no relation to the Chicago Bears linebacker. He was a by-the-book officer full of scientific jargon for every odd twist of mind ever recorded. He only left Nico feeling stuck between worlds, unable to plant both feet in any one. His professional detachment so frustrated him that Nico broke down and cried, "Kiss my ass!" Behind the doctor's back, he referred to him as "Buttkiss."

Any mechanic could understand the difference between fixing a driveshaft and monkey-wrenching around with an organ as complex as the human brain. So Nico tried to be flexible, made an attempt to be a partner in his healing, stretching his own belief to consider the shrink's explanations. Explanations like how the soldier had been in another bed in the same room when he died.

Buttkiss went on to explain what happened to Nico in physical terms. His blood pressure had dropped from loss of blood. The decreased flow of oxygenated blood to his brain induced these hallucinations like the soldier dying in bed next to him. While admitting modern medicine couldn't fully understand the mental functioning of patients in his condition, Buttkiss nevertheless kept asking, "Tell me again. What happened on the road from Kon Barr?" He jotted down notes about his narrative. The shrink suggested maybe he'd also hallucinated the soldier in the road, in that moment before losing consciousness. In some states of mind, an injured soldier might experience thoughts as reality. "You suffered a serious head injury. You nearly died."

Though plausible, Buttkiss wasn't convincing. Nico sympathized with witnesses of the unexplained, witnesses of UFOs browbeaten by investigators into believing they'd seen swamp gas. That's how he felt. Even if the soldier hadn't been present, there was still the vision, which Nico decided might not have been real, but it certainly meant something. A soldier did die in the bed and he was trying to communicate with him.

Lack of oxygen to the brain or the need to restore damaged neural connections didn't explain why, with eyes wide open, Nico still flashed on the wounded soldier coming through a crowd of angry voices.

Okay, maybe insanity was one possibility.

* * *

The Pleiku Evacuation Hospital was a makeshift nucleus of prefab quonset huts and wooden buildings. Screens separated the wards: emergency room from operating rooms to pharmacy, laboratory, X-ray to mess hall to headquarters. Hospital staff were housed in wooden-framed cabin tents surrounding the hospital's nucleus.

Once up and trundling around in slippers and robe, IV attached, Nico visited Parker in her quarters. She lived with six other nurses. He read her invitation to mean she wanted to be alone with him. Parker's private world consisted of a 6x10 cubicle with separating walls of bamboo mat tacked to the tent's inner frame. She slept on a metal cot enclosed by mosquito nets. Her belongings were kept in a narrow wall locker, except for a photo on a crate beside her cot. The young man in graduation robes was her brother back home in Stockton, California.

"I saw you once," Parker confessed. "The White Tiger. You were dickering for elephants." The White Tiger was a local hotel and the owner, Nyugen, had two Cambodian wooden white tiger sculptures in the lobby. Nico thought they'd make good dressing for The Splendors. They'd been in Nyugen's family for generations and the barter went on a long time, over many days and many visits. But Nico couldn't take "no" for an answer. Nyugen's sense of their worth was inflated with sentiment. War had a way of changing the value of things, even human life.

When alone with Parker, Nico brought up the subject of the wounded soldier who died in the other bed.

She surprised him, taking hold of his hands in earnest. "He was only here a few days."

"Yes, but he died here, didn't he?" Nico probed without sensitivity. "What'd he look like?"

"Young. They're always young." Parker's eyes misted. "Handsome. Reminded me of Troy Donahue."

"You're kidding. Well, did he have any distinguishing features?"

"Like what?" Alyssa looked puzzled.

"Maybe his face was disfigured in the crash?"

"You were hallucinating."

"What else can you tell me?" He wouldn't let it go.

"He had just one visitor," she said.

"Who?"

"A Warrant Officer with the First Cav. His shoulder patch had the black horse's head against a yellow field."

"I don't remember that."

"You were behind a screen."

He pressed for more details. Parker grew impatient. "You're obsessed." She stood up. "You want a soda?"

He declined. "Got any beer?"

She reached into a crock of ice and pulled out a bottle of Bier 33, opening it with a church key. "Not Pabst Blue Ribbon but it's palatable."

He gargled before swallowing.

"So, was I hallucinating before I hit the landmine?"

"*Before* you hit the landmine?"

"Yeah. That's when I first saw him."

"Who?"

"But his face wasn't burned."

"Who?"

"The soldier in the bed next to me was the same soldier I saw on the road from Kon Barr. Same guy."

"The soldier who died was a SPC-4 with the First Cav. He came in when you did. After the crash."

"What crash? You said there wasn't a crash."

"The chopper crashed after they picked you up." She patted his hand. "You arrived at the same time."

Nico drank the beer in silence. She didn't understand.

Her gaze was a long and agonizing assessment of his confused mental state.

Finally he said, "Look, I saw this guy on the road from Kon Barr, right before we hit the landmine near Route 19. I believe he pulled me out of the wreckage, in spite of his own mortal wounds."

Parker arched her eyebrows.

"You don't believe me." Nico's eyes dropped, voice faltering.

"No, I believe you." She was courageous but not very convincing.

"Where did the chopper crash?"

"Mang Yang Pass."

"Close to where I hit the landmine. Was he conscious?"

"Sometimes."

After another long silence, Nico held the still-cool empty bottle of beer against his hot cheek.

"But it's not possible," she added.

"Why not?"

"The Huey was diverted from a mission to medevac you. They were bringing you here when they were shot down. Word is the crew fought off NVA until another chopper arrived. It was quite heroic."

"I can't imagine it," Nico answered, setting the bottle on the crate. The air in the tent was heavy. His brow tickled with sweat.

"He did mention a girlfriend," Parker's eyes blinked. "They wanted to save themselves for marriage. I'm not sure why he told *me* that."

"You don't?" Nico laughed too loud. "He was a *virgin*, wasn't he?"

"Oh, come on," she said, blinking away the sadness.

"What about you?"

"What about me?"

Nico realized from the shocked look on her face that she'd misunderstood the question. "I mean, do you have a boyfriend?"

"Yeah," she glanced at the photo on the crate, squeezed

Nico's hand, and said, "every one of our boys who come through here." She wiped her nose with the back of her knuckle, then leaned over to kiss him on the cheek. He turned so that her kiss planted on his mouth. She let him kiss her, but her eyes remained clear.

"I'm sorry," he said.

She was quick to switch the subject. "You'll get medals, you know? Service Medal, Purple Heart. Bet you never thought you'd be a war hero."

He laughed again and a sharp pain shot through his skull.

She looked offended. By the time she led him back to the ward, he realized she really meant it. The mere fact that he was in-country meant he was a hero to her.

"Is that what I tell my mom when I see her? Hey mom, look, I got this Purple Heart transporting fresh hostesses for The Splendors of Bangkok? It insults the real heroes. My parents should be proud of what exactly? That their son helped turn bargirls into professionals?"

"They'll just be glad you came home." Parker's radiant smile broke through his gray mood. She was the hero, not him.

4.

Milo strolled onto the dock, his right cheek bandaged and painkillers numbing his whole head. Still no boats. Around two in the afternoon, Bill Brown called him and Geo into the cooker room. "Things are slow." The supervisor pinched a wet Camel from his lips and flicked it into the river. "Why don't you call it a day—'less you wanna tail-off for a while?"

Milo wasn't tailing-off again. He took the opening on the docks to get off the tuna line. He much preferred hosing fish bins, dumping brine, unloading boats and boxcars to the soul-crushing monotony of the line. He didn't know how anyone could work the line for ten or twenty years.

A tailer stood at the end of the tuna line and guided still-hot cans into iron racks, row by uniform row. When each rack was full, it was the tailer's job to slide the rack on to a stack on a wooden pallet. When the stack was waist-high and any more would force the tailer to lift the racks, the jitney came by and took the pallet to the warehouse, and the tailer would start another pallet of racks. Standing all day under the big clock as hour ticked through hour and passed from day to day, row after row, rack upon rack, pallet to pallet, you live for mechanical breakdowns. Milo never knew time could pass so slowly. The crawl of the second hand over the clock face marked the relativity of time. The more he tried to slow it down the faster it went; the more he tried to hurry it up and more it slowed down. He was caught in this eternal tide of daydreaming, creating whole worlds in his head in minutes, worlds that popped suddenly at the sound of the lunch whistle.

Milo tossed his slicker over his shoulder. "Call us if a boat comes in."

* * *

Milo and Geo slogged down the wooden alleyway in oversized rubber boots. Several butchers in white wrap-around smocks, hair pushed up under white headscarves, huddled around a co-worker who'd just severed her thumb. Butchers, on hands and knees, groped into gutters between wet floorboards under stainless steel tables and came up with nothing. Her thumb was missing. The woman sat calmly on a stack of empty pallets, smiling at no one in particular. No blood gushed from the wound. Not a spot soiled her white smock. Her co-workers started opening cans.

A yellow and black Bumblebee Hyster stood at a stall in the alleyway near the labeling line. Balanced on the jitney's forks was a pallet of white albacore in 12-ounce tins. Wilfred Limon pushed the ignition button again and again, cursing when it didn't start up.

Limon saw Milo and Geo coming down the alleyway and threw up his arms.

"Where's Brown?"

Milo barely heard the driver over the *chunk-chunk-chunk* of the labeling machine.

"Accident on the butcher line. They lost a thumb," Milo answered, raising his voice over the machine. "No boats. We're outta here."

"Shit, man," Limon whined. "Yesterday the dock she gave out on the west side. Bad rot there. Gettin' damned dangerous to work here, no? Sweet Jesus."

Limon thumped the hard seat of the Hyster with the ball of his hand while grinding the ignition, neck veins bulging.

The engine wouldn't turn over. "C'mon, you sick bumblebee. Start! What a piece of shit!"

Limon cuffed his ears in frustration, dislodging his left eyeball. The eyeball popped out and dropped onto the wooden driveway. His other eye watched as it rolled through a crevice in the planking. Limon stuck a finger into the empty socket and stirred. "Damned doctors." He pulled a clear marble from his coveralls and plugged it into the eyehole as a replacement, and kept on cranking that ignition until the Hyster started up. He made a thankful gesture to heaven, double-clutched the jitney and made it lurch down the alleyway.

Milo stepped back as Limon jerked by.

"Didn't know Limon had a glass eye," Geo noted.

Milo shrugged.

Limon went skidding around the corner on wet planking, lost control and drove forks clean through the wooden wall. The abrupt stop popped Limon's right eyeball out. His hands fluttered, fingers probing the cracked vinyl seat. "Damn doctors!"

Geo scratched his shoulder absently. "That proves it."

"Proves what?"

"A blind man can drive a jitney."

Limon stumbled from the forklift, feeling around on the floor. "Yeah?" Milo said. "Then how come he gets paid more?"

"Experience."

Geo stopped, mid-thought, reaching under his collar as if being bitten by ants. He tried to scratch this unreachable itch on his back, below the shoulder blade. His antics made Milo laugh.

"This rash is driving me crazy," Geo glared.

Shot like a bullet from the labeling machine, a tin can struck Milo in the neck, just under the already wounded right cheek. He cried out, spun around and dropped to one knee—a move he hadn't done so impressively since he died at the age of twelve, playing war.

Geo shouted at the Filipinos on the labeling machine. "Hey, watch where you're shooting, you guys!" The seasonal workers couldn't hear over the *chunk, chunk, chunk*. So they just smiled and waved when they saw Geo's mouth moving like a fish gulping the air. The shortest of the three had this sparse mustache and stood by the machine yanking a lever, shaking his fist when the machine fired off another round.

Geo helped Milo to his feet and handed him the evidence. Milo inspected the round. He marched over to the machine and shoved it into the Filipino's face. "Solid White. It's dated 1968." The Filipino gave a thumb's up. "Reject!"

Geo was too busy spanking his itch, unable to reach it. "Fucking itches, man."

Solid White was the only decent tuna in a can. Milo slipped it into his pocket. Strict policy on rejects let workers take home tuna, but never smoked sturgeon. The company kept count of them. Milo hated tuna in a can, but Solid White was edible. Once you've seen steaming flanks of fresh tuna crushed into a tin, you lose your appetite for anything in a can.

The labeling machine stopped. The Filipino's hand got entangled in it. A co-worker shut the machine down and yanked his arm free. The operator's forearm was plastered with the label: SOLID WHITE.

This brought tears to Geo's eyes. He laughed so hard, he forgot about the itch. Geo didn't like Filipinos and resented the way Bumble Bee brought them on to strip the chum and black sturgeon of eggs for caviar, and now they were taking over the labeling machine. They'd be running the company soon and he'd be out of a job. Corporate was plugging in foreigners wherever they needed to save money. Geo worked with one in the cold room and the poor unfortunate man dropped a block of ice on Geo's foot. He ended up with a broken toe.

* * *

They slogged in silence to the locker room, Milo clutching his bruised neck, bandaged cheek shrunken over the bone, and Geo, raking nails over flaking skin trying to reach the unreachable itch.

The drowned man appeared again: a blanched and puffy, waxy sheen still dripping wet. A bump on its newly-formed and featureless face poked out like a ball-bearing under a rubber glove. A nose was forming. The thin film over the man's eyes split and blinked open. They locked onto Milo with keen interest. A naked man by the retorts was staring back at him. Behind the man was something heavy like an anchor and chain. He couldn't see it well enough as the torpedo-shaped retort cooker blocked his line of sight. Milo stepped back for a better view.

The man was dragging a sledgehammer. Not that strange in a cannery. Milo once used a sledgehammer to band barrels of salted salmon. When the man lifted the sledgehammer and swung it round and round over his head like Thor, Milo had second thoughts. When the man released the hammer and it crashed head-first through green-painted steel machinery with enough force to shatter eardrums, Milo didn't hear anything.

The man vanished. Not a single dent marred the machinery.

"See anybody 'round the retorts?" Milo asked.

"Yeah," Geo responded, "Happy Harrison."

Milo regarded the man pulling racks of pressurized cans out of the retort cookers on a narrow track. He shook his head. "No," he said, "the naked guy."

"You're looking for naked guys?" Geo raised an eyebrow.

Milo couldn't explain. The drowned man's face was still featureless. What if he wasn't a man at all? He still hadn't developed any genitals or breasts. What if this resurrected creature was the product of Milo's own mind? He instinctively knew the unformed creature was a man that might be possessed by some demon. It was only a matter of time before evidence began to take shape. A few hours ago the naked man was a corpse rising after being underwater possibly for years, bloodless limbs gnawed-away, strips of rotten clothing on grubby white, bloated skin. Now look: he's throwing hammers.

Geo waved at Harrison. "Ain't nobody stranger than Harrison, Sunny, and if *he's* naked it's a probation violation." Harrison waved back. He was a good-natured guy but he was slow in processing anything that wasn't strict routine. It was a break in routine when he was court-ordered to steer clear of children. He showed up for work every day and performed his routines cheerfully, without complaint or incident. A model of the company man.

"Poor bastard," Geo said, shaking his head. "He's happy working here. Ain't that depressing?"

"No, what's depressing," Milo noted with deadpan, "is that he gets paid more than we do."

Geo nodded in agreement. "Experience. You need more experience." He pulled a hand from inside his coveralls where he was scratching. He sniffed his fingernails and wrinkled his nose. "I think my skin is flaking off."

"Yeah. Well, you live in Astoria."

Geo shrugged, wiping fingernails on his coveralls.

Milo gazed back at the retorts. Maybe it *had* been Happy Harrison all along. Maybe he was the shadow man, moving through the steam like a ghost in the fog.

5.

Nico's '64 Comet Cyclone backfired as he gunned it up 28th Street to Foothill Road. Ritual Sunday dinner with the folks. It was a beaten path. The sound of his tuned engine resonated in his body like a tuning fork. It was missing and in need of adjustment. The Cyclone wasn't showy like some but held its own with a 289 c.i. engine, yellow exterior, white trim, pleated white vinyl interior, bucket seats. He rode in style with a Hurst 4-speed on the floor, tach mounted on top of the dash, immersed in a bubble of sound from the Pioneer AM/FM/8-track and four good speakers.

He pulled into the driveway of the two-story farmhouse where he grew up. The evening sun filtered through the hardwoods in the lot his father acquired for a feeling of being close to the woods. Nico's dad once told him "Boise" was French for trees or woods. The valley was like a paradise for those tortured souls in a great migration wandering off the desert into the cool shadows of native cottonwoods. He could imagine the pioneers falling to their knees at the edge of the Boise River, giving thanks to God for leading them to water. They watered the trees they brought with them, shade trees like maple, black locust, dutch elm, sycamore, box elder, horse chestnut, even the sturdy oak. They named Boise a City of Trees, an almost Biblical "Promised Land."

Sunday dinner was a peace offering. Nothing short of relapse excused him from this family commitment. When Nico returned from Vietnam, his parents expected him to move back home. His mother wanted nothing more than to fatten him up and smother him in good Catholic blessings. That was what he really needed, but Nico spurned his mother's wishes. He chose to live on his own. It wasn't because he'd outgrown the need of a mother, but because he'd grown into a man needing his own space. After basic training, tech school and troop barracks, he'd barely had any privacy outside the privy. That's why he read in the bathroom.

Sunday dinners were stressful enough. A couple of weeks ago his parents invited his oldest sister, Jean, and family (her building-contractor husband and new baby girl). Last week they brought in Father Michael for a barbecue with the Wallaces from next door. These gatherings were engineered to prevent Nico from burning up on re-entry. His mom wanted things back to normal. After the war, Nico's normal found little consensus in any community, except with other vets. Nico had seen and done too many things to believe his country was always a force for good in the world. Never again could he be made anybody's instrument of war. This made him another outsider.

His parents feared being alone with an outsider. They still lived in the afterglow of the Eisenhower years, the Golden Age of America. Actions in Vietnam were not in their vocabulary. They stepped back and let dinner guests engage their son in talking out his war wounds so as to sustain some conversation. Otherwise, they'd sit at the dinner table in silence, not looking at each other, afraid one let the other down. Even Nico's father, who'd walked through Italy into Germany and liberated Jews from death camps, utilized vague refrains when talking about it: "War is hell." It was a necessary evil sometimes to be endured in defense of liberty. Liberty did not include the right not to go to war if your country needed you. Nico simply avoided the subject.

Tonight would be one of those nights when there was no way to avoid it. Uncle Frosty was an Air Force lifer, a Technical Sergeant for the Reconnaissance Wing at Mountain Home Air Force Base. The Feds let his uncle make a career of failure, passed over more times than the bombing range. Married once. Ex-wife. Two kids. Frosty's invisible disdain became visible from the moment he opened the screen door to find Nico standing there in Buddha beads, paisley shirt tucked into bellbottoms, broad white belt, black Beatles boots, long hair held in a headband, daypack slung over his shoulder.

"The hippie's here," Frosty called back into the living room. The harsh announcement burned Nico's ears. The one who taught him to dress that way was Mr. Josh Brownton, who stepped right off the streets of London magazines. Nico recognized the unease of his uncle in the tone of his voice. Nico felt a sudden advantage. Frosty could sense it and it made him a little self-conscious. Nico had been in Vietnam. Frosty had been in Korea.

His cousin Shelly was the first girl Nico ever felt up. The folks didn't realize why he and Frosty didn't like each other. He pulled off his headband and shook out his hair, black locks tumbling over his ears. He swept long bangs out of his eyes like d'Artagnan and deflected his uncle's cold stare.

The kitchen fan clattered so Annabel Bilbao didn't hear him come in. She dropped her oven mitt on the counter when she saw him inside the swinging saloon doors. She threw her arms around him. "Nicky," she cried, sage, onions, green pepper and garlic her perfume.

The aroma of baked pork chops on a bed of potatoes and vegetables permeated the house as it often did. It was one of his mom's favorite dishes. There was nothing better than a three-course meal prepared in a single pot. Thank God for casseroles.

His mother was small in stature but energetic, like Nico. In her mid-forties, she dressed sensibly in a mid-calf navy blue dress with Peter Pan collar under a full white apron. Her pluck well compensated any lack of stature. Her optimism was only reinforced after surviving three older brothers on a dairy farm in Caldwell. "You hungry?"

Nico nodded. "Does a bear snore?"

* * *

Nico's dad reclined in his La-Z-Boy. "Sorry I don't get up." Maury shifted his Camel cigarette to his thumb and forefinger, flicking ashes into a beanbag ashtray balanced on his stomach. The tobacco smoke spread into a thin cloud near the ceiling. In his trademark faded green EZ-Flush Plumbing coveralls with "Maury" stitched in red over the chest pocket, his father shifted his dentures with his tongue. He had three different colors broken in, some worn so thin they looked like his lungs. Purple veins on paper-white skin in flannel slippers. "I'm saving my strength to digest your mom's pork chops."

Maury rumbled some phlegm into a cloth held to his mouth, folded it over once and stuffed it back into his pocket.

A late game between the Detroit Tigers and Boston Red Sox was on television. The sun hadn't even set in Boise yet, but there in Detroit the game was under lights. Pat Dobson took the mound for the Tigers. The right-hander gave up back-to-back home runs in the first inning. Not a good start.

"Nicky, tell your uncle about Bob Hope," his mother prompted, eyes gleaming. Then she turned to Frosty, "It's how he earned his Purple Heart."

Lies come back on you. You've got to be ready, when they do, to tell a bigger one. Nico lied his way through war wounds with real intention. With his dad already sick, he didn't want to give his mom a heart attack. So he told a story, one they could accept. He was driving a band of Army musicians to the USO show at Tan Son Nhut to perform with Bob Hope. He was their driver. He was responsible for them. After the show, Ann-Margret kissed him on the cheek and thanked him for being such a good driver. That was the story. He embellished a little in the telling but there was the core truth of hitting a landmine that made for a lot of grief. He wanted to spare his parents and retreated into half-truth to cope with it. "Mom," he shook his head.

"I loved the Road movies. With Bing Crosby and Dorothy Lamour. They don't make movies like that anymore." She flopped down on the sofa beside him, worn out as usual, the lines around her eyes a little deeper than last time. She closed her eyes as if imagining one of their movies.

"Thank God." Maury rolled watery eyes toward the ceiling. Anyone like Nico's dad who spent as much time as he did cleaning sewer pipes didn't waste time romanticizing what can come out of humans. Maury even used shit as an excuse to smoke Camels. You needed some strong tobacco to purge that smell.

Emphysema shredded Maury's lungs. At fifty-two, he'd inhaled enough dust, fiberglass and insulation to kill most men. He ripped into walls with a Sawzall without any masks. His short trial using filters ended when he compared them to something retrieved on the end of a plumbing snake. It was too late anyway to clean out his clogged pipes. Let him have another one. At least he's happy.

"So what's the score?" Annabelle slapped Maury's knee. She might have been asking about the game, but she didn't care about baseball. She just wanted to see if he was paying attention. He always knew the score even when falling asleep in his recliner.

In the bottom of the first inning, after the Tigers' second baseman Dick McAuliffe went down, Tom Tresh hit a solo home run. 2–1 Red Sox, one out.

Maury was a damn good pipefitter, a journeyman who cut clean threads. His joints seldom broke or leaked. Yet after years of dedicated service to EZ-Flush, they let him go after the hernia operation. EZ was a non-union shop with minimal health coverage and no pension plans. Maury dragged Nico under houses, through spider webs and dead dust until his son grew so accustomed to crawlspaces he could curl up in the cool and dank dark and take a nap. When

Maury finished a job and needed help gathering his tools he could never find that boy. Where did he go?

Nico grew up loving baseball and kept a collection of baseball cards in the garage. Maury knew the lineups of all the major-league teams, cited batting averages and ERAs with the same aplomb as Nico showed in identifying rock groups.

"Ann-Margret kissed my boy on the cheek." Annabel looked like she was ready to tear up.

"Wow!" Frosty's grin betrayed his neatly contained contempt. He shouldn't have said any more, but he'd already had a couple of beers. "Isn't that like a golfer saying he got the ball onto the green but couldn't find the hole?"

"Frosty." His mother glowered at Maury. Maury shook his head at Frosty, cautioned his brother with his eyes.

"We're all adults here," Frosty reminded them.

Nico wasn't a little boy. He could handle profanity and Uncle Frosty just fine.

"Cup of Maxwell House, Nicky?" His mother pushed herself up with a smile.

"I'll get it." Nico started to rise.

"No, no dear," Annabel touched his shoulder to keep him down. "Stay and visit with your uncle."

"Thanks, mom."

The saloon doors were still swinging when Frosty leaned in with a wink and a nod, eyes getting bleary. "You ever try that Asian stuff?"

Asian stuff? Nico's mind flashed on Chu Len and Lu Bien. He fought the impulse to ask Frosty if he meant whores or Cambodian Red? His fingers itched to pinch the joint from his pocket and light up. Take a great big hit and pass it over to Maury. Here, try *this*, dad. It's really good shit. Beats the hell out of those Camels. Instead, Nico pretended not to know what Frosty was referring to, reflecting back a puzzled look that forced his uncle to clarify.

"Pussy? You know?" He licked his lips and said in a low voice, "Hear they can't get enough white cock."

Maury fidgeted in his lounger. His brother was going too far. His eyes flashed *caution, caution. Go slow. Wreck ahead.* Nico ignored the flags and stepped on the accelerator. "They're also pretty good at faking it."

Maury clicked his cheek and hacked up a green gobbet. He wiped it off his tongue with a white handkerchief and inspected it, folding it over and pushing it back into the front pocket of his coveralls. Good for at least one more use. He kicked back in his chair and lit another Camel.

Top of the third: Tigers 6, Red Sox 2.

"Well, at least you didn't run off to Canada," Frosty offered as a concession.

"We're all heroes here, Frosty. It doesn't matter who's leading the charge." Nico remarked under his breath.

"What's that?" Frosty's teeth chomped at the bit, jaw muscles working overtime.

Annabel stepped between them with a steaming cup of Maxwell House in a mug Nico had used since high school.

Nico took the heavy mug and tasted it. Good as any restaurant. "You didn't have to get it, mom. I know where the pot is."

"No trouble, dear." She patted Nico on the knee and turned a critical eye on her husband. "Don't go giving your son ideas."

Maury ignored the reprimand. "He's got plenty of his own."

In Detroit's half of the sixth inning, Northrop hit a two-run homer for the Tigers. Then Freehan, the catcher, tagged a fast ball. "Kiss that one good-bye," Maury said as the camera followed the ball up and out of the stadium, a solo shot to centerfield. The ball bounded out of the glove of a fan and bounced on concrete in the aisle below. The camera zoomed in on a tall, broad-shouldered man who trapped the ball in his Tiger cap. The man held the home run ball up to applause. The camera moved in. The man's face was a shadow, but Nico knew him. The ballpark organ played the tune the wounded soldier whistled on the road to Kon Barr. He shut his eyes tight. When he opened them, Freehan was crossing home plate.

"What's that make it?" Frosty called from the kitchen, reappearing with a beer bottle in each fist, handing one to his brother.

"11–2," Maury answered. "Tigers are roaring."

Nico heard the sound of china so went to help his mother in the kitchen. Annabel's kitchen was a glossy ad with *Good Housekeeping* stamped all over it. She was proud of the middle class conveniences that cluttered the counter: automatic coffeepot, blender, electric can opener, four-slice toaster. She always complained that Nico and his sister had been corrupted by these conveniences. She was very constrained but still managed to keep up with the Arritolas and the Navarros.

On one of Nico's all-too-frequent "bad mood" Sundays, he motioned toward the sparkling dishwasher. "Now you get one." A convenience he and his sister, Jean, never had.

Annabel smiled knowingly. "Well, I lost two dishwashers."

The new Amana chest freezer was a monument to America. We should be thankful for the sacrifices of those that made our Amana possible. Sacrifices were made for him. Be grateful! Nico stood on the shoulders of giants. Look how far they'd come since Enrique immigrated to America from Spain in 1920.

"We eating at the table tonight?" he asked, starting to set out places with silverware.

"Of course," his mother said. Dinner every Sunday was in the dining room. Most other nights they ate off TV trays so Maury could watch his primetime favorites. Nico set out the silverware and came back to pick up the glasses. Annabel stepped in front of him. "Give us a hug."

"I already gave us one."

"Well, give us another." He let himself be embraced, holding onto glasses. He set the glasses down and gave his mother a big squeeze.

Maury pitched forward in his recliner and pushed himself up. He hobbled to the dinner table. Family night was Annabelle's show, but hearing Maury say grace was something amusing to behold.

"It's good to have you home, Nicky." Annabelle patted his hand.

"Thanks, mom." Maury was right. She would never leave her world of Bing Crosby, Bob Hope, and Dorothy Lamour, Donald O'Connor and the Three Stooges. Just like Maury's fantasy world of Westerns with Audie Murphy, James Stewart, and John Wayne, riding over the ridge with colors flying, bugles blowing. The good guys always saved the day. But no cavalry could save Maury from the rapid break-down of his paper-thin lungs under repeated fits of coughing.

Nico didn't believe his parents could stomach the truth about Vietnam. They had been insulated by propaganda and false patriotism. Americans weren't the good guys in this one. You can hold the mirror of reality at odd angles and reflect a different truth, but it came down to Nico having served his country, contributing to the war effort, or at least helping a little with troop readiness.

He made it through dinner on small talk. While he cleared the dinner table and loaded the dishwasher, his mother brought him a news clipping. It was a serviceman update from *The Idaho Statesman*. Nico sat on a stool at the breakfast bar and pressed the wrinkled paper flat:

Local hero awarded Silver Star

Jesse Walker, 23, of Boise, Idaho, was awarded the Silver Star for Conspicuous Gallantry in Action during a ceremony in the office of Idaho Senator Frank Church at the State Capitol Building on Thursday afternoon. Senator Church, in presenting the award, commended Warrant Officer Walker who "distinguished himself for exceptional valorous action" while serving with the

First Cavalry (Airmobile) in the Central Highlands of Vietnam. According to the citation, Walker's actions saved several lives and represented the highest traditions of military service reflecting great credit upon himself, his unit and the United States Army.

"Wow!" Nico was impressed. "What did he do?"

"I don't know," Annabelle answered. "The paper never followed up."

* * *

Frosty set up TV trays for dessert and Nico carried in the almond tart with sweet Basque cream and Annabelle brought fresh coffee. In the Bilbao home, hot coffee brewed 12 hours a day. It was not just a morning drink.

Halfway through the tart, Nico retrieved his daypack. When he heard Uncle Frosty was going to be there, he decided to bring Maury his Vietnam Service Medal and Purple Heart. "Will you keep these for me, dad?" he asked. Maury held the medals in one hand, his cigarette in the other, smoke trailing up, shredded by the ceiling fan. Nico reached again into the daypack and pulled out the NVA F-1 grenade given to him by Colonel Jefferson Hedges.

Annabel fluttered her fingers nervously, voice tightening. "Is that a *live* grenade?"

"No, mom," Nico reassured her, "it's disarmed."

Maury laid his Camel into the ashtray and held out his hand. Nico dropped the grenade and Maury weighed it against the medals. He set the grenade down on the tray and studied the medals.

Frosty, who didn't have either of those medals, picked up the grenade. "Where'd you buy this?"

"It was a gift from a colonel."

As a Korean War veteran, Frosty considered himself an expert on war. He'd read an article or two about the Tet and May offensives. He quizzed Nico on how Charlie got so close to the embassy in Saigon. Nico shook his head. Didn't anyone check for tunnels? Nico shrugged. Everybody knows gooks dig tunnels. If politicians like Frank Church, Wayne Morse and Eugene McCarthy kept their noses out of the military's business we could win this thing and bring our boys home. We can't let some backward communist country of Munchkins force America to withdraw. Frosty's face was pink with passion. "Our hands are tied," he said. "Church is a god-damned traitor. I ain't voting for him again."

"You never voted for him in the first place," Maury pointed out, setting the medals down and picking up the still-burning Camel, waving it like a pointer.

"Somebody must have."

"At least Church stands for something," Nico blurted.

After four beers, Frosty's true warp showed through the veil of family tolerance. "Like those long-haired protesters? The government ought to pluck every one of those over-privileged middle-class deferments off the picket lines and ship their asses straight to 'Nam."

"Yes," Nico said, "so we can save the Vietnamese from the Communists by blowing up their villages!"

Maury clicked his cheek impatiently. Things were getting out of control and there weren't any more games on TV.

"It's about honoring our word to an ally," Frosty hissed. "It's about containing Communism and supporting Democracy."

Nico borrowed from his father's professional lexicon. "That's a load of shit. We're not interested in democracy for Vietnam. We opposed free elections in 1956 because we were afraid Ho Chi Minh would win."

Having seen firsthand the outcome of his country's involvement in Southeast Asia, Nico didn't sit still for lectures. But his mother did not stand for her son being disrespectful to a relative. "I don't know who *you* are, but I want my son back."

Her words stung the breath out of him. Who would have thought such a sweet and petite French Catholic girl curled up inside the thick shell of her heritage could have such an impact. He wanted to scream back, *Look deeper, mom. Underneath all the cynicism and lost faith, I'm still here!* But Nico held his silence because he, too, felt the loss.

"I was in Korea," Frosty lectured. A chunk of almond shot off the track of his tongue with the plosive *k*.

"I meant no disrespect." Nico opened his eyes. "I've just heard so much propaganda."

"The North Koreans backed us up 'til our butts dipped in the Sea of Japan," Frosty went on. "We would've ended it quickly if the Chinese hadn't entered it. You guys have been fighting a guerrilla war of ambushes and small skirmishes. In three years, the North Koreans and Chinese suffered one and a half million dead or wounded. We were fighting for inches. You guys are counting bodies."

Nico thought some Asian wisdom might be useful. "Cut off the head of a dragon and two grow back."

"What's that supposed to mean?"

"We're occupying their country."

"And now you all come home and we're supposed to treat you like war heroes? What did you do? Kiss ass and play chauffeur to your Colonel? Now we owe you an education? G.I. home loan? For what? So you can join the demonstrators?"

In managing The Splendors, Nico ran into guys selling off supplies with a handshake and justifying it as good old American capitalism. Name of the game: *Let's Make A Deal.* It got the United States Manhattan Island for a handful of beads.

Nico didn't claim to be a hero, but he'd known some. They were just guys who drank too much and told scary stories to children. They walked straight out of the bush, dragging sweaty asses onto a cool stool in some dark interior, shaking red dust out of their hair. They'd been touched somehow. After downing straight vermouth over ice, they washed the blood off their fatigues. Some had an air about them. They resonated with another frequency like shamans beating drums as they walked in two worlds. A deep silence settled over them like thick fog. Their eyes made him feel uneasy then, just as he made friends and relatives feel uneasy now.

Coming home to Boise from Vietnam was like coming back from Mars. His mother worried about what had possessed him. She kept trying to recover her son, one hug at a time.

6.

"Return to Sender" came through the speakers in the locker room. Milo shed his rubber boots and yellow slicker, hosed them down and hung 'em up in the locker. He knocked a *Kool* from the pack and lit up. The menthol hacked his ragged lungs.

Geo chided Milo about smoking. Milo called him a hypocrite. A pretend model of good health practices. He consumed junk food like a buck in a campground, yet never gained a pound. If there's a lesson there, it's that life was unfair. Milo accumulated so much crud in his pipes he required regular appointments with Roto-Rooter. Unusual dry weather had dislodged some gunk from his lungs he could only cough up. Milo might be a member of the Finnish Brotherhood, but he seemed maladapted to Astoria. That's why Geo called him "Sunny."

Geo's locker door slammed open and he unbuttoned the white coverall. He was shorter than Milo, but stockier, broad chested and had a thick neck that could hit you like a linebacker. He may be a tough guy, but he wasn't nearly as self-assured as he looked. His father was an asshole who bullied him all the time. The day was coming when Geo Kaartinen wouldn't leave his rage on the football field.

Milo, by comparison, was the golden boy, over six feet tall, blond hair and lean body. He attracted girls but didn't know what to do about it as he was also bashful, reticent and susceptible to dark moods. It was Geo's perception that Milo brought out a woman's need to nurture. He said Milo could use that. Use his soft voice that aroused the feminine heart. Let his gray-blue eyes reveal the civil war in a poet's soul.

Elvis gave way to Sedaka. The locker room banter turned into a bitch session. Milo was repeating the latest conspiracy theory: John F. Kennedy was an alien. Milo preferred verbiage over reality. You could shape reality with enough words and an aptitude for puzzles. You could make fun of anything if you had enough words.

Geo winced as he sloughed the coveralls from his shoulders. His rash was spreading.

"How long you had that?" Milo asked.

A red patch forked down under Geo's left shoulder blade just out of reach. He backed up and scratched against the door jamb with orgasmic relief.

The Hangover Twins, Hank and Jim, hobbled in from the boxcars, arguing over who was responsible for a stack of canned tuna cases coming down on Jim's ankle. Jim's wide beam dropped onto the wooden bench. Hank kneeled in front of his brother and cut off the rubber boot with a butcher knife from the tuna line. Jim's lower fibula protruded through the skin above the ankle. Hank elevated his brother's leg on an upside-down plastic bucket with a rolled-up towel. The foot dangled, barely held together by a skein of skin. But he was smiling and there was no blood. Milo thought of the butcher who lost her thumb. Neither felt pain.

"If you'd listened..." Hank shook his head.

"Can you put it back?"

Hank jammed the broken foot hard onto Jim's ankle, wrapping it in gauze and taping it tight. There was little in the first aid kit that would help much.

"Thanks, bro."

The Hangover Twins were actually younger than Milo and Geo. Side by side, they were two-year lettermen anchoring the Fishermen's defensive line. Tough guys too;

stoic, with a high pain threshold. Milo wondered if a high pain threshold made for better sex. You know, getting the job done even when it hurts. You'd think he was a wuss, face and neck throbbing, cheek stiff with emergency room stitches, coughing phlegm into a coffee cup.

Geo contorted his body to "Little Town Flirt" standing in front of the full-length mirror trying to glimpse the rash on his back. "Man, it wasn't so bad this morning."

"Maybe it's a heat rash," Milo teased, "from rubbing up against Gayleen?"

"Just my luck if I was *allergic.*"

Geo squeezed the thick muscle at the back of his neck.

Hank and Jim stared.

"What ya gawking at?" Geo bared his teeth.

Hank stepped closer, inspecting Geo's back.

"Wow! That's some rash, kid."

"*Kid?* When I was with your momma last night she screamed *Man, oh Man.*"

Taunting didn't ruffle Hank. "You're struttin' hot stuff there, Lone Ranger." He kicked off his boots, lifted his right foot up onto the bench and pulled up his pant leg. Dark splotches afflicted his calf. "I was just curious...then maybe I got this from your girl?"

Jim opened his coveralls and parted a thicket of chest hair, scratching with the backs of his nails. "Yeah, Geo, your girl's giving us all an itch."

Geo stayed cool. "Bite me, King Kong."

The broken ankle didn't faze Jim much; it was the rash that was driving him crazy. The three compared their rashes. Milo stood off in an uneasy silence as they sized him up.

"Guess I'm the only one who *wasn't* with your girl last night, Geo."

The Hangover Twins laughed at that.

Geo wagged his finger. "That's real funny, Sunny."

Milo's reflection in the mirror, in damp Fruit-of-the-Looms, blond bangs falling onto his forehead, wavered. The drowned man materialized behind his back in the glass in front of him, rising from a briny deep. His reflection warped as the drowned man stepped through and displaced him in the mirror. For a second the drowned man's restored body appeared swaddled in white bandages, neck swollen from flying rounds of white albacore. Milo glanced back but saw no one behind him. In the mirror, the drowned man swung his sledge-hammer and the mirror exploded into glittering glass. Water poured through the breach, spilling gray bodies onto the floor.

Milo blinked hard. The glass was still intact but the reflection wavered.

"I feel dizzy," he said, turning away from the mirror and closing his eyes. "Do I look warped to you?"

"Don't worry, Sunny, it's your normal." Hank sniggered. He'd changed into street clothes and was guiding his socks over the bloodless foot, leaving them bunched at the ankle.

"That's what I told Monica. She wants you to prove it. How warped can you be?" Geo said, pulling on stretch Levis.

Milo's reflection oscillated in perfect time with his breathing. "It feels like a mirage."

"A mirage is something you see, not feel," Hank said, snatching up a pair of dirty briefs from his bag and tossing it at Milo. They landed on his head. He elbowed Milo. "Hey Sunny, you and skinhead there should work the boxes. I think the sun's gettin' to ya."

"Yeah," his brother chimed in, "you're lookin' pale. Better ask Brown to get you out of the sun."

Milo snatched the briefs off his head. "Like I need advice from the Tweedle-twins."

Geo placed the back of his hand on Milo's forehead. "You get whacked on the noggin with that boom? Just ignore them."

Hank and Jim exchanged glances, eyebrows arching together.

"I'm fine."

"We should double tonight. Look here." Geo produced a box of Trojans from his sports bag. "Boy Scout motto. *Be Prepared*. How far you gone with Monica?"

The Hangovers leaned in.

Milo shook his head. "None of your business."

"He's dating one of the most beautiful girls in school and doesn't know what to do with her," Geo winked at Jim and Hank.

"Yeah?" The linemen chimed in unison, sitting half-dressed on the bench with arms around each other. "We can show ya."

"You can share with us. What can we help you with?" Geo coaxed.

Milo wiped his armpits with a towel, reached for his Right Guard. "It's nobody's business."

"Tag. You're out! Caught sliding into second base, huh?" Hank speculated.

"Sunny can't find second base," Jim said.

The Hangovers laughed and punched each other in the shoulder.

Hank unlaced Jim's tennis shoe and helped slip it over the swollen foot. It at least helped to hold the broken ankle together a little longer.

"Nobody here's had less sex than Sunny," Jim teased, standing up on one leg. "Except maybe Brown. Brown's not been laid since the Korean War. Did you notice if he had a rash?"

Geo shook his head.

"See. There you have it," Jim concluded. "Mystery solved."

"That filly of yours looks ready for breeding, Sunny," Hank replied, clicking his tongue. "If you're not man enough, just let me know. Glad to step in."

Milo reached deep for a comeback but his pockets were bare. "Assholes."

Hopping up on one leg, Jim turned to his brother. "What'd he call us?"

Hank placed a calming hand on his brother's shoulder. "He was only joking, right Sunny?"

Milo nodded. "Yeah, just joking."

Jim leaned on his brother and limped through the door. Hank muttered, "Hope that ankle's better by the time we open the season."

Geo slapped Old Spice on his cheek and switched off the radio. *That blue ball blindness drives me off the road*, he crooned without a tune, scratching his armpit and watching white flakes fall onto his pant leg. He splashed more aftershave into his palms, rubbed them together and sniffed his hands. He slapped some on his chest for good measure. "So what do ya say? Double tonight after sauna?"

The Finnish Brotherhood owned a sauna and it was ritual for Geo every Friday night. Milo went along because Geo claimed it would sweat the sludge out of his lungs. Just look at Eino Mattson. He smoked and drank and chased women and still had a powerful set of lungs. Milo respected Eino as a fisherman and a man with tradition, but now that he was dating Milo's mom he was more circumspect when it came to Eino and women. Eino sat up there, high in the steam, on a cedar bench, beating his back raw with a juniper and yanking the cord over and over for more steam until Milo and Geo bailed.

"I'm picking up Monica. We're going to the A&W."

"Yeah? What about after that? Ain't your mom on graveyard? I get it. You wanna be alone." Geo ran his comb through butch hair and wet his finger to lay down his cowlick.

"Can't be alone if you're there."

"It's a big house."

Milo made a deal with Mindy, his sixteen-year-old sister. If she did an overnighter with Francie, he would give her two 45s, The Beach Boys' "Surfin' USA" and Orbison's "Leah" with "Workin' for the Man" on the flip side. Plus, he'd do her dishes for a week. She wanted Orbison's "In Dreams," but that would have been a deal breaker.

At the cannery door leading out to the parking lot, Milo checked the sky. Storm clouds stacked up over the ocean, growing darker by the minute. Ominous thunder rolled across the sky.

7.

Major Whitney Pratt gently massaged Nico's scalp. The hair had grown back ghost gray where the neurosurgeon at McChord performed surgery on the fractured skull. Hot shrapnel from the landmine crushed and depressed part of the frontal lobe and bruised his brain. He suffered no permanent damage, but didn't trust his memory. The sequence, from jeep to Chu Len and Lu Bien, Pleiku evacuation to Tan Son Nhut, then to McChord, blurred together. The Air Force expedited his medical discharge at Fort Lewis. Now he was in an outpatient program through the V.A. Regional Hospital in Boise.

Nico couldn't read what the Major jotted down on a pad, but it didn't look like a prescription. "The wound is healing nicely, but let's get a picture just to be sure." He patted Nico on the shoulder. "Since the Government's paying for it."

Nico headed to x-ray. Just to be sure. He couldn't be sure of anything—except maybe the fact Boise had changed. America had changed. He no longer identified much with either. He confronted the day with psychic numbness, voluntary isolation and visions of the unwelcome wounded. It took conscious effort not to surrender to depression. He sometimes wanted to pull out his own hair. His only companions were daytime television and classic movies. Ennui became Nico's training partner who lacked passion and compassion, who left him sitting on the couch in front of Queen for a Day.

All over the country, vets in V.A. hospitals, still looking for a way home. Boise was no different. Viet vets in wheelchairs, in drug rehab, engaging in rap sessions to talk out the ghosts among brothers, sharing whatever capacity they had to cope as they coughed up lungs into handkerchiefs. We come through a gauntlet of the wounded and the forgotten. Nico glimpsed a handsome young man with blond hair. The man turned into the light of the x-ray waiting room. One side of his face was disfigured—pink from grafts, scarred pate wrinkled with patchy implants, ear gone, nose reconstructed. When Nico looked again, there was an empty chair.

Nico crossed the lobby and sat down opposite the empty chair. He picked up the most recent issue of *Time* and started reading an article with one eye, the other watching the empty chair. The U.S. was withdrawing 25,000 troops. That would leave a mere half million in-country. The war was winding down. The withdrawal marked the first decrease in the escalation of American troops in Vietnam since 1950. The war was shifting to incremental withdrawals as the news magazines reported on a conflicted America in the throes of dissent and political upheaval. The country was a war zone.

***

The road back to the real world was marked with sharp curves including the rap group that met in a clinic on Thursdays under the watchful eye of the group leader, "Doc" Mayfield.

Since coming back to Boise, the numbness spread from Nico's body into his mind and back into his body twofold. When he couldn't stand the pain any longer he'd numbed himself and collapsed inward. When he couldn't stand the numbness any longer he'd sought out mutual therapy. That was when he was referred to Mayfield's group, which called itself the Peace Action Strike Team.

Mark Mayfield didn't get his nickname for bedside manner. He wasn't even a real doctor. He was a therapist by virtue of having survived in the bush. He was a straight-shooter who prescribed to the 5 Ps: **prior planning prevents poor performance.** Doc didn't fit the stereotype of a bush Marine. Despite a good education, he passed on officer's training, went in the draft and volunteered to become a Marine. Doc earned respect as a savvy combat squad leader, a Lance Corporal for the 26th Marines.

Doc believed you're the sum of your choices. Those choices created a deep pattern analogous to a well-established streambed. Now gravity flowed into a path of least resistance, followed the "easy" way. Doc insisted being human wasn't about the easy way. The struggle for greater awareness was like the salmon swimming against the current, overcoming obstacles, all the way, without surrendering.

"Awareness precedes change," Doc said. "Change requires intentional acts of liberty against the habitual pull of gravity. You see, change means going *against*, not *with* the flow."

Without question, these ideas were revolutionary and the two most militant members often set the tone for the PAST: Doc and Pat.

Pat Parsons was scrappy and muscular. He carried the M-79 in Doc's rifle squad. When he smiled you didn't know what the brother was thinking. Parsons' discharge came only days after Martin Luther King's assassination and it brought him to Black Power. Doc was discharged six months before Parsons, but he kept in touch. When Parsons got out, Doc rode his Harley down to Oakland to pick him up. The first thing Parsons did was buy an Electra Glide and return with Doc to Boise. Parsons didn't fight for America to come home and become anybody's nigger. He was open in group about his hope in coming to Boise, that it would be a color-blind brave new world with hippie brothers and sisters, all part of one big village. His *Soul on Ice* did not come without a cost. Parsons told good war stories while Doc kept pointing to the map and telling us how to triangulate and follow the right directions home.

Doc and Pat were solid partners. They fought back-to-back on nameless jungle trails. They had a battle-tested friendship. Nico envied that. Martin Luther King once said, "We have been repeatedly faced with the cruel irony of watching Negro and white boys on TV screens as they kill and die together for an America where they can't sit together in a classroom." Doc and Pat were beyond any of those artificial boundaries.

Another of the group, Donny Sunderman, reminded Nico of Mick Jagger. He was homely and awkward, until he ripped off a riff on his Telecaster. By then everybody was listening. Nico heard him perform as lead guitarist for Charity Drive and the guy underwent some freakish transformation on stage. Girls flocked to him like he was the Pied Piper. The group, Charity Hope, was named after the front vocalist who had a rich alto voice and bad girl angst that won her a modest following in the valley. But Donny's energy-charged leads so competed for attention that he finally broke off and formed Double Barrel with a 17-year-old guitar phenom, Terry Clancy.

Josh Brownton, another founding member of the Peace Action Strike Team along with Mark Mayfield and Pat Parsons, saved his family embarrassment by choosing against a career in the military. Only an error in replication of Brownton DNA—the same DNA that produced his grandfather, Colonel Jedediah Brownton, a hero in the First World War, and his dad, a judge in Adams County—could explain offspring like Josh, an ex-clerk typist, stoned more often than not. Already a disappointment to the clan, Josh decided to play the gadfly, promoting peace and love with impeccable dress and a good recipe for marijuana brownies.

Then there's Manny Hernandez, who came into group about the same time as Nico. He was a former tight end with the Nampa Bulldogs. The t-shirt he wore could not conceal the muscles underneath. On the t-shirt was a grinning skull inside a Nazi helmet. *Born to Be Wild* writ in lightning shot through the helmet. Manny's bicep touted the tattoo: *3/27-Vietnam.* He was a radio operator with the 3rd Battalion/27th Marines, stationed north of Da Nang in '66-67. Sheltered in a command bunker, he never saw any real action, but a hung bomb dropped once too close for comfort, killing three. His obsession with skulls and zombies and the color black actually pre-dated the War, but he liked that people had the impression he might have fought the Cong hand-to-hand.

Two strong views were the high and low tides of the PAST. Doc and Pat fed them a kind of cowboy pessimism in the face of power that rebelled by throwing the gauntlet of life as constant struggle. "Peace is just another word for sleep," Doc said. "The comfort of the norm is self-indulgence. Strive for self-realization. The Warrior's active engagement with the *now* reaffirms his role in choosing a more difficult path. Live more fully on the journey to selfhood. That's what we have."

Nico wasn't quite ready to concede any guru status to Doc. The Veterans clinic was not part of the hospital but they had comfortable couches, plenty of coffee, cookies and a good stereo for their sessions. Sometimes they just listened to music. In some ways it felt like a quiet revolt because you couldn't talk about Vietnam without expressing feelings about the government. Doc was a smart guy, but his politics left little room for reconciliation.

Until Vietnam, Nico never feared the dark. He could lay awake in the dark and imagine anything without ever feeling threatened. Now darkness teemed with presences, some hostile. The PAST had become his new family. He hung out with them, played cribbage with them, lounged in the grass under shade trees with them on a hot day sweating in a G.I. jacket. He watched with a sense of nostalgia as those untouched by war floated by, lighter than air.

Nico agreed with a lot of what Doc said, but sometimes he felt obligated to challenge his ideas. This was the very basis of a two-party system. "What could be more revolutionary than the People choosing their own leaders? Doesn't revolution always result in a new order? How long will it take for the new order to start its own army?" he said.

When Nico was in Pleiku he learned a distinction American Buddhists called 'big boat' and 'little boat' in relation to the search for truth. Little boat was a philosophy for hermits, focusing on saving yourself, in hopes that one at a time the world would save enough to save itself. Big boat philosophy could be compared to the captain of a ship refusing to launch until everyone was on board. Both visions had negative aspects—the negative hermit might commit suicide; the negative captain might sink with everybody on the ship.

Nico didn't know which way Doc tipped. He was a natural leader who refused to lead. His opinion meant everything to a few. He didn't like the idea of leaders. The war could not be fought without support back home. The PAST should erode that support. American casualties in the Tet and the media coverage afterward steeled public sentiment against the war. "Are we to be counted amongst Nixon's 'silent majority'?" he asked. "Or is it time for a revolution?"

Sometimes Nico could see how the clinic was a good place for these sessions. A safe environment in which to hang out, drink your own beer and play cribbage. The PAST was contributing to revolution about as much as a ladies reading circle contributed to the behavior of young women.

Even in Bermuda shorts and Hawaiian shirt, with one eye on a cribbage board to keep Parsons from cheating, Doc looked mercenary. He wasn't just smart, but decorated.

"I think it's time we made some kind of statement," Doc said.

Pat nodded in agreement. "Yeah, let's blow something up--anything. You can pick."

"I mean we need to bring the war home to the average American reclining in a La-Z-Boy while watching the war on the evening news."

Nico's father rode the recliner through war one minute then *Bonanza* the next. There was no reality anymore, only good guys and bad guys. Still, his father wasn't the enemy.

"The Black Panthers," Parsons explained, "turned down the sound on the boob tube during coverage of the riots in Watts and read the Declaration of Independence *out loud* from the back of the room. It was effective, man."

Doc nodded and pitched again. "Thomas Jefferson wrote that the new always struggles against the old. But the new always wins. It's taken a century since the Civil War for blacks to finally declare their freedom. Freedom is liberation."

"Yeah but we're already getting a bum rap in the community." Nico was having second thoughts. "People think we're a bunch of druggies."

"We *are*." Josh opened a plate of his famous brownies and passed it around.

"Okay then, they think we're a bunch of *losers*." Nico countered, as if there was a distinction to be made.

"So?" Mayfield shook his head. "Fuck the community!"

Parson took up the chant, FUCK THE COMMUNITY! Donny and Manny joined in. FUCK THE COMMUNITY!

Nico stuck to his guns. "We can't alienate everybody. We gotta move beyond this posture of opposition and stand *for* something."

"Who alienated who?" Doc interjected.

"I'm just saying we should at least operate within the law..." Nico argued.

Mayfield chuckled. "There's a lot of *we* in there, sarge."

Josh chomped on a brownie and spit out crumbs. "Sometimes the laws are just *wrong*, man! Aren't we obligated to do something?"

"The chocolate's addictive, dude." Manny lifted his shirt, showed his hairy belly.

"If we break a law," Nico tried to reason, "aren't we still responsible for breaking it?"

"And we *should* be responsible," Doc confirmed. "Responsibility needs a person who makes his own choices instead of letting someone else make them for him."

Donny put The Beatles' White Album on the stereo. He then pulled around a folding chair and sat down backwards, chin on his arms. "*Representative* democracy. We choose the people we want to make fun of us."

"A lot of *we* in there." Doc said, scratching his chin.

Parsons scratched his ear. "Okay, just 'cause you vote don't mean you give up your voice the next day. Sometimes you break a law to draw attention to it when it hurts people. It's called raising consciousness." When nobody laughed, he went on. "I'm not being represented. You're not being represented. There is no representative government. We live in a military-industrial complex."

In the great war, Nico's dad walked through ruined land and bombed-out towns in France, cheered by the liberated and welcomed as liberators. Freedom was liberation. Maury couldn't imagine America as an invader in Vietnam. Nico knew he had been part of an occupying force. As the conflict wore on, borders had as much meaning as restraint. North and South Vietnam didn't exist, only an enemy, an enemy that came through Cambodia. The Vietnamese people blamed America, and America blamed the Communists.

Nico's never-in-combat wounds taught him to trust his instincts. Maybe conflict could be avoided. You could have a *feel* for things without always walking point. He didn't trust appearances. He treated what he saw on the news or read in the media as pure fiction.

Everywhere Nico looked, the American Dream had washed into gray. The sameness of Nico's hometown was an easy illusion. On the surface, the old neighborhood hadn't changed. The Union Pacific railroad depot still overlooked Capitol Boulevard and ran straight to the lighted dome of the state capitol building. The lure of the Highlands brought adventuresome kids to assault bike paths in the foothills of North Boise. Each day more tri-level homes appeared on paved cul-de-sacs around Camelsback Park. Ann Morrison and Julia Davis Parks, lying in cool splendor beside the Boise River, were still the havens he remembered. The groomed manors of Warm Springs Avenue still pointed with pride to the privileged. That much had not changed

Familiar landmarks wouldn't bring Nico back to where he once was. He couldn't change the fact he now possessed second sight when it came to home—saw the deep shadows tugging the edges of reality, the uncovered manholes more felt than seen.

At the check-out stand in the M&W market on State Street, the white-haired clerk, Bo, was still checking. Nico went through the line to buy a six pack of Coors. "Ain't seen you around for a while," Bo remarked.

Nico didn't mention the war, but said he'd been recovering from an accident.

"Sorry, son. What happened?" Bo asked, curious.

Nico pointed to his ear. "Head injury. Can't remember much."

Back with the PAST, "As My Guitar Gently Weeps" carried Nico to a place he'd never been. He took a breath and closed his eyes. But he couldn't stop thinking about how to respond to Doc and Parsons. They were taking the PAST in the wrong direction. He might not see fireworks on the backs of his eyelids like Doc, but he'd gazed over the smoking slag of his life and found some answers. He looked out the clinic window and saw a familiar landmark.

Jesse Walker walked down the sidewalk.

Jesse Walker had been Nico's competition for Coco Bird since they'd attended Lowell Elementary. On and off over the years through North Junior High and Boise High, the threesome revolved around each other in a strange dynamic.

Nico recognized Jesse's stride. He leaned forward at the waist like the White Rabbit in a rush to nowhere. Short brown hair. Thick neck. Unmistakeable gait. Nico rubbed the nostalgia out of his eyes and rushed out the door to catch up to him. "Excuse me," he called. Jesse kept walking. "Ex-CUSE me!" It must have sounded like a sneeze.

Jesse turned around. He was wearing a black turtleneck under a Stinker Station black and yellow racing jacket. The solemn brown eyes caused Nico to pull up short. It *was* Jesse Walker, wasn't it? Maybe, but not the one he knew.

"Jess, hey man. How ya been?" Nico forced a smile. He stepped up and touched Jesse's shoulder and offered his hand. Jesse extended a prosthetic that opened with a whir. Nico could only stare. He finally grasped the plastic hand and squeezed. When the plastic squeezed back, he wanted to pull away. "Wow! What happened?"

Jesse stared over Nico's shoulder. "Too long a story for a brief visit." His voice was unruffled by Nico's silent panic.

"Read somewhere you were flying slicks for the First Cav?"

"That's right," Jesse said.

"We were practically neighbors," Nico cracked a lame smile. "4th Infantry. Pleiku."

"Yeah? So why're *you* here?" Jesse nodded to the clinic door.

"Check-up. They want to inspect my head." Nico touched his scalp and winced. "They put a plate in it."

They faced each other in silence. Jesse stared out through these black holes surrounded by an intense field of gravity. *No Trespassing* signs were nailed onto his eyeballs. Too many combat vets returned from 'Nam still missing in action, war casualties pulling the trigger by reflex long after the ammo was gone. Most of the guys Nico knew weren't that way. Some were otherworldly calm after being awakened, as if a mask insulated their true self from any psychic numbness. Whatever happened within the group reached into the soul, something they did not show people much. Jesse spared them the madness of where he'd been.

Nico stumbled around small talk as Jesse looked anxious to move on. Nico pinched the arm of Jesse's silk jacket. "You take to the track?"

"Like I was born to it."

"Win any?"

"Some. You still a crack mechanic?"

"I suppose so."

"Good." Jesse's interest piqued.

"Heard from Coco?" Nico asked. "She wrote for a while, then the letters stopped coming. Seen her since you got back?"

Jesse raised his head. "Yeah, yeah, I married her." He felt for his jacket pocket and pulled out a business card. "Give Harley a call. Team's looking for an engine man."

Team? Nico glanced at the card: Harley Cavanaugh, Chief Mechanic, Stinker Station Racing Team. "Thanks. I'll do that. Say hi to Coco for me."

Jesse got into a GTO and drove off.

In group, Nico showed the business card.

Doc said, "Yeah, Walker. He's been referred to the group."

Manny said, "I'm on the team. I told the owners I was in a group. They thought maybe Walker might need one."

8.

Milo drummed the steering wheel of his '57 Bel Air in time to Del Shannon, following the flight of the organ down a dark and rainy night.

Question: Which drew more attention at the A&W? His sweet Cherry 2-door hardtop or his girl, Monica? Milo felt like a lucky bastard.

"Does it hurt?" Monica touched the bandage on his cheek.

"Quit changing the subject," he said.

"You're weirding me out."

Monica cozied up, white-pleated skirt riding over plump knees, legs in red tights straddling the emerald gearshift knob. Foreplay was Monica squealing as he down-shifted on the back road to Seaside, as he rammed his fist up between her thighs. He could still feel her gripping his leg at the sudden acceleration of the 350 cubic inch engine.

Milo was feeling pretty important with Monica beside him, her blonde hair in a Sandra Dee flip, A&W frosted lips sipping from the frosted mug. He couldn't read all the signs so had to trust his feelings. There was always the risk of doing too much or too little. He was supposed to know. Shouldn't he know these things? She laid her head on his chest, nudging him with her chin. Was she asking for a kiss? Milo had no father or uncle to give him advice, only Geo.

"So now the hammer man is dragging this sledgehammer around behind him." Milo dropped his head back and bit off successive chunks of steaming fry. "I'm serious. Then just like that—he's gone. I mean he crosses over."

Monica pinched the last quarter of burger between painted nails. "Crosses over what?"

"I don't know. A bridge maybe? Or like a ship crossing the bar into another dimension."

"You're scaring me," Monica complained. "I don't like ghosts."

"Don't you think fear is just God's way of helping people appreciate what they have?" Milo set the empty mugs on the rubber matting of the tray. "Take Cuba..."

"Please don't," Monica sighed, knowing where this was headed. "I hate politics."

"I thought you hated ghosts."

"I just don't like politics. Now ghosts I hate," she said.

The carhop skated over to the Bel Air. She was wearing a short orange waitress dress with black apron, black headpiece and knee-high orange socks. One of her skates gave out, crashing the poor girl in a heap. She sat up on the blacktop, bare knees scraped from concrete. Her name was Gayleen. She was Geo's girlfriend. After removing the skate and inspecting it, Gayleen got up and tried to smooth a bloodless flap of skin back over her knee, but otherwise none the worse for wear. She limped over to the car, one hand holding the ruined skate, the other pressing the flesh into place.

"Need anything?" Gayleen asked. Her funny lips were smudged, the little black cap knocked akimbo.

"Where'd you learn to skate, the roller derby?" Milo joked. He realized too late that it sounded cruel. Monica looked embarrassed.

Gayleen blew a tangle of red hair from her eyes and set the skate down to pull the tray off the car window. When the tray was balanced, she picked up the skate again and limped back to the pick-up window.

Monica reprimanded Milo, "That wasn't nice."

"I didn't mean to make fun of her," Milo said. He leaned in for a kiss. Monica pecked his cheek.

"She *did* look silly."

"That's all I was saying." Milo cranked the ignition key. Cherry started up. The engine revved and they rocked with a low rumble.

Monica stroked his thigh as he backed out of the parking spot. Her touch was soft and distracting. He didn't notice the hammer man slip into the rear view mirror. By the time he saw his slimy skin and snake eyes, sledgehammer on its head by his side, Milo's foot was slow to the brake.

Milo swore he heard "If I Had a Hammer" come on the radio as the hammer man hefted his hammer. He wore a floppy hat and slicker like some whaler from the 19th century. Smoke from a black stogie curled into the air as from a steamship.

"WHAT?" Monica's eyes flashed with alarm.

Milo stomped the brakes again and again, but Cherry didn't stop. He cranked the wheel, heard a *whump*. The car kept rolling until the back bumper struck the A&W signpost and jolted to a stop.

"What's wrong with you?" Monica's ashen face turned crimson with anger.

Milo climbed out of the car. The hammer man crossed over, singing "If I Had a Hammer," light pouring in around him.

* * *

Milo leaned against Cherry's back bumper considering the hammer man as Sphere in Flatland. One night before school let out, this local, Johnny Evenfall, and his California surfer buddy, Monterey Jack, initiated Milo into their secret sect. They had access to the old bunkers at Fort Stevens so made a special night of Milo's initiation. They drank beer and talked about the supernatural, mused about the meaning of life in the face of nuclear war and UFOs, the opportunities of unexplored dimensions in the footsteps of Charles Fort. The strangeness of frogs raining from the sky, vanishings, abductions, and the lanterns of Atlantis led Johnny to tell Milo about The Ghosthole. The Ghosthole, it seemed, was the real reason the Columbia Bar was called the Pacific Graveyard. An interdimensional portal appeared now and then, he said, at the mouth of the river.

A '62 Ford Fairlane pulled into the A&W parking lot way too fast. The Fairlane's brakes failed. The car jumped the curb, ramming the passenger side of a red Pontiac. Hamburgers, fries and milkshakes hit the blacktop. This angry Neanderthal with flat nose and low forehead emerged from the Pontiac. He grabbed Tiny Carlito, a skinny kid of sixteen, by the scruff of his windbreaker and punched him in the gut. Milo wanted to intervene, but a voice told him, *It's not your fight.*

"Do something!" Monica admonished.

By the time Milo acted, Tiny was writhing on the ground and the pugilist was running flat hands over his damaged Pontiac whimpering, "Look what you did."

"Do something," Monica repeated.

Milo climbed back into Cherry, fired up the engine and drove away.

Minutes later, Milo and Monica mounted the steps of a 65-year-old two-story Queen Anne with a plaque out front. The house was on a hill overlooking the Columbia River.

"Why didn't you help Tiny?" Monica wondered aloud, unable to hide her disappointment.

"Because it *was* his fault."

"So he deserved to get beaten?"

"No. But it was on Wallace's property and he called the cops." Wallace owned the A&W and he tolerated a lot of teen behavior, but never a fight.

At two hours before dusk, the sun was high in the west. Sunlight torched the top edges of a bank of clouds, the clouds with dark bellies letting down squalls on the horizon. The leading edge of the cloud bank stopped three miles offshore. North wind stirred the hot July air.

Milo felt like he'd failed an important test.

9.

Nico's tour of duty amounted to little more than mind-less routine and banking a welfare check. Who was he to criticize his uncle? He was privileged with discounts at the PX, bought new stereo equipment, the latest LPs, a Nikon camera. He drove an officer's jeep as if it were his own. He gave little thought to less fortunate draftees hunkered under mortar fire in sandbag bunkers.

In one moment his life changed in ways he couldn't have imagined. Instead of a secret handshake from the Colonel for scoring two gorgeous bargirls, Nico landed smack dab in the middle of bedlam. There were no safe places in Vietnam, but Nico cultivated a false sense of security under the Colonel's protection. If he couldn't see the enemy, the enemy couldn't see him. The mission to Kon Barr, the Colonel assured him, would be a field trip.

Nico never understood the concept of war. Though it often brought out precious human qualities—courage under fire, death with dignity, a national identity and a desire to get the job done—war fed off blind trust in leaders, blind trust in God. The most reliable alliance one ever had was one's comrades, fellow warriors who journeyed through hell for blind trust in leaders and blind trust in God. The PAST re-membered together how intensely they'd lived under fire—

bumping blasted hills in downpours, brains too fried from blind trails dead-ending in a firefight.

Facing civilian life with few prospects, Nico felt like a *no-body*. He was nobody until he joined the group. The PAST helped him see his work with The Splendors achieved so much more than crawling under a gun truck to pull the plug on an oil pan. He'd helped a lot of soldiers find brief respite from the bedlam. Now at home he avoided quiet moments when the forward tide of time flowed backward. Alyssa Parker was right. Nico's knack for unconventional acquisitions, brown-nosing, brokering uncommon skill sets and pulling strings laid a solid foundation on which he could build a great career. What he'd learned in war *could* have a practical use.

Nico's first job lasted all of two weeks: Assistant Night Manager for Big Boy Restaurant on Capitol Boulevard. The road seemed clear for easy ascension. He took a draw the first week and set up a smart bachelor pad within walking distance to the job and to campus where he would throw in some classes on Cubism, Herman Hesse, and the cowboy fascination with bucking Broncos, all in an afternoon, before stepping into upward mobility in a competitive enterprise at night.

The reality wasn't equal to the fantasy.

Few Bronco co-eds took summer classes, unless they were married. The co-eds were too busy earning tuition for the fall. The ladder of success at Big Boy dissolved under blistering lectures from his boss, Rodney Fortunata. Rod-God was this slick NY Italian transplant, a Jets refugee from *West Side Story*, dense black hair combed back, molded into plastic fantastic with a half tube of Brylcreem. The home of the famous Big Boy double-decker hamburger was Rod-God's unassailable turf. If Corporate dropped him into red-checkered overalls and slapped on a smile, he'd make a disgusting older version of the chubby cheery mascot himself. As Nico's father might put it, Nico's job was to clean shit out of the pipes, working late hours for salary and taking orders from everybody, customers and management.

The only thing Rod-God loved more than his own image was tradition—chain of command, policy, and worst of all, *uniforms*. Nico'd seen enough uniforms in the Army to last a lifetime. So two weeks later, he was gone.

He rented a small house in his old neighborhood on the north side—land of the free and home of the Braves. One good move followed another and he landed his dream job: night manager for The Enchanted Forest and The Castalia Lounge. The owner, Tomas Aguirre, an old Basque friend of Nico's father, bought this red brick building downtown in the warehouse district for a song. Tomas reopened the Front Street-level lounge within two months as it promised quick returns. He decided the large, open-spaced, second floor with its own street entrance would make a perfect dance club. Managing an 18–25 rock club fell outside his expertise so Tomas hired Nico to put it together. His experience with The Splendors and his handyman background made him a good choice for the job.

Former owners removed the interior walls but left all the support beams. The solid structure would support a small crowd of bouncing bohemians. Tomas saw the opportunity to fill a void left when the Miramar Ballroom went up in smoke in '63. It must be said, the Basques do love their dance. Tomas wanted a place to host the community's *jotas*, Basque traditional dances, and then let Nico try his hand in getting college kids on a Saturday night.

Within budgetary constraints, Nico contracted for a new wooden floor, an updated electrical system that could carry a load, along with a sturdy stage. The separate entrance with a narrow flight of stairs provided good control of who could enter the club. It also denied minors easy access to the lounge. Nico designed a tile facade, a neon light sign and art boxes for black light posters at the entryway—and Josh drew a fantasy tree from his enchanted forest.

The Enchanted Forest's location was central to both high schools and close to the college. The loud music didn't violate noise ordinances as there weren't any residents nearby.

Nico did the hiring and firing for both lounge and dance club. He set up menus for the bar & grill, booked bands and reconciled accounts. At the youth club, in addition to the non-alcoholic drinks offered at the refreshment bar, there was a half-wall alcove of several tables set up near the dumbwaiter that had been updated to a small elevator from the bar & grill below. The job called for a shit-load of responsibility, poor pay and too much fried food, but it came with amenities: no boss breathing down his neck, lots of unattended young women, and, maybe most of all, live music by the best regional bands.

Nico had missed the hippie movement, having joined the Army in mid-1966. The flower children bloomed and wilted by the time Nehru jackets, bell-bottoms, paisley shirts, tie-dyed simple shifts and mini-skirts brightened the dun landscape of southern Idaho. When Nico graduated in '65, boys were wearing checkered button-downs and bleeding Madras shirts.

The grass-fed upper-middle-class anti-war free-love post-hippie culture that congregated at Julia Davis Park, spilled into streets and head shops, and seized the dance floors mesmerized by strobe lights. The Boise Braves and Borah Lions, cross-town rivals, found in The Enchanted Forest something in common—war protest, marijuana, free sex and tribal music.

Nico was a quick study. The Enchanted Forest lived up to the name. After a few Saturday nights, the place was a swaying forest of young fir reaching out to the cosmos, finding their senses, enchanted by Northwest garage bands. Every weekend the joint was hopping with late bloomers, radical Yippies, vets in G.I. jackets and outlaw bikers swimming through mind-numbing rock, swaying in trance. Even on the rare occasion when one of the bouncers was busy, The Enchanted Forest was a cake-walk compared to Vietnam. Nico never once had to take the long way home to avoid a landmine.

* * *

One morning after a shift at the dance club, Nico found a blue pastel envelope in the mailbox. Nico didn't get mail—mostly overdue notices with late charges. So he felt jubilant when he pulled the envelope out of the mailbox. Hand-lettered in dark blue ink. No stamp or return address. Maybe Coco Bird wrote it. Maybe she wanted to see him. He slid his forefinger under the flap and ripped along the edge. Inside he found a half-sheet of matching blue pastel stationery. The note read:

Captain Karl Neumann, M.D., Psychoanalysis
V.A. Hospital, Room 135
Tuesday, June 17th, 10:30 a.m.

Nico never asked for any appointment. Did Dr. Pratt make an appointment for him? That didn't seem right.

* * *

Room 135 was in a dim hallway with stained walls. Neumann's door had a natural wood finish—walnut maybe. All the other doors in the hallway were dirty white. Neumann's name was etched on a black and white plaque on the door. Nico hesitated at the threshold, nervous as a paratrooper on his first jump. His confidence in a talking cure was severely undermined by reasonable doubt. Was psychiatry even a science?

The waiting room offered two straight-backed chairs with book tables lit by reading lamps. A stern-looking receptionist behind a maybe-walnut desk guarded the entrance to Neumann's inner sanctum. A large unframed painting covered the entire west wall—unfocused and luminous rectangles floating in orange and yellow mist. The mist evaporated Nico's sense of self. A slight vertigo overwhelmed him as if the room tilted a few degrees. The painting defied conventions of perspective—no foreground, no horizon line. The calming effect unwound minutes into hours, or hours into minutes.

Nico remembered this dream he had in high school. He was making love to a girl. They seemed to be made for each other. Then the next day at school he waltzed into choir class and there she was, high in the risers among the sopranos. How could he not have noticed her before? Sixty members in *a cappella* choir and he'd not really seen her until the dream. Had she always possessed this strange aura or was it just him? They'd been dream lovers, connected on another plane. He wanted to ask her if she'd had the same dream, but he feared rejection. He lacked the conviction that dreams came true. Consequently, the dream evaporated into just a dream, the girl into just another soprano. Now, in remembering, he wondered if he'd missed his one chance.

What Nico knew about war was second-hand until Kon Barr. In Pleiku he woke every morning with a sour stomach from the toxic guilt of having been spared. Sure, he'd endured hardship cracking knuckles on engine blocks, but he rose to the bait when old Iron Horse dangled the temporary duty assignment. The transformation of Vu Chi's little club into The Splendors of Bangkok didn't need medals. Nico won friends in high places; they in turn helped him perform the magic of making war disappear. Toxic guilt in the comfort of clean sheets, air-conditioning, electricity, good food and hot showers was worth the price of admission. He danced with the locals and paid them off in black-market booty. The taint of Thai stick and smoked oysters hung about him like inherited wealth.

Neumann's secretary could smell the privilege on him as she peered over horn-rimmed glasses. He handed her the pastel blue letter. She studied it, chewing her lip, smearing the red lipstick, running her finger over the appointment book. "I don't see any scheduled appointment for...what did you say your name was?"

"Bilbao. Nicolasa Bilbao. People call me Nico."

"Well, I'm sorry, Mr. Nico," she handed the pastel blue appointment envelope back, "but I never sent this." She returned to typing.

"Could you please check with the doctor? Perhaps he sent it?"

The secretary stopped typing. She folded her arms over her bosom. "I set up his appointments," she bit off the reply. When she saw confusion rising in Nico's eyes, she softened. "Okay, take a seat."

Nico took a seat.

Maybe-walnut bookcases loaded with esoterica and fantastic art covered the south wall, except for the door, of course; there had to be a way into the office. The bookcases wrapped halfway around the east wall. Books so insulated the room that outside noise was nonexistent. Nico felt sequestered in a monk's cell. Books on Perennial Philosophy, Buddhism, Mysticism, Native American religion and shamanism. Oversized art books with color plates by Max Ernst, Jackson Pollock, Wassily Kandinsky. Writings of P.D. Ouspensky, D.T. Suzuki, Madame Blavatsky, Alan Watts, Ramakrishna, C.G. Jung, Krishnamurti, Eric Fromm. Nico suspected Neumann displayed them to command respect, to lend credence to the practice of a mind doctor, or maybe just to distract his patients from the long wait.

Nico picked a book off the shelf and thumbed it open. It was *The Hero with a Thousand Faces*. He started reading Joseph Campbell's preface:

> *The old teachers knew what they were saying. Once we have learned to read again their symbolic language, it requires no more than the talent of an anthologist to let their teaching be heard. But first we must learn the grammar of the symbols, and as a key to this mystery I know of no better modern tool than psychoanalysis.*

Hah, Nico thought. These books were ads selling a fantasy called normal. He was lost in Campbell's description of a hero when Captain Neumann suddenly towered over him. The analyst stood over six feet tall with raven hair combed back in a copious wave. He wore rumpled brown slacks, wingtips, black turtle-neck and tweed jacket in a perfect stereotype of an Ivy League professor. Neumann's youth surprised Nico after the litany of gray-haired paternal types who'd probed his scalp since the blast. Despite the Germanic name, Neumann could've been of Basque descent. The analyst thumbed the hook of his nose.

"Ah, heroes and monsters, some of my favorite stories." Neumann nodded toward the book in Nico's lap. "Encounters with the underworld." Intense brown eyes focused on Nico, analytically. The doctor's skin looked transparently thin. He extended his hand. "I'm Captain Neumann."

Nico placed the bookmark and laid the book on the table. He grasped the doctor's hand. His fingers were long and elegant, the skin callus-free. Neumann had what Nico's dad called *girly hands*. But the grip was firm, the gaze deliberate and grounded. In spite of Neumann's stature, he didn't seem to be the outdoor type. He invited Nico into his lair with a small gesture. "Let's talk." Nico followed his round shoulders and willowy frame into his office. The light wasn't dim so much as subtle. An adjustable lamp on a polished maybe-walnut book table shone down on a leather-bound notebook next to a captain's chair. Neumann beckoned for Nico to sit across from him so he sat down on the edge of the couch. "Should I lie down?" he asked.

"If you want," Neumann said.

Nico chose to remain sitting.

The book lamp threw a shadow across the doctor's face that gave him bird-like features. Neumann picked up the notebook and began reviewing notes. This struck Nico as odd as he'd just met the man. Instead of the usual display of framed advanced degrees on the wall, behind him was a large stuffed owl hovering on fishing line, suspended over Neumann's desk. It felt like two sets of predator eyes were watching Nico, as he steadied himself, two feet on the floor and arms over his chest. Next to the owl, there was a framed M.C. Escher print that turned proportion and direction on its head with these strange dreamlike creatures marching up and down stone stairways.

Neumann thumbed his nose again. "The owl is a messenger from the unconscious. Did you know that?"

Nico's eyes must have widened as Neumann arched thick eyebrows to invite a response. "He symbolizes for me the need to listen for news from the dark."

Nico kept quiet, but the words "news from the dark" started echoing in his skull.

"And Escher," the doctor nodded toward the print. "Escher reminds me of how the human mind defies limits."

Nico wasn't sure if this was science or fantasy. Neumann's eyes grew larger with subtle light, the whites expanding, pupils contracting. Many Vietnam vets, he explained, suffered flashbacks and repressed memories. Some, like Odysseus, lost their way home from the battlefield. All too common in the history of war, he said, ignoring the symptoms only lead to even greater isolation. "No reason to be alarmed, but your case presents some tantalizing features."

Nico was beginning to blame Doc for this unwanted visit.

"We don't know much more about how nature forms the content and character of our minds than ancient cultures did," Neumann explained. "We pin and label the parts and never know why the butterfly takes flight. We kill beauty to understand it. Physiology and biology have not determined why we see what we see and not something else, why we dream what we dream instead of something else. The owl is specially equipped to work in the dark."

Neumann blinked. Or maybe it was the owl. "You sustained trauma to the frontal lobe. Would you describe yourself as someone who likes to make plans, Nico?"

"They never work out, but I keep making them." Nico said, drumming fingers on his biceps.

"Patients with injuries to the frontal lobe have reported a sense of being held captive in the past, unable to learn new sequences. Have you felt disconnected or frustrated with being unable to repeat simple steps in learning situations?"

"Have you been talking to my mom?" He shook his head. "Can't you just prescribe something?"

"You reported having visions. Are you using any drugs?" Neumann asked.

"Only for headaches," Nico lied.

"What are you taking?"

"Excedrin Extra Strength."

"Don't overmedicate. We don't want to suppress your vision; we want to find a threshold."

"To what?" Nico knitted his brows, eyes becoming slits.

"The way home."

Nico's hands twitched in his lap. "Can I be cured?"

"Cured?" Neumann rose from his chair and squeezed Nico's shoulder. "We don't know there's any illness now, do we? You're going through a *normal* process. You might need to re-balance your life a bit. For the time being I suggest you reconnect with the past. Seek out familiar places. Remember how you felt there. Contact old friends. Listen to the thoughts that come from the interaction."

"I'm doing rap sessions." Nico pointed out.

"Good. Keep it up. What I want for you now is to be more secure in coming home before we delve too deeply into the content of your character."

With a simple flagging of Neumann's index finger, time expired.

Neumann guided Nico to his feet and steered him toward the door. "Remember, Nicolasa, right now it's all about making connections."

Halfway down the hospital corridor, Nico remembered he'd forgotten to set up another appointment, so he went back.

The door to Room 135 was no longer maybe-walnut. The plain white plaque with black lettering read: *Dr. Willis Campo, Internal Medicine*.

Nico stepped inside. Several people sat on couches in a totally different waiting room, a different secretary peered up from behind a glass window.

Confused, Nico hurried to the parking lot and drove home. When he got there, he searched his pockets for the appointment notice on the blue stationery, but couldn't find it anywhere.

10.

"C'mon Mindy!" Milo pounded on the door. "Get out of the bathroom." His sister was stalling, looking to spoil his fun. Mindy and her girlfriend, Francie, were always hanging around, asking stupid questions. Have you guys done it yet? What's Blue Balls? Why do they call it that?

Mindy opened the door a crack, water running in the washbasin. "What's the big hurry? You gonna take Monica out to the bunkers?"

"None of your business."

His reflection in the hallway mirror looked solid enough in bleeding madras shirt, white stretch Levis and black Converse high tops. He looked cool on date night. Sweeping his long blond bangs back with his fingers, an old song popped into his head. He whistled it as he bounded down the stairs, leaping from the third step to the floor.

THUD. CRACK.

His foot smashed through hardwood up to the knee. He yanked the leg out of the hole; the calf was scraped. Oh God, he thought, mom will kill me.

"Anything wrong?" Monica's voice trilled from the living room.

"Nothing," he lied, "just a simple misstep. Be there in a minute."

Milo went down to the basement. The ceiling was low. He cracked his skull on a joist. The blow staggered him. He worked his way in a crouch to where his foot broke the floor. The subflooring had rotted. He blamed it on Astoria weather; it rotted and rusted everything. He scrounged and found a piece of plywood, took it upstairs to plug the hole for a temporary fix and threw a rug over it. He'd have to come clean. If mom tripped over the bulge in the wee hours after her shift, he'd be a dead man.

He dropped onto the sofa next to Monica. His head ached and his cheek was stiff. The sight of his pretty girlfriend softened the pain. She had a remarkably good personality for a majorette whose duty, it seemed, was to bedazzle. Milo didn't like her friends much; they were immature, not interested in the spheres of Flatland. His arm snaked around her.

"You look like a ghost," Monica swirled the ice in her Dr. Pepper.

He sang Dion into her ear, tickled it with his lips.

She laughed and shrugged him off. "Your sister's still here."

The Detroit Tigers and Boston Red Sox were playing under the lights. By the top of the third, the Tigers led 6 – 2.

Monica seemed to like the game. She preferred it over football. "At least you don't freeze your tushy off." She pulled a compact from her purse, applied blush to her cheeks and batted eyelashes at the small round mirror.

The next batter ended the inning.

Mindy tripped on the rug at the bottom of the stairs and cursed. A moment later she appeared in the living room doorway—hair ratted, sloppy green sweatshirt half off her shoulder, black knit skirt hitched up above her knees, wearing black mesh stockings. Her skin was splotchy orange.

"What's that lump in the floor? You hiding a body?" she asked.

"What lump?"

Mindy smirked. "Better fix it, Milo. Mom might trip."

Overnight bag slung over her shoulder and lipstick applied, Mindy turned to the door. "I'm going to Francie's now."

"Just a minute." Milo followed her into the foyer.

Monica shifted positions on the sofa, leaning back and stretching out her arms.

Milo pointed at his sister's splotchy orange shoulder. "Is that a rash?"

"No, stupid," Mindy pulled the sweatshirt up to cover the bare shoulder. "It's Coppertone Quick Tan."

Milo laughed.

"Oh, shut up," Mindy said, "I followed directions."

"Yeah?" Milo looked her up and down. "Since when does mom let you dress like a beatnik?"

"Since I grew up, bonehead." She flipped him off and slammed the door behind her.

"Ah, sweet little sixteen," Milo muttered.

PART TWO

It is peculiar that when one expects some horrible,
incalculable and devastating thing which does not
materialize, one is more disappointed than relieved.

—FLANN O'BRIEN, *The Third Policeman*

11.

Boise High School was a three-story white brick and stone main building with Grecian columns. The complex included an industrial arts building, gym, and music building. Nico's favorite classes—English, shop and music—were all in different buildings.

Nico's senior English teacher, Mr. Keith, hunched over his desk grading summer class papers. He was a stubby man with a handlebar mustache and thinning hair. He jumped to his feet and pumped Nico's hand like a long-lost relative.

After pleasantries, Nico mentioned the summer class on Hermann Hesse. He could identify with Emil Sinclair and his revolt against his *bourgeois* upbringing in Hesse's *Demian* and his encounters with the bully, Franz Kromer. Mr. Keith listened, hands fussing with paper on his desk, pushing a blue pastel envelope under some other papers as if to hide it. Mr. Keith jotted something in a wire-bound tablet, tore out the page and handed it to Nico. "*Steppenwolf.*"

"Thanks. We'll be reading it later in class." Nico slipped the folded paper into the front pocket of his shirt.

After they shook hands, Mr. Keith backed into a ground fog as if he'd never existed in the first place.

* * *

Ira Skye or 'Big Skye' as his students called him, stood at a long conference table in the band room and sorted sheet music into folders.

Big Skye was a talented horn player and inspired teacher. High school music teachers like him didn't teach for easy money. They wanted to give back to the community for supporting their passion. Teaching kept Big Skye whole. He loved it. Bent over the task, his bald head reflected the fluorescent lights. "Lawrence of Arabia" blared through the music room speakers. A skinny drummer in wire-rimmed glasses practiced snare drum in the back, playing along. When he looked up, Big Skye's green eyes sparkled. He met Nico with a wide smile. It was how he welcomed the most untutored musicians into his family. The size of Big Skye's heart equaled his girth. Nico waved and walked down through tiers of amphitheater. Big Skye's leprechaun grin and flushed pixie ears made Nico feel at home.

"You ever get that Conn Constellation?" Big Skye asked, voice booming over the recorded music.

"*Silver* Conn Constellation," Nico clarified with the shake of his head. "No. Haven't touched a horn in two years."

"That's a shame. You had splendid tone," Big Skye remembered. "That's why I chose you for herald trumpet."

"I thought it was because I played so LOUD."

"Yes, you *did* play loud," Big Skye confessed. He stepped over to the recorder/tuner and took the volume down, motioning the drummer. "One tomorrow," he called. The kid nodded, put sticks in his back pocket and waved goodbye.

Big Skye graduated from a fabled Texas jazz program. He was Boise's own Al Hirt and fronted the local combo, "Big Skye and Terra Firma." They played gigs in Garden City. His high school stage band performed at local proms every year. In spite of his jazz training, Big Skye's Irish eyes reflected the color and sound of Texas marching bands. He loved the game, the music, the celebratory mood, the colors of the season, and he loved the Boise fans who supported his program with a roar whenever they took the field at halftime.

Big Skye's passion shone through everyone he taught. Playing herald trumpet with him at the Veteran's Day rivalry game between Boise and Borah was one of Nico's most cherished memories.

An awkward silence gripped the room but Big Skye broke it with the natural volume of his voice. His rich baritone was conditioned to rise over the daily cacophony of kids with instruments. "I'm working with the community band now. Wednesday nights. Come sit in. Could use another horn on the Sousa."

"Hah," Nico said. "It'd take a month to get any lip back, but I'm grateful for the offer."

"Well, we'll be around," Big Skye assured him, "if you find time." He directed Nico's attention to the table. Next year's compositions included old standards: "Maria" and "Tonight" from *West Side Story*, "The Lonely Bull" by Herb Alpert and the Tijuana Brass and Nico's own favorite, "Malaguena." In the band's mix was an arrangement of Richard Berry's hit song, "Louie, Louie," recorded at the same time by two groups, The Kingsmen and a local group, Paul Revere and the Raiders. That would get the crowd going.

Nico thanked Big Skye for supporting his love of music and described how it fit so well into his new job at The Enchanted Forest. When Nico got up to leave, Big Skye gave him a big hug. "Oh, and Nico…"

Nico turned, lifting an eyebrow.

"…thank you for your service."

* * *

Nico dropped by the gym. A couple of kids were playing basketball. He remembered playing first trumpet in pep band the year the Braves made the state playoffs in basketball. Exciting times. Cheerleaders stomping and clapping, fierce with fight song, swinging their hips to the beat,

Braves in warmups swishing one after the other. Coco Bird somersaulted onto the polished hardwood, skirt wilting over her ears as Nico stumbled up the bleachers, eyes on the wrong step, coming back late after halftime. He sat on the hard wooden bench and raised his trumpet, joining in "On Wisconsin," the swing beat of his brass Bundy like a jawbone cracking skulls. Trombone slides kicked high in a chorus line, stepping up bass on "Peter Gunn." Boise fans whooping up war cries. A lightning bolt of sax and trumpet bringing down the house of the Braves.

Near the end of the game, between songs of the hit parade, Nico's sheet music slipped the folder and dropped through the space between the seats, gliding down into the shadows under the bleachers. The uplifted face from below was that of Jesse Walker.

"What're you doing there?" Nico shouted in a hoarse voice. Jesse went under the bleachers to scare up some Scarlet Skirts in the cheering section, in the right place when they rose to cheer at the countdown of the clock.

"C'mon down!" Jesse called through cupped hands, mischief in his eyes.

The Braves' all-star forward blocked a shot, passed ahead to the bullet-quick guard mid-court who laid the ball in on a fast break, nice and easy, in the ruckus and roar as time ran out. Nico squeezed through the gap between seats, straddling the angle irons in careful descent to recover the lost music.

Above him, this Chinese-American doll started to descend when she saw the boys below in the shadows. She clutched her skirt tight against her legs. Her white oval face floated like a bright full moon above him. "Could you hand me my coat, please?" The girl pointed to the coat on the floor.

Jesse handed the coat up and Nico, with sheet music between his teeth, handed it up to the girl. Her round face dissolved into Chu Len's. Her mouth opened and closed soundlessly like a fish out of water.

"Did we win?" Jesse called up.

The lights in the gym blinked out and Nico stood in the dark, hearing the echo of a door closing. "Doesn't feel like it."

* * *

Late afternoon light lay across the radiator of a bright green '57 Pontiac with #90 painted on the doors. The auto shop teacher, Mr. Roosevelt, ducked under the open hood. When he heard Nico come in, he kicked back to his feet, wiping grease off his mitts with a cloth. He recognized Nico immediately. "Welcome home," he said with a crooked smile. "Your dad mentioned you were back."

"Still tinkering with racecars? I thought you'd be retired by now."

"Couple more years to bolster the pension," Rosie said, busting open a package of spark plugs and pulling them out one by one, lining them up on a clean cloth.

"Whose car?"

"Whitey O'Riley. We're prepping for the Firecracker at Meridian."

Whitey O'Riley was a real hotshot. Graduated a year ahead of Nico. One of Rosie's best students, he was running well at the Speedway.

"What brings you here?" Rosie placed a spark plug. "Looking for work?"

"Memories." Nico popped a socket onto a ratchet handle.

"Crack your knuckles," Rosie invited.

Rosie opened a pouch and pinched tobacco into his pipe, tamping it down. His hands were scarred, his knuckles knobby from being smashed against engine blocks.

Nico applied steady English on the plugs until they broke loose. Working side by side with Rosie silenced Nico's overactive mind. It was a good silence, not the silence of Vietnam after a bomb blast. The kind of silence that is never really silent as it invites a wider listening. Rosie's tough, dry skin from years of using wire brushes and Borax made him look older than sixty-two.

"You seen that hooligan, Walker, around?" Rosie ratcheted the last spark plug into the engine block. "He's been chewin' up Riley's ass. But he doesn't listen to anybody."

"Never did." Nico plucked the radiator belt to test the tightness, flicked the fuel pump with his finger, and looked back over his shoulder.

Rosie continued. "You two worked well together once..."

"Yeah," Nico reflected, "he wrecked the cars, and I fixed 'em."

"Now that's what I'd call a symbiotic relationship," Rosie said with a show of hands. Oil and grease formed a carapace around stiff joints. Blue-collar hands like his father's, hard and callused from a lifetime of working with tools.

"Ever heard of Harley Cavanaugh?"

"Yeah. Good engine man. He was with NASCAR once. Harley's the other reason Walker's eatin' up the track. Too bad he never finishes."

"What brought this Harley to Boise?"

"Don't know. You'd have to ask him."

Nico lined up the used spark plugs and checked them for carbon buildup. Some were in decent shape. They'd work in his V-8.

Rosie leaned over the fender of O'Riley's Sizzling Shamrock, feet off the floor, reaching through brackets and belts. "Going back to school?" Rosie asked.

"Why take classes just because I got the G.I. Bill?" Nico shrugged. "Still don't know what I wanna be when I grow up." Nico quit college after the first year and joined the Army when he lost his deferment. Volunteers got some preference over draftees in terms of station. Rosie was disappointed after Nico dropped out. He'd always told him not to waste his talent. Nico just thought Rosie was overestimating him.

"At least you know you're not grown up yet. Too many never get to *grown up*." Rosie drew on the pipe and blew a stream of Cherry Blend into the air. He rubbed the coarse gray stubble on his chin as if ready to pontificate. "See?

You're ahead of the game. Riley's got an entry level opening at Capitol Transmission."

"Thanks, Rosie, but I got a job."

* * *

Captain Neumann essentially gave Nico license to wallow in nostalgia. There were summer picnics, Thanksgiving and Christmas holidays, ballgames, carnivals, the dream of suburban America before it was shot down at Mang Yang Pass.

Nico recognized faces in the yearbook, but felt strangely detached.

Mrs. Tupper, for instance, his sophomore history teacher. He'd never liked her. That woman was a scowler with bad temperament. Nico once molded a defiant "finger" out of clay in art class and dared Jesse to leave it on Tupper's desk. They both visited the vice-principal's office, separately.

The time Jesse broke up with Coco Bird, he and Jesse muscled Mr. Bird's Volkswagen onto the sidewalk, the front end on the third porch step of somebody's house two blocks from the school. When Coco backed the car off the concrete porch, she scraped the undercarriage and scratched the front fender. Mr. Bird blamed Jesse. He always did. Nico enjoyed immunity. He was the *nice* boy. Nico could disassemble and reassemble an engine. He liked math. He had a father. Unfortunately, Lenny Bird did not choose Coco's boyfriends.

His other friends from high school seemed stunted in their growth. It was like time stopped in Boise while Nico went to war. Everyone seemed preoccupied with trivialities and small talk. The old crowd had broken up, gone separate ways, and only by happenstance did he run into one on the street or in the grocery store. He was lucky to have the PAST as they all felt like they'd returned from another dimension, come home bearing the mark of Cain.

12.

Milo slipped his arm around Monica's shoulder. Alone at last. Her sweet neck was perfumed sculpture. He reached to turn her face and she shot off the couch, snatching her nightbag. Her shoulder busted his jaw in haste. He bit his tongue.

"Awwwk," he croaked, cupping his jaw.

"Be right back," she said, rushing upstairs to the bathroom. "Don't go anywhere."

"Watch out for the hump in the carpet." Milo's tongue throbbed in his throat but his thoughts swept the unknown territory ahead, looking for signs, not knowing the landmarks of sex. The toilet flushed. Monica returned with a naughty grin, no longer wearing tights. She slid beside him, white pleated skirt riding up her bare thighs. Milo understood that to mean she had expectations. He felt the pressure building.

Her warm body pressed against his. They kissed. He winced. "Oh, did I hurt you?" she asked.

"No, no," he said, "It's okay."

She kissed him again, deeper this time. His tongue writhed like a slug. They came up for air, gasping. "Now we're *communicating*," she said.

In the sixth inning, a new Tiger Milo hadn't ever seen before stepped up to the plate, number 5, Jim Northrup.

The tall right-hander who batted lefty tagged a two-run homer.

Monica cooed into Milo's left ear and Tiger fans roared into his right. Rookie catcher, Bill Freehan, followed Northrup's two-run homer with a solo shot. Monica feigned interest. He felt her soft breast against his elbow, nesting there under red cashmere. "Home run derby," she said. She nibbled his earlobes and her body moved against his. Live wires in his brain snapped. Milo kissed her neck, glimpsing the game over her shoulder. The baserunner rounded the bases, waving to fans. As he headed home, a strange popping sound made Milo blink. He thought maybe the Zenith had short-circuited. Then he thought his own rising heat was so immolating his body that the whole house was going up in smoke. His life would be reduced to a blackened husk as primal horses dragged him through the street. He unwrapped himself from Monica's arms and sat erect on the edge of the couch.

"What's wrong?" she asked.

Freehan's legs buckled between third and home, momentum carrying him into a somersault, ending up flat on his back in the baseline, short of home plate. The collective in-rushing of air by thousands of fans sounded like the backwash of a tidal wave.

"Milo, come back," Monica pleaded.

"What?"

"We were just getting warmed up." Monica shifted on the couch. The skirt rode higher.

The roar of Tiger stadium dropped into still shock. The cameras zoomed in. A spreading pool of dark flowed from under the downed catcher. The Red Sox sprinted into the dugout covering their heads with gloves. Screaming fans rushed exits, pushing, shoving, trampling whoever got in the way.

A test pattern popped up on the TV screen.

Please stand by, we are experiencing technical difficulties.

"What's going on?" Monica bolted upright.

Milo moved to the Zenith-in-a-cabinet, switching channels, twisting the fine tune knob. All three networks displayed test patterns.

> *We are sorry to interrupt this program. What follows is an important message from the Emergency Broadcasting System and the President of the United States.*

"Damn," Milo slapped the TV with his open hand. "I'm missing the game for news?"

A grim-faced President John F. Kennedy appeared on the screen, sitting at his desk in the Oval Office, American flag behind him. The President spoke:

> *My fellow Americans, our nation has come under attack. Snipers of undeclared allegiance opened fire on unsuspecting crowds in several cities. American citizens are being killed and injured. I have mobilized the National Guard. Do not go outside. Remain in your homes and stay tuned to this network.*

A crackling sound interrupted Kennedy's speech. A thickening snowstorm eclipsed the President's face. The screen went black then burst suddenly into light. From the white light emerged the image of a new president, Lyndon B. Johnson, sitting in the Oval Office:

> *I shall not seek and I will not accept the nomination of my party for another term as your President. But, let men everywhere know, however, that a strong and a confident, a vigilant America stands ready tonight to seek an honorable peace...*

"An honorable peace? What happened with the invasion?" Milo asked. Monica reached for his hand and squeezed it.

President Johnson's face came through static as through a storm, like an anchored rubber mask filling with water. The mask burst and another face appeared—Richard Milhous Nixon—shaking loose jowls like a bulldog:

> *They will be mourned by their families and friends; they will be mourned by their nation; they will be mourned by the people of the world; they will be mourned by a Mother Earth that dared send two of her sons into the unknown...*

"Something terrible has happened!" Milo declared.

Nixon's eyes suddenly shifted from the camera to a blurred shadow. The shadow passed in front of him. The shadow was the Hammer Man in a black shirt and white tie. As he lowered his head and came eye to eye with the camera, Milo noticed he now had thick dark hair. His rheumy eye grew larger until a black pupil bounced in the static. In the background, Nixon droned:

> *In ancient days, men looked at stars and saw their heroes in the constellations. In modern times, we do much the same, but our heroes are epic men of flesh and blood...*

Men of flesh and blood.

The picture blinked out.

"Do you want me to take you home?" he asked Monica.

"I want to be with you." Monica kissed him quickly.

Another test pattern appeared.

> *One moment please, we are experiencing technical difficulties.*

The network returned, this time with a popular game show. The host flashed perfect teeth. A panel of contestants stood behind podiums on stage.

"I think we lost the game," Milo muttered, turning the fine tune.

Monica tugged him back, batting her eyelashes. "The game's not over."

Milo stared at the contestants: a dark-haired barbarian in a bearskin, a petite cheerleader in pigtails, a woman who looked like a librarian and the Hammer Man. The Hammer Man pushed black horned-rim glasses back up his nose with his forefinger. He gripped the front of the podium and waited for the first question.

"Are we ready to play Jeopardy? Okay then, today we have the following categories: Politics, Music, Movies, Fun Places and Undeclared Modern Wars. Professor, as our champion, you go first."

"Music for 100, Bill." The Hammer Man brushed long black hair back from his high forehead, waiting for the answer.

Professor Hammer? Milo watched, entranced.

"This three-day festival of music and peace held on Max Yasgur's farm near Bethel, New York, with an audience of over 400,000 was one of the greatest and most pivotal moments in the history of rock 'n' roll."

"What is Woodstock, Bill?

"That is correct."

"Woodstock?" Milo shrugged to Monica, and she shrugged back.

"Movies for 100, Bill."

"Scoring cocaine in Mexico, two free-spirited bikers in this famous movie resell the drugs in California, and set off on a trek from Los Angeles to New Orleans for Mardi Gras."

"What is Easy Rider*?"*

"That is correct."

"Easy Rider?" Milo blinked at Monica.

"What is *Easy Rider*?" Monica corrected, pulling his shirt out of his pants.

"Politics for 300, Bill." Professor Hammer held the stage.

"This famous political writer, philosopher and educator died several days after the publication of his Message *to Young* People *in which he said, 'Some of you may already have fallen*

in love with an actual world of the past. Not realizing that a past actual world, although it was once possible, is now an impossible world, you may even seek to defend it with your life'."

The barbarian brought up a leg of roasted lamb that hit the buzzer. When he realized the host was waiting for an answer, he said, "Ah...what is Genghis Khan?"

"I'm sorry; that's incorrect."

The cheerleader hit the buzzer, jumping in place. "Did I win? Oh, oh, who is Thomas Jefferson?"

"I'm sorry; that's incorrect. Professor, do you have an answer?"

The Professor peered into the camera, dark eyes gazing over his glasses. "Who is...Scott Buchanan?"

"That is correct;" the host said, "from an article that appeared just days before his death in 1968."

"1968?" Milo cast a quizzical glance at Monica.

"*What is* 1968?" Monica corrected.

"But that's five years from now." Maybe the world *was* ending, he thought. Maybe it had already ended. Not even Monica's hot breath on his neck could break the spell of this future broadcast.

"Undeclared Modern Wars for 500, Bill." The Professor faced the camera, cool and collected.

"This offensive, which began on January 31, 1968, though a military victory for the United States, turned the tide of popular support at home against the war in Southeast Asia, leading to eventual American withdrawal."

The barbarian slapped the buzzer with open hand. "What is Genghis Khan?"

"I'm sorry; that is incorrect."

"Mayday, mayday." The Professor hauled up his sledgehammer from behind the podium and brought it down full force, splintering the barbarian's podium.

Scan lines rolled on the screen. The image rippled. Figures twisted, distorted, stretched and warped. Milo adjusted the rabbit-ear antenna. The picture only rolled faster and faster. Another burst of light collapsed into black screen. They'd lost the future.

"Thank God," Monica sighed.

Milo checked behind the TV. It wasn't even plugged in. They had been witnessing an impossible telecast. He tried not to tremble.

"Put something on the stereo—Dion or Roy Orbison?" Monica said, kicking off white slip-on tennis shoes, tucking bare legs under. "You like Orbison, don't you?"

"What?" He stared at her legs.

"Orbison. You like Roy Orbison, don't you?"

"Yeah." He stepped over to the stereo and he looked back, worried. "What if the world is ending?"

"Let's worry about it tomorrow," she pouted.

Yeah, he agreed, life was too short. It was time to be a man.

Milo climbed onto the couch and placed his hand above Monica's knee. Her skin felt electric. In spite of renewed intent, his mind drifted away as they kissed. He fought to stay on task. The dull ache in his neck pulsed. Suddenly he broke away. "1968."

"What about it?" Monica sagged back into the corner of the couch.

"The tuna can." Milo got up and retrieved the can from his jacket.

Her helpless gesture begged for explanation.

"The can's dated 1968. The *Jeopardy* host said 1968. It's 1963."

"Okay."

"I'm sorry." His face flushed. "Maybe I'm dreaming."

Monica leaned over to kiss him again. She took his hand and placed it on her soft breast. "Pinch me if I'm dreaming."

He tried; he really did. His perception misaligned diagonally like interference waves on the TV screen. The cannery. The weather. The Hammer Man. He again gently pushed her away. "What if I'm having a mental breakdown?"

Monica slid her hand up his thigh. "Then I wonder what I'm having?" She reached for his buckle.

Two virgins groped in the dark under the haunting falsetto of Roy Orbison. He pushed her back onto the couch and she welcomed him with open arms, throwing her leg over his, grinding against his hip. He tried to concentrate.

"We have the whole night," she whispered.

Even with Chanel short-circuiting his brain, his nerve-ends snapping, he managed to blink. "You don't have to go home?"

"Sleepover." Monica's breath scorched the back of his neck. "Hi, Zelda." She unbuttoned his shirt, pulled it over his shoulders and kissed his chest. "I need you inside me," her breath burned. "I want to have your baby."

BABY?

The world stopped spinning and Milo kept going, flying right over the handlebars. Did she say, *I want to have you, baby* or did she say, *I want to have your baby?* Milo panicked as he saw himself working full-time year-round at the cannery, dropping out of school, cradling a baby in his arms, a small helpless human depending almost totally on him as provider. He gazed into Monica's soft eyes. He could do worse. She made him feel light-headed. She took away the heaviness. She was always telling him that he thinks too much, that he needed to listen to his body. Milo's greatest worries revolved around things he couldn't control.

A voice came to him from far off.

C'mon, man. She wants it!

Milo lifted his head from her shoulder and gazed into her eyes. "Do you want it?"

"With all my heart, love," she panted, her skirt falling away, exposing the delicate lace of white panties. Her eyes kept daring him. His hand reached her buttocks. No voices came with more advice.

Gotta do what a man's gotta do, he said to himself into her ear, and let his fingers probe the elastic of her panties.

Monica touched his cheek.

Her boldness took Milo by surprise. Her finger teased the hair on his chest. "Zelda and I are at the show now. We won't be coming in until midnight. Do you have an alarm clock?"

The stiffness in Milo's cheek and neck relaxed as it migrated to his groin. His eyes rolled. Monica hummed at just the right pitch, her engine was revving. He felt like a Tiger ready to hit one over the fence.

Blue Moon, this is Blue 4. How do you read? Over.

He tried to sit up, but Monica pulled him back down. "Don't think so much," she said, crossing her arms and pulling her sweater over her head. She reached back and unfastened her bra. The bra fluttered down over the white enamel of her breasts. Instead of fixating on her natural endowment, Milo's eyes went straight to her flat, creamy belly, to the splotch of red rash. Monica pressed her upper body against his, pulling his belt out of the loops. All he could think about was the rash crawling across her skin.

Mayday! Mayday! We're going down.

The rash crawled on to him, spreading all over the house until it became one big pulsing red rash ready to crack and bleed.

13.

Nico picked up Josh Brownton and drove northwest on West State Street past Collister Shopping Center, halfway to Eagle. He turned onto Highway 44 just beyond the Stinker Station with the billboard: *Cattle Country—watch out for Bum Steers*. He took a right onto North 5 Mile Road and proceeded north to the Hill Road merge.

The Walkers lived in a wood-framed white farmhouse with screened porch that faced the dry sage-covered foothills. A windbreak of poplars lined the back property. Dutch elms screened the house from the road. The pungent smell of lilac and manure after a rain drifted through Nico's open window. Behind the house stood a faded red barn with peeling paint, a junked car on blocks and a small pasture with barrels. A dun buckskin with chopped black mane and an Appaloosa mare stood side by side watching Nico pull up the drive.

Boise Valley fanned out to the west and south in green pastureland, dairies and cornfields. Each year development swallowed more native ground with colorless blight.

Nico and Josh got out of the car and a shadow pushed open the screen door. "Found us okay?" Jesse called from the porch. A black t-shirt stretched over his thick chest. Watery red eyes blinked as if cloud-dimmed daylight was just too much to bear.

"Not too hard," Nico said, offering his hand. Jesse reached across his body with the left in a backward shake. He was wearing a hook instead of the molded hand. "What happened to the other hand?"

"Kept breaking glasses."

Nico's anxiousness gave way to visible relief when Jesse said Coco Bird was off shopping until lunch. He nodded Josh and Nico toward the barn. "C'mon, I'll show you our Little Stinker."

Nico followed Jesse through a wooden gate, grasshoppers breaking in waves ahead of him. The smell of damp wood and motor oil greeted him with cold comfort. A conservative-looking thirty-something man with close-cropped hair and thick eyeglasses rattled a can of paint and sprayed over a stencil onto the rusting body of a wrecked Buick Special. The car was up on blocks with wheels removed. Dry stalks of yellow grass grew around and through the chassis.

Jesse introduced Joe Samples, the manager of the Stinker Station back on West State. He reminded Nico of Buddy Holly in a button-down checkered shirt, threadbare jeans and tattered tennis shoes spattered with white paint.

Mr. Stinker checked them out head-to-toe before extending his hand. He walked with them to the sliding barn door. Jesse pulled it back enough for them to enter. Just inside, a black '55 Chevy Bel Air with two white stripes down its back resembled a cross between a panther and a skunk, made sleek with trim and emblems removed, number 8 painted on the hood and doors. The stockcar was parked over a greasepit. The hood yawned, held open with an iron rod. Squatting in the pit to install a new universal was Jesse's engine man, Harley Cavanaugh. Harley was the other owner of the West State Street Stinker Station.

Jesse pointed to some cups on the workbench. "You boys help yourself." Harley went about his business in the greaespit as if unaware anyone had come into the barn.

Nico heard tires in loose gravel and his stomach fluttered. Manny Hernandez walked in. Josh flashed a wide smile. "Hey man."

Manny set a plate of brownies on the workbench. "Brownton Brownies. Don't tell his granny but he fudged on her recipe." He turned his attention to Nico. "Hey Nico. What does Josh know about engines?" He snatched up a brownie in each hand. Two bites and they were gone.

"Should have worn old duds, dude." Jesse nodded at Josh.

Josh glanced down at himself in ruffled blue shirt and paisley bellbottoms. He shrugged, "I am."

"Shit." Jesse shook his head. "Give him some coveralls."

Manny's unzipped faded green coveralls exposed a hairy chest. As a Marine, Manny never saw combat, but the former tight end for the Nampa Bulldogs struck an imposing figure at six-three, 230 pounds. He disappeared into a stall and The Doors erupted from mounted Pioneer speakers. When Manny came back, he shrugged at Josh. He wasn't impressed with the brownies. "Maybe you got the recipe wrong."

"Don't worry," Josh warned, "it sneaks up on ya." He zipped up the coveralls and slapped his hands together. "Okay, I'm ready to work."

Within minutes, Manny was shit-faced, smiling, pupils dilated, nodding to himself. "Good shit, man. Really *good* shit."

In spite of Neumann's caution against voluntary altered states with a serious brain injury, Nico couldn't resist the soothing effects of rich dark chocolate.

Jesse's strict adherence to a diet of beer and Jack Daniel's Black waved away Josh's hand. He took a long pull on his Coors.

"You got beer?" Josh asked.

"If you're buying."

Josh handed Jesse a ten-dollar bill and Jess handed him a beer.

After two brownies and three cuts by The Doors, Nico's lips had loosened a bit and his hands were itching to get dirty.

Harley ducked out from under the Stinker Bomb. "Christ, turn down that music. Can't hear nothin'."

"Like that'll help," Manny answered. After "Break On Through" he turned the music down.

Harley was in his late thirties, maybe early forties, with a slight tic in the left eye. He wore black and white coveralls, name embroidered in yellow over the right chest pocket. The crew reminded Nico of a little league team when they first get their caps and shirts. In the middle of the back was the *Little Stinker* logo, a skunk, and the words "West State." Harley looked like a raccoon, come out of the greasepit—graying at the temples, grease smudge under his eyes, looking uneasy as if a flashlight found him going through the trash.

"Harley's our secret weapon. NASCAR pro." Jesse gave his secret weapon a manly hug. "Harley once worked with Ralph Moody's pit crew. The sound of a finely tuned engine is his first love. Ain't that right, Harley?"

"First, but not my last." Harley offered Nico a greasy hand, turning his head slightly to hear better. "Glad to meet ya. Nick, was it?"

"NEE-KO." Nico raised his voice over The Doors and the NASCAR engines revving in Harley's damaged ears. They shook hands. Nico picked up a rag and wiped off his palms.

Harley pointed to his ear. "Doan hear so much anymore. Been listenin' for ticks in too many engines. Jesse says y'all know sump'n about machines, that right?"

"A little," Nico answered humbly.

"Ya say what?"

Nico held up his hand so the thumb and forefinger pinched the air. "A LITTLE! Never worked on race cars before."

"Stocks are a nice place to start." Harley squatted, turning a valve cover soaking in gasoline in a pan, stood the cover on end and scrubbed away the grease buildup with a wire brush.

Nico checked under the hood. The Stinker Bomb had new valve springs, seals and gaskets, plugs, points, hoses, distributor wires, carburetor. The V-8 gleamed. "Some serious rebuilding."

"Y'all know why they call 'em stockcars, don't ya?" Harley raised an eyebrow. Nico didn't know if he was asking him or someone else. Harley went on. "Well, Big Bill France sold the public on this vision of comin' to the races to see the spittin' image of what you drive off the showroom floor. You know, marketing. Used t' be you only used parts from the factory. None of these cars are really 'stock.' Parts are retooled, sanded and shined up 'til they fit snug as stretch pants on a whore."

Jesse downed the Coors. "Harley was at Charlotte the day Fireball Roberts died."

Harley fitted a new gasket and replaced the valve cover. Nico anticipated what he'd need and handed him the socket wrench. Harley took it without looking, like a surgeon taking a scalpel from a nurse.

"That's why he gave up NASCAR." Jesse looked on as Nico handed Harley the oil pan bolts. Harley ratcheted them in nice and tight. "But the track always called you, didn't it, Harley? The call of the wild, leading you away from home."

Harley called back from under the Stinker Bomb hood. "Walker, you're so full of crap you fart when you think."

Harley backed out from under the hood, straightened up and pressed fists into the small of his back. "The dude thinks he's Elvis." He was referring, of course, to Elvis' role as Lucky Jackson in *Viva Las Vegas*. The title song provided for lots of crashing, burning, speed and women. It summed up Jesse's whole life. Harley wiped his hands off with a rag and limped to the refrigerator. Years of crawling under cars had wreaked havoc on his hips. He chugged from a quart of milk, his Adam's apple bobbing up and down inside a loose-skinned southern turkey neck. Harley set the carton down on the workbench next to greasy hose clamps and wire clips. "Ulcers," he confided, "brought on by stress, booze, and drivers like this who won't listen to their elders."

Nico and Josh laughed.

Joe Samples walked into the barn. "What's the joke? Ain't I payin' you guys enough to work?"

Manny turned in surprise. "We're getting paid?"

"Fuck no, Manny. That's called a sense of humor."

Manny looked perplexed.

"Drawin' on my vast experience here," Harley explained to Nico, "you gotta make a race of it." His attention focused on Jesse. "Y'all can't go out there and win by two laps and draw a crowd. And Jesus you don't even finish half the time."

"Maybe they come out to see me crash."

"Yeah, but if you keep it close, folks'll come back. They wanna believe the other guy can beat ya right up to the finish line. Then you take 'em on that last lap. Give 'em a show and everybody wins—owners, drivers, sponsors, the track. That's what NASCAR taught me, bud."

Jesse jerked his thumb towards Harley. "Yes, *mother.*"

Harley kissed his fingers and slapped Jesse's cheek. He then knocked a Salem Menthol from the crush-proof pack and offered one. Nico declined. "Yeah, I know," Harley nodded, "My wife, Margo, she's been tryin' to get me to quit. Sometimes only a good kick in the ass gets me goin' in the mornin'. It's too late to reform this old sinner. She keeps tryin' though. Bless her heart."

* * *

Come 10:30, Jesse, Joe, Josh and Manny piled into Joe's brown and white '68 Ford Bronco and dashed to West State for crankcase oil and new tires.

Harley lit up and stepped into the stereo stall to change the music. He put some jazz on, something with lots of sax. He leaned against a post and watched smoke rings dissolve in the air. "Ah'll tell y'all this much. Most drivers here are weekend warriors. No future for them on the big tracks. They're too reckless or too local. Got no clue what it takes to succeed. Now Jesse—and if you tell him I said this I'll deny it—he's an honest-to-God throwback to Curtis and Fireball. He has this internal need to push to the brink of breakdown. He goes harder when everybody else is backin' off. He knows how to get more out of a car than his crew does. He's all-out but smart enough not to get too reckless."

"Did you quit NASCAR because of Fireball Roberts?"

"What's that again?"

"I said, did you *quit* the track 'cause Fireball died?"

"Nah, I quit 'cause he didn't have to."

"Die?" Nico fetched a Coors from the refrigerator, popped the cap with the church-key tied to a string on the door. The beer foamed up into his nostrils. He shoved the bottle neck into his mouth to catch the overflow.

"I was working for Ralph Moody—Holman and Moody. Moody had designed safer cars but NASCAR wouldn't run 'em. He designed this rubber bladder for the fuel tank, to prevent the tank from leaking in crashes. But that wasn't stock, ya see. That's how Fireball died. Fuel tank ruptured, car caught fire and exploded. Didn't have to happen. That bladder wouldn't have made that car run any faster. Folks come to see crashes but no reason drivers gotta die." Harley took a long drag off the cigarette, let the smoke drift up his nostrils. "Didcha know they named him Fireball 'cause he had one helluva fastball? Ironic. Fireball goin' up in a fireball that way.

"It was thrills and spills when those tough ol' boys in the Depression were drinkin' and haulin' moon. It's a rush to have the law on your tail. Can't do that nowadays, what with owners, sponsors, factories. Nobody dares risk bad press. Don't know if Jesse's got the mettle for NASCAR. He's a cocky son-of-bitch. Not a good fit with the money men. But to my mind the cocky ones make the best drivers. He'll drive the wheels plumb off a machine."

Harley bought into West State Street Stinker with retirement money and became Joe's partner, and it wasn't long before they were partners in the Stinker Bomb.

Joe Sample had gotten all fired up on Harley's glory-days. He started to fantasize and they invested in Stinker Bomb so Joe could race it at the Meridian Speedway. He wanted to experience those thrills and spills for himself. Harley missed working with racecars. So he left the business end to Joe and worked on the Stinker Bomb's engine. He thought maybe he could recapture the fun if the money didn't matter. It was the pressure of winning at the super-speed-ways that caused drivers to take unnecessary risks. They started breaking down as often as the cars. Joe only raced the Stinker Bomb for two seasons. He didn't have the in-stincts and realized it himself after getting tangled up with Whitey O'Riley. Sometimes you have to let people do their own thing or they'll never learn. Joe crashed into the south wall on the backstretch and he realized the benefits of own-ership didn't require him to put his life on the line. His wife wouldn't stand for it.

Harley caught Jesse racing a jalopy and recognized innate ability even with his handicap. They weren't really looking for a driver, but Jesse won twice and finished in the top three several times their first season. He got a share of the purse. Joe envisioned this rapid ascent to bigger tracks and more money with Jesse at the wheel. Unfortunately, Joe forgot to include Harley in all this planning. NASCAR wasn't Har-ley's dream; he'd already dispelled that one. He raced for fun, not for money. Harley feared losing the fun again.

* * *

Harley's war stories conjured a few of Nico's own, like when he dared Jesse to ride down one of the steep roads up by Camel's Back Park. They were fourteen. Mister Evel Knievel straddled the red Yamaha, cranking the throttle. Neither Jesse nor the motorbike had any kind of license. Chad Summers blindfolded him with Coco Bird's scarf and Nico counted down. He remembered the ecstacy on Coco's face, inspired, Nico thought, by Jesse's gallantry—even though a sophomoric feat. Jesse always needed that attention, not just Coco's. Everybody's. Somehow he ex-tended his senses to feel the road through the motorbike's tires. The drift of grilled onions rising in the air from the Dairy Queen reached his nose. Each bump in near-suicidal descent catapulted him halfway down the next block and he landed with legs up, hanging on to the handlebar, shouting, "I love you, Coco!" One block short of the impossible he crashed. He ripped open his left arm and fractured his left foot. A police car climbed a curb on Hill Road to avoid hitting him where he landed in the gutter. Some old coot was crossing the road, startled by the breeze of a near miss and dropped his sack of groceries. Milk and eggs mixed French toast that congealed in the warm air. Several ruby red grapefruit rolled down the street bumping the wheels of cars stopped in the intersection. Jesse pulled off the blindfold and the cracked helmet. Two cops stood over him. "Afternoon, officers." He winced. "I must have made a wrong turn."

* * *

The Clown walks on hands at the edge of a cliff, one is flesh and the other is soft plastic. His legs are pumping, his feet treading air. "How's this for being handicapped?" the Clown calls to the Hermit sitting in a fire-lit cave.

Below them, the ocean boils, waves bash into rock face.

The Hermit wears an amulet and it starts to glow as if from pure thought. Omens fly up in embers. Shadows play across the cavern wall. The Hermit beats on a bearskin drum. Sings himself calm. "If you don't change," he warns the Clown, "you're gonna fall."

The painted red smile of the Clown twists into lunacy and the specter of apocalypse spoils the Hermit's view of forever. He leaves the cave and comes to the ledge, paces back and forth. The more he frets, puffing on his feathered pipe, the more he blows smoke up his ass. At last, he wets his forefinger and holds it high. The wind comes up and throws an angry rain. "We're all going to fall, we don't let go," the Hermit laments, waves smashing rocks below, rain in his eyes.

The Clown and the Hermit walk on hands at the edge of the cliff. The morbid crowd in the rocks near the waves points up as if they were jumpers. Chained to a bracelet on the Clown's ankle, a Cave Woman whimpers, "Can we go home now?" By the time the

Hermit realizes he's chained to the ankle bracelet worn by the Cave Woman, she is falling.

* * *

Nico popped some Excedrin and washed them down with Coke. His face stiffened as he reached back, pinching the tight muscles in his shoulders.

Jesse, Manny, Joe and Josh were back from West State before noon.

Still no Coco Bird.

Two hours later they had checked fluid levels, mounted new tires, adjusted fuel injection and checked the Stinker's timing. Harley's exacting attention to every detail in the service of purring engines belied his easy-going hillbilly persona. His Southern drawl left the impression he was slow in the think department, but he wasn't.

Harley took another cigarette break and sat on a toolbox watching Nico work. "Y'all know racing cars ain't nothing like baseball or football. You don't get big money upfront so you can afford to miss a race here and there. Drivers have to win on the circuit and keep winning or they don't get paid. That means nobody on the crew gets paid. Without the money boys, 20% of nothing is nothing.

"I've seen lot of cats out there driving over their heads. Ya cain't trust 'em. They try to go faster and faster until they take out other drivers, ending somebody's dream."

Jesse took a can of brake fluid from Manny and shrugged it off. "There he goes, talking as if I'm not here."

Harley went on. "Few cats waltz away from a bad crash. When you're lucky enough to be spared the trauma, ya don't remember. Jesse gets right back on the track and runs wide open. It's the rememberin' that slows ya down."

Nico shrugged. "Jesse's always gone all-out, does that mean he never remembers?"

"Jesus!" Jesse glared at Nico, "now *you're* doing it."

"Doan do no good to talk *at* ya," Harley challenged back, "Might just as well talk *about* ya."

Harley wiped a socket wrench with a rag, took another swig of milk and dragged on the filtered menthol. He leaned toward Nico, confidentially. "He can give ya a rundown on every driver on the track. Has instincts for knowing when to ride their bumper and when to back off, when to make a move. That boy's fearless as a drunken Scot in a skirt and it's instinctual. Hopefully, it'll keep him out of trouble."

Nico tightened the fuel pump. The wrench slipped, busting his knuckles on the engine block. He leaped up, cussing, and cracked his head on the Stinker's hood. A light flashed behind his eyes. The jeep hit a landmine. The soldier on the road from Kon Barr stood beside the front fender whistling a haunting tune. Searing pain shot through Nico's skull, his knees buckled, and he slumped to the ground. Helicopter rotors sounded overhead—*whop, whop, whop.*

14.

Milo started at the sound of the front door. Monica dropped her bra behind the couch and slipped the sweater over her head, fluffing out her hair. Milo buttoned his shirt. The clock in the living room read 6:45.

"Did we interrupt anything?" Mindy called from the foyer where she peeked around the corner. Francie, a skinny brunette, grinned like a Chihuahua.

"Jesus Christ, Mindy!" Milo's voice climbed a whole octave. "What the hell you doing here?"

"Came back to pick up the hair dryer. We're giving each other perms."

Francie bit her lower lip, keen eyes dropping to Milo's shirttails.

Monica was cool, her arm on the back of the sofa. Her cheeks were a little flushed. "Sounds fun."

"Yeah? Want us to do yours?" Francie invited. She was waiting for Mindy at the bottom of the stairs, pondering the covered lump in the rug.

Monica's pleasant sing-song responded, "Oh, that would be cool, Francie, but not tonight, okay? Maybe another time."

"Sure," Francie replied, wide-eyed. "When you're not so busy."

A growl formed at the edges of Milo's mouth as he glared at Francie. "Thank you, Francie. You can go anytime."

Francie averted her eyes. "It was Mindy's idea."

Mindy trotted down the stairs with the hair dryer and a bag filled with shampoo and beauty aids. She bounced into the living room. "You got five dollars so Francie and I can go downtown?"

"Hell no! We had a deal." Milo's face burned in sharp retort. He yanked Mindy by the arm toward the door. "Time to go now."

"You're hurting me!" Mindy dropped the beauty bag and swung the hair dryer case. Milo ducked, wrenched her arm behind her and shoved her face into the wall. The *Blue Boy* reproduction rattled in its frame. When Milo spun his sister around to face him, she left a lipstick-print on the flowered wallpaper. "I'm gonna tell *mom!*" she blubbered.

Francie looked on in horror as Milo raised an open hand. Mindy covered her head with her arm. Milo held back.

"Milo!" Monica intervened, gripping his shoulder. "What has gotten into you?"

Francie slid by, back to the wall, picking up the bag and opening the door. Milo released Mindy and she stumbled out onto the stoop. She pivoted with tears streaming. "I'M GONNA TELL!"

"Go right ahead." Milo slammed the door. He walked briskly into the kitchen leaving Monica standing stunned in the foyer. By the time she caught up with him, Milo had knocked dishes into the sink, breaking a saucer or two.

"Milo, you're scaring me."

Blue Boy, this is Blue Moon. You're loud and clear. Over.

Milo turned, disoriented, and spoke into his collar. "Come in. Over."

This is Blue Boy. There's movement in that sector. Do you copy? Over.

"You could have hurt her." Monica took an involuntary step back.

This is Blue Moon. Hang on, Blue Boy, the Cavalry's comin'...

Milo blinked and rubbed his eyes. "I didn't mean to." He leaned against the sink and hugged himself.

"It's okay." Monica stroked his sore cheek. "You just lost it. She *can* be a brat."

Sedaka drifted in from the living room. Milo wiped his eyes with his shirt sleeve.

"It's okay," Monica repeated, her arms encircling him. She kissed his cheek to heal the split. Milo ducked into her arms.

After a few minutes, he extracted himself and retrieved a Jiffy Pop from the cupboard. He switched on the stove and shuffled the aluminum pan in a circular motion over the red-hot burner. Monica poured 7-Up into tumblers with ice. The tinfoil on the Jiffy Pop expanded with a popping sound and Milo thought of the Tigers' game—that popping sound. He closed his eyes. Even as the world disintegrated, he held onto Monica as his one and only truth.

His eyes opened to concerned eyes studying him. He pulled the Jiffy Pop off the burner holding the top with a large oven mitt. The popcorn stopped popping, but the tinfoil continued to expand. Holding the wire handle with the mitt, Milo punctured the hot foil with a fork. There was an explosion that dropped them to the floor. Monica's red cashmere sweater and white skirt were splattered with blood and guts.

"Blue Moon, this is Blue Boy. We're taking heavy fire. Over."

"Oh yuck!" Monica gawked at the ooze on her chest. "What's this?" She snagged a washcloth from the kitchen rack, held it under her chin and retched into the sink. When done, she turned on the faucet and let it run.

Milo lifted himself off the floor and dabbed at her sweater, smearing it all the more. Monica's blank stare needed some guidance, hand on elbow, back into the living room, back onto the couch. The television blinked on and the Hammer Man sat behind a news desk, mouthing without sound. The scene shifted to a camouflaged soldier in slow motion racing down a narrow trail toward a helicopter surrounded by tall grass. He changed into Wile E. Coyote, his face black and smoking after miscalculating the TNT.

The telephone rang. Milo answered.

"Hello," he said.

"Hello," the voice answered.

"Who are you calling?"

"Who are *you* calling?"

"I'm not calling anyone. You called me." Milo heard music in the background. It wasn't anything he'd ever heard before but it had a lot of sax.

"No, you called *me*," the voice echoed.

"No, you called *me*."

"You didn't call anyone?"

"No. Who is this?"

Mayday! Mayday!

"Maybe it's the storm," the phone voice spoke with plenty of sax.

"What storm?" Milo asked.

Thunder rattled the eaves.

Mayday! Mayday! This is Blue Boy.

Milo hung up the phone and turned to Monica who stood, shivering, color draining from her face.

The phone rang again.

"Hello," Milo answered.

"Fuck you, G.I." *Click.*

"Who was that?" Monica asked, holding onto his arm.

"Wrong number."

He took Monica upstairs to Mindy's room, went through his sister's drawers and found a floppy blue sweater and short black skirt. It was a total turn-off to see Monica in his sister's clothes. He could only laugh: the majorette became a beatnik.

"I hope you don't get in trouble." Monica pinched the sweater, pulling the fabric away from the rash on her belly. The wind pressed against windows, voices rattling against the pane. *It's the storm.* Outside, leaves on the trees didn't even flutter.

"I'm always in trouble," Milo shrugged, aware she now wore only three items of clothing. He took her hand, led her back downstairs to the couch to where she huddled, small and vulnerable, inside his arms. Whatever happened in Detroit, New York, and Hollywood would eventually find its way to them.

15.

A cool hand stroked Nico's forehead. He pulled the fingers to his lips and kissed them.

"What the fuck!" A voice cried. The hand yanked away.

Nico blinked awake. Josh Brownton turned to the shadows behind him. "I think he's asking for you."

This radiant angel stepped from the shadows and hovered over him. She wore Coco's perfume. Her misty blue eyes reflected his surprise. Thick henna hair streaked with blonde tumbled onto her delicate neck. A sense of loss jolted through him. He recognized the gold heart pinned to a black choker from their senior year.

"Coco Bird?"

"Feeling better, Nicky?"

Nico eased into her voice like a wounded animal. He let her lay him down supported by several fluffy pillows. The stain on the ceiling formed an umber frottage with long dripping fangs. Psychedelic posters covered cracked and yellowing wallpaper. Jimi Hendrix glowed in black light, his hair on fire. An expensive stereo system with Pioneer speakers was centerpiece on a cinderblock bookshelf.

Coco could have stepped out of a dance cage on *Hullaballoo.* "Got quite a bump on the noggin." She gently touched his head. The blinds in the living room were pulled and the only light came from a low-wattage floor lamp. "Jesse never told me you were coming."

The lump under Nico's scalp pulsed mere inches from his head wound. "Surprise!" he said, gritting his teeth.

Over the stereo hung a realistic portrait of Coco at the age of nine. Vincent Vandermeer, Coco's father, painted it in loving detail. Coco's freckles seemed to blossom like tulips in a Van Gogh field. Vincent died shortly after finishing the painting, dropped over dead in his studio from a silent heart attack. Vincent had struggled as an artist, but Nico always liked him. With the artless convenience of cameras, too little demand existed for good portrait painters. He earned his living as a sign painter. Vincent never complained but his work grew dispirited. Money was tight. His generous spirit refused his daughter nothing, even to the detriment of his marriage.

Nine months after Vincent died, Coco's mother Caroline married Lenny Bird, owner of a hardware store in Meridian. Coco never finished mourning Vincent before a new father stepped into her life. Somehow they brokered a deal though and Coco assumed the Bird name in exchange for a nice bedroom.

Lenny Bird was rigid and possessive. The three pillars of success in any business were independence, work ethic and customer service—with a smile. Vincent's gentle spirit and refined sensibilities inhibited his market value. Lenny flourished as a capitalist and Caroline made a show of Lenny's prosperity. It sickened Coco as she saw this as critical of her father. By the time she reached puberty, she battled her mother constantly. Caroline recruited Lenny as an ally in this fight and they told Coco she was selfish, warned her Jesse was a delinquent. "Why don't you go out with that *nice boy*? You know, Nico, the son of a middle-class working stiff." Nico passed muster with Lenny, but Coco wanted a guy who didn't. Lenny Bird had fed Coco so much sugar-and-spice it became her poison. He'd convinced her men like Vincent Vandermeer never grew up, and therefore failed to assume their birthright as the natural heads of households.

"Was I out?" Nico asked, cool washcloth easing the throb. The watchful eyes of controllers like Lenny Bird and Jesse Walker hadn't really stunted Coco's growth.

"Like a light," Coco answered. "So, who's this Alyssa?"

"What?" How did she know about Alyssa?

Josh tore out the back door, screen slamming behind him.

Nico watched the easy swing of Coco Bird's hips as she parted a curtain of beads and stepped into the kitchen. The beads were still clacking when she reappeared with a tall glass of ice water and two aspirins. "Here, take these."

Coco's fingers brushed his palm about the time The Electric Prunes were having too much to dream in stereo. Nico downed the pills. The lump in his throat was nearly as big as the one on his head. He hadn't expected how hard it would be to accept Coco as Jesse's wife.

The screen door slammed again. Jesse, Manny and Josh joined Coco in a semicircle around Nico as if he were some patient in a surgical theater, his entrails hanging out for doctors to read the future.

"I swear," Jesse said, "Cuckoo thought you knocked yourself out trying to avoid her."

"Jesse Luke Walker, you're such a liar." Coco punched her husband on the shoulder. "Why didn't you tell me?"

"Surprise!"

Nico felt his body floating, his heart pounding. One moment he was on the couch, the next cruising low over tepid jungle. When his vision returned to the small circle around him, there was one extra: a nimbus warrior. Nico wasn't even surprised. The Kon Barr soldier had been hanging around of late. The likelihood of encounters increased as everyone in the PAST carried ghosts. After a while the soldier felt like everyday normal. A hard shadow crossed Jesse's face and his shoulders slumped involuntarily. Nico wondered if Jesse had sensed Nico's ghost or maybe Nico had sensed his.

"Flashback?" Manny's lopsided smile summoned Nico into *crazy*, a world where the inmates were in charge of the loony bin. "Imagine trying to explain to folks how you made it through the war only to end up knocked dead by the hood of a car?"

Jesse's playful headlock brought Coco's face to his. Nico shut his eyes as they kissed. What he couldn't see couldn't hurt him. When his eyes opened again, Coco's lips had drawn tight. He tried not to read too much into it. "We're such poor hosts." Jesse winked. "Coco, we got some grub for these headcases? Joe, Harley and I gonna trailer the Bomb and take it to the track."

Nico tried to sit up. "I'll come." The room began to spin. Jesse's hand on his shoulder restrained him. "No, take it easy, Little Engine. We'll be back. Manny, can you help Coco make sandwiches?"

"Sure, boss." Manny followed Jesse to the screen door, nodding in quiet complicity, glancing over to Nico and Coco side-by-side on the couch.

Minutes later, Joe's Bronco and the Stinker trailer pulled out. Josh came in, throwing open the screen. "What can I do?" Josh squirmed out of the coveralls, dropping them like a sloughed skin on the floor by the back door.

"Put something on the stereo," Coco said, unpacking groceries onto the kitchen counter.

Josh strolled into the living room and found the Steve Miller Band. He danced back into the kitchen, took Coco by the hand and gave her a twirl. She bumped into Manny who'd just pinched some Gold from a baggie, missing the bowl. "Shit," Manny scowled at Josh, then got down on hands and knees, dabbing at dried leaves with a wet forefinger. He bubbled up a good hit and exhaled a stream. He offered the bong to Nico. "El-Kabong?"

Nico shook his head. "Got a headache."

"Wow. And we're not even *married*."

Now Neumann's point about reconnecting with the world made some sense if you didn't include the PAST in it. Their motto was *Excess in all things.* Warriors throughout history have lost their way home from the battlefield. For Manny "Ten-Mile-High" Hernandez, there were plenty of reasons to self-medicate. He'd taken to a worldview, you might say, of being connected to the earth through his favorite plant. He had a green thumb and gave Josh everything he needed for his grandmother's recipe. The PAST almost daily gave witness to the refined sensibilities of Vietnam vet stoners. Legalization was Manny's religion; horticulture his worship. God will provide with a little help from technology, Manny often said, in deference to his family who went to church every Sunday. He was more of a medicine man than a churchgoer. He believed the plant existed to divinely inspire and he needed a lot of inspiration. *Cannabis* taught humanity to find God in nature, God in man. Who could object to that? The Church, of course. If people found God in themselves, who would support a priestly class?

"Nico, are you okay?" Coco asked. "I gotta go to work in a couple of hours." She steered Manny toward the kitchen. "Aren't you getting the munchies by now? Wash your hands and peel some oranges." Coco lit a stick of patchouli incense and set it in a holder on the book shelf.

"I can help," Nico volunteered, rising to his feet.

Coco Bird came back through the beads and helped him up. She assessed his acuity. "You sure?"

Nico nodded, following her into the kitchen. "Let's make sandwiches."

Manny bellied up to the sink, scrubbed his hands with Lava and, after ten minutes, inspected his fingernails. Coco Bird took a small bowl from the cupboard and set it on the counter.

Manny's blunt nails shucked the rind in small chunks. The greater challenge, Nico thought, would be to remove the rind in one piece. Peeling one orange took Manny an eternity; he removed the rind in little pieces as if time slowed down.

"Here, open the tuna." Coco Bird tossed Nico a can of Bumble Bee solid white. She pulled sandwich fixings out of the refrigerator—crisp head lettuce, mayonnaise and relish. Manny held a naked orange to the light for inspection then arranged the separated segments in a neat circle on a paper plate. A work of art. Coco Bird ripped open a bag of chips and emptied them into a bowl. Josh poured Coke into glasses. Nico clamped the can opener onto the 12-ounce tin and twisted. He loosened the meat with a fork. The fork struck something hard. Nico pinched from the can a chunk of bony meat and examined it carefully. It was a finger—more precisely, a thumb.

Nico laid the thumb onto his palm, rolled it first one way then the other. He held it up to Manny and Coco. "Look, I think it's real." He held up his own thumb for comparison. Skin and bone and flesh pad. A thumb cleanly severed at the joint.

"How awful!" Coco covered her open mouth, trying not to gag.

Manny sniffed it. "Smells like tuna."

"How can you tell?" Coco asked.

Manny poked the thumb with a finger, plucked it out of Nico's hand. "It's not so thick as a slug. Seems fresh, as if canned yesterday." Manny picked up the can and peeled off the label. "Solid white albacore canned in Astoria." His eyebrow went up. "Can I have it?"

"Oh my God, Manny." Coco Bird belched her disgust.

Manny ran out the back door like a little boy who'd caught a toad.

"What's he doing?" Coco Bird wondered.

Nico shrugged, tossed the rest of the tuna into a bowl.

"Oh God, no." Coco said, taking the bowl away and tossing the tuna into the garbage, washing the bowl in the sink. "We have potted meat." She went through cupboards, opened the refrigerator door "...and Kraft cheddar slices." She reached overhead to fetch the potted meat. Her mini climbed the backs of her legs. Nico stared.

He blinked hard, a little embarrassed, but reached around her to find the cheese.

Potted meat and cheese slice sandwiches weren't so bad. Josh excused himself to take a plate out to Manny in the barn. Nico pushed through clacking beads and sat down on the faded flower couch. Coco Bird put a group called Quicksilver Messenger Service on the stereo. Nico was reading the album notes when she sat down beside him, her thigh touching his. They ate and listened to "The Fool." Nico never heard anything like it. Instrumental jams were getting longer with more improvisation, from Bushy's drum solo in Iron Butterfly's "In-A-Gadda-Da-Vida" to the album versions of The Doors' "Light My Fire" and "The End." The jams in Quicksilver's "Gold and Silver" and "The Fool" conjured visions of San Francisco light shows and turned-on crowds. Nico fantasized about groups like Quicksilver and Mothers of Invention and Dr. Hook coming to The Enchanted Forest.

Coco Bird knocked on the invisible glass of Nico's sound booth. "Earth to Nico," she called.

"Yeah?"

"Still in there?"

"Where else would I be?" He cracked a weak smile of embarrassment.

Coco shrugged. Their shoulders touched. She turned to him. "I just wanted to say," she hesitated, hands dropping into her lap, "that I'm sorry."

Her eyes were sky bright. Nico wasn't sure what to say. "For what?"

"For not writing."

"Ah, why is that?"

"It's complicated." Coco's voice shifted.

"It always is."

"But Jesse seems different," she said.

"What do you mean by different? We've all changed; everyone except Jesse. Harley says if Jesse crashes, he climbs back into the car like nothing happened, like he has no fear. He lost an arm and acts totally unaffected by the war."

She avoided his gaze. "When Jesse came home," she disclosed, "he seemed grateful to be alive. He'd survived the worst. He was ready to begin a new life. But he doesn't talk about anything with me…about the war, about the crash. When he took up racing, it was like a fresh start. Nothing could hold him back, not Jesse Walker, no siree. Harley's convinced him he has a future in racing cars. But I think he's drinking too much."

"Maybe he should join our Vet's group. We all talk about all kinds of things. It helps. Jesse *always* drank," he reminded her, unable to disguise a lack of sympathy.

"Not like this. Used to be mostly beer." She led him into the kitchen and opened a cabinet. Inside was a glass carnival of liquor bottles. "Jesse drinks from the time he gets up in the morning to the time he goes to bed at night. He's never falling-down drunk, but he's always drinking. I left my job at the nursing home," she confessed, "after Jesse dropped by one night and he told this harmless old guy, 'Tonight's your night, old man.' And Sammy died that night."

"C'mon Coco, you work in a nursing home. People die in nursing homes, for God's sake."

"They end up there because there's no one else to take care of them. How could Jesse know Sammy would die that night…on my shift? He didn't even know the man. I found Sammy's body."

The last body Coco saw was Chad Summers who died in a rollover crash in the spring of '64. The accident occurred on a dangerous stretch of road coming from a wrestling meet at Mountain Home. Jesse was driving Chad's '62 Buick Special, the same car up on blocks out back. Jesse suffered only cuts and bruises. Chad had been asleep in the passenger seat when Jesse lost control. The Police believed he dozed off at the wheel and Jesse swore he hadn't. They were all going to be seniors—it should have been the best year of their lives.

"He wakes up crying sometimes. If I bring it up, he just gets angry."

"You think the war's responsible, not just his personality?" Nico slipped on the proverbial dangerous slope and invited a shoulder-cry. "Guys tell war stories," he soothed her with a hand on her head.

"Yeah, like your wounded warriors club." Coco blinked away a tear, wiped her eyes dry and checked herself in the living room's full-length mirror. "God, look at me now. I need to fix my face." She went back into the bathroom.

The very fact that Coco fell apart when an elderly gent died in the nursing home suggested to Nico she wasn't cut out for that job. He thought of the dead and dying grunts Jesse flew out of hot LZs; it was possible he could recognize a ghost when he saw one.

"So you goin' to school?" he raised his voice over water running in the basin. "I thought you wanted to be an R.N." Coco wouldn't be able to handle an emergency room. She wasn't Alyssa Parker, living in a six-by-ten cubicle in Pleiku. Coco didn't have her strength.

"No, I'm working at K-Mart in their women's department."

"Ah. Sounds less stressful. So why'd you quit writing?"

Coco reappeared from the hallway with a pained expression. "It wasn't only you. I quit writing Jesse, too. I couldn't handle the war. It was overwhelming me—in the newspapers, magazines, television, movies, music, everywhere soldiers dying, demonstrators getting their heads bashed in."

"Yeah, I can't blame ya." He lied. He *did* blame her. If he were honest he would say: *So turn off the TV, don't pick up the paper. At least you had that option. You could turn off the war.*

"So you forgive me then?"

"Sure."

"Friends?"

"Friends."

The screendoor slammed. Coco let go of his hand. Manny pushed through the beaded doorway and stood, hands on hips, modeling his new prize—the severed thumb hung on a cord around his neck.

* * *

One April afternoon after co-ed softball, the lights in the west wing blinked out. The hush of dark hallways in the high school erupted with echoes of hoot-owls. Boys in the locker room paraded outside to the practice field wrapped in white towels, their showers interrupted. Sunlight cascaded through budding trees and the boys kept their eyes glued on the outside door to the girls' locker room. They were hoping the girls too would file out wrapped in white towels. No such luck. Nico dared Jesse to go into their locker room in the dark and bring something back as proof. Minutes later, he came back with a pair of white lace panties. He sniffed the crotch which had *Tuesday* etched in red, and shared it around, declaring they belonged to Tawnee Phillips. "Wanna bet? I can smell her sweet cherry a mile off."

After history class, Jesse approached Tawnee in the hall. "Feeling a bit drafty, Tawnee?" Jesse pulled the panties out of his pocket and passed them under his nose. Tawnee looked down at the floor and headed to the principal's office. Jesse ran them up the flagpole where they fluttered half-mast, ruby Tuesday snapping in the breeze. Mrs. Gronowski, the girls' P.E. teacher, complained to Mr. Ball, the vice-principal. As he was lowering them from the flagpole, a gust of wind came up and blew ruby Tuesday from his hands. Her panties took flight like a startled dove and landed inside the wooden fence that surrounded the MacIntyre place. Their large cross-eyed boxer sniffed them out immediately and carried them into his doghouse to shred blissfully.

16.

Milo was on his feet at the sound of the doorbell. That Mindy didn't know when to quit, he thought. Monica tugged his arm. "It's okay," he assured her. "I'm cool." He opened the door.

A shiver of mud and blood haunted the front porch with iridescent snakes writhing from its body cavity, crawling over the welcome mat. A soldier stood wide-eyed as the wetness of his life's blood oozed down his sleeves and pants legs. He opened his mouth like a fish and static crackled the air.

Blue Moon, this is Blue Boy. We're taking heavy fire. Over.

Milo's brain stuttered and the door opened on Geo, sports bag in one hand, a brown paper bag in the other, Gayleen Cooper under his arm.

"*Que pasa, amigo.*" Geo saluted with the brown bag. "Are we late?"

"Hope we're not intruding," Gayleen said.

"No, no," he lied. "Please, come in." He held the door for them. Gayleen wasn't limping. That was a good sign. She'd always struck Milo as stand-offish, a National Honor student and all that. But he had to confess she had a style all her own. She was more conservative than her hipster parents who loved poetry and jazz and wrote letters to the editor, and hoped to one day succeed in business. She couldn't be more different than Monica. They both were smart, but Gayleen was book smart. On Geo's arm, she looked a little plain.

The sun dropped behind the storm clouds. Cloud shadow fell over the house. No writhing snakes slithered on the welcome mat as Milo pulled shut the door. The storm could move in during the night. His watch read 6:45. He held it up to his ear. The watch was still ticking.

I say again. Heavy Fire!

Milo hooked Geo's arm, dragging his friend inside. Geo in turn dragged Gayleen, whipping her through the foyer into the living room where she glided to the La-Z-Boy, and dropped into it with a grand gesture, arms thrown wide. Geo either couldn't tell or didn't care if they were interrupting anything. Milo's anger mellowed into a strange sense of relief.

Gayleen's red hair was bound back with an orange ribbon. She left sweet curls to frame her eyes and cheeks. She looked chic in brown capris, green jester shirt with notched hem and slip-on white tennis shoes. When she smiled she showed a little too much space between her teeth.

Monica's weak smile was nothing but tolerant. She and Gayleen hardly knew each other. Gayleen was from Alderbrook, at the edge of town, back up-river. They ran in different crowds. Monica's dad was a bar pilot and made good money. She lived in a historic house on Astoria's Nob Hill overlooking Young's Bay. Gayleen's parents ran a local bookshop and earned a modest living. Books were stacked everywhere in their house. Gayleen shared a copy of *The Autobiography of Frank Harris* with Geo and called it Victorian fiction. Milo had never seen his friend so enthusiastic about reading before. He read the juiciest bits out loud.

"Does your TV work?" Geo asked.

Milo shook his head. "Interference and test patterns."

"What about the phone?" Geo lifted the receiver. "No dial tone."

"Worked a minute ago."

"Sit tight, girls." Geo's anxiety stemmed not from *coitus interruptus* but something larger; Gayleen had already enlisted Monica into a witness program. Monica sat up straight, with keen interest, eyes blinking in Morse code. Gayleen sometimes talked way too much to mask her insecurity.

In the kitchen, Geo pulled two bottles out of a brown paper bag and set them on the counter: Boone's Farm Strawberry Hill and Annie Green Springs. His contribution to a good time was usually himself, so Milo counted himself lucky to get two bottles of ghetto wine. He wondered what his friend carried in the sports bag, besides a box of Trojans? Milo understood what it meant to be prepared. He carried a kit in Cherry's trunk: a half-case of beer, chips, transistor radio, battery lantern, some blankets and two pillows.

Milo read the date on the wine label. "Isn't wine supposed to be better the longer it's aged?"

"Not this stuff," Geo answered.

He opened the Kelvinator door and retrieved an ice tray from the freezer. The kitchen sparkled just the way his mom had left it. No evidence of shrapnel in the cupboards. Then why was Monica wearing Mindy's sweater and skirt?

"It's better warm." Geo twisted the cap—cheap wine doesn't come with corks. Milo pulled four long-stemmed goblets out of the hutch. Even ghetto wine could be made to look expensive. The Jiffy Pop still sat on the shelf unopened. "How's popcorn go with wine?"

Milo broke loose ice cubes in the ice tray and dropped one into each glass.

In a low voice, Geo buzzed, "Monica's ready, man. You know how cheerleaders are."

"She's a majorette."

"Same dif," Geo said.

Milo met Monica through band. The first time he saw her in that short majorette skirt with those great legs he was smitten.

"Bet she'd put out for you."

"Shut up! She might hear you."

"Did you notice?" He winked, conspiratorially. "She's not wearing a bra. You can see her nipples." Geo arched his eyebrows lewdly. Milo only frowned. "Okay, then, but you know the story about the girl who asked her grandmother if she wore lipstick if she thought her boyfriend would kiss her, and the grandmother said no, so the girl wore no panties on their date?"

Milo watched the tinfoil on the popcorn expand. Nothing happened this time. He pulled it off the burner, popped the foil and poured popcorn into a large bowl. Then he added melted margarine and several brisk shakes of salt, stirring with a wooden spoon.

Geo rolled the wine goblet under his nose like an official taster for Annie Green Springs. "Ahh, sweet nectar!"

Milo corralled the popcorn bowl under his arm and headed to the living room. Geo brought the goblets with Strawberry Hill for the girls. Milo went back for Annie Green Springs for the guys.

"I'd rather have Annie Green Springs," Gayleen said, so Geo switched with her. He didn't care as long as it was wine.

"So when we broke down." Geo started.

Milo interrupted. "How'd you break down?"

"Just toolin' down Marine Drive." Geo sat on the arm of the La-Z-Boy, sliding his arm around Gayleen. "We passed this cold storage truck loaded with frozen albacore on the side of the road."

As Geo told the story, Milo realized his eyes were on Monica's nipples.

"Dan Marshall's driving. So we pull over. Dan's checking underneath. The truck's got a broken axle."

Monica picked up Geo's stare and covered her breasts with her arms. Milo flopped on the couch next to her, sipping apple wine and listening to Geo tell the story.

"The truck broke down while Dan was just driving along. He swears he was going easy because minutes earlier he'd seen this car by the Marina lose control and plunge into the bay. The axle suddenly broke. I said to him, isn't this International a '60 or '61? The undercarriage was rusted out. Sure, cars rust out in Astoria, but after only two years? Then I remembered the cable that snagged you at the cannery. That was a new cable. Right?"

"So I offered Dan a lift over to Hanson's so he could get a tow. Then *my* car wouldn't start. I turned the key and nothing happened. It won't so much as turn over. I opened the hood and, you wouldn't believe it." Geo scratched his shoulder, nervous nails raking his shirt. "The engine's like overgrown with moss. Moss and creepers. The carburetor's choked with vines. So we hoofed it. All these people were stalled by the side of the road, cars breaking down everywhere in Astoria, their parts dropping onto the road."

Gayleen conjured an eerie sound like a UFO or Outer Limits. Milo checked the windows. The leaves outside on the trees were windless still.

Was it nuclear war? He wondered. Or maybe some galactic overlord was tickering with the timing chain on the cosmic engine? Possibilities pureed in the curiosity blender of Milo's mind.

"What if the world blew up and none of us in the outer reaches heard the sirens?" Gayleen shivered.

"That's hopeful." Monica smiled tolerantly.

"You guys are depressing!" Geo said.

"Or what if somebody just wants *me* to accept all this?" Milo expelled a flatulent blow through loose lips. Not even the Hammer Man—lurking tall, dark and ominous in the back of his mind—could convince Milo this wasn't some joke being played on only him.

Thunder rumbled in the distance.

"If the world were ending," Geo said, rolling off the arm of the La-Z-Boy into Gayleen's lap, "I'd wanna go out with a *bang*." She pushed him off, spilling a few drops of wine.

"Watch the wine," Milo warned. "Ruin mom's carpet and I'm a dead man."

Gayleen was embarrassed.

Something struck the house, a whump like a jet breaking the sound barrier. It rattled the house on its World War One foundation. It was the wind, Milo decided. The storm was coming in. The glass in the window vibrated with wind current, yet the leaves on the trees barely stirred.

"Yeah, let's go out with a *bang*," Monica agreed, lifting her leg over Milo's, wrapping her arms around his neck and kissing him hard. She surprised him. When they came up for air, Geo applauded.

Gayleen ducked under Geo's arms, blushing, smoothing her jester shirt where it bunched up, showing her midriff. Geo slapped her ass.

Milo straightened his shirt. He wondered if Gayleen felt the kind of pressure he felt.

The TV came on and off. Out of a snowy screen an indistinct figure emerged, slogging up the snowy street. He still dragged his hammer. The Hammer Man grew with each step until his dark face menaced the whole 24" screen and a finger ticked the glass. Bright light spilled in around him as he sputtered in the flux. Still, Milo understood him to say, "Don't give up. Hold on."

The Hammer Man from the edge of his vision hoisted his hammer and the TV screen shattered. Milo blinked at the poof of smoke but didn't react. The TV was only shattering in his head, until Monica screamed. Gayleen's face turned pale. Geo's jaw dropped. They gawked at the smoking Zenith-in-a-cabinet.

"Did you *see* that?" Milo asked.

"Christ, Milo." Geo huffed. "Your TV exploded."

"Yeah," Milo checked the shocked faces again, "but did you see *him*?"

"Who?"

"He must only want *me*."

"Oh God." Geo rubbed his head with an open hand. "Here we go again. Everything is happening to *you*. Forget us. We're just figments of your imagination."

A rhythmic pounding like a drum beat reverberated

through every beam of the house. Milo looked up the dim stairwell to the second floor where the pounding came from. Late sun pooled on the landing under stained glass. The house warped with the stairs twisting into a spiral. He felt drawn upward, so he mounted the stairs slowly, singing "If I Had a Hammer" in his head.

"Where ya going?" Geo called, close behind. At the head of the stairs, Milo stopped and listened. Geo drew up beside him. They peered through the hallway toward the north side window. The glass spasmed in the pane, but there was not a whisper of wind outside. It was like the whole house was shivering. Milo walked down the hallway in a cold sweat. The pounding sound came from behind that door. His bedroom door. The panels were vibrating with every percussive blow. Milo studied the doorknob. "Do you hear that?" he asked, uncertain.

"Of course, I hear it," Geo shouted. "I'm not deaf."

"Don't be afraid." Milo reached for the doorknob.

"I *ain't* afraid," Geo stammered, his conviction breaking as each beat rattled his bones.

Milo pushed the door open. The pounding stopped. His room had been recently ransacked: his record player smashed, a stack of 45s broken and strewn in black fragments, his bed busted, its posts splintered, clothes shredded, mattress torn, stuffing still adrift in the air. The house's outside wall had blown clean off.

Another loud bang shook the house. Walls swayed, dust sifted through cracks, the floor buckled beneath their feet, beams and rafters split.

The girls screamed from down in the living room.

Milo and Geo raced to the stairs. The whole house shuddered. Geo grabbed his sports bag, the unfinished bottle of strawberry wine and herded the girls out the front door. Milo blasted through behind them, car keys in hand.

Behind the wheel, Milo's hands shook as he cranked the key over and over in the ignition. The car wouldn't start. He kept grinding and churning and it finally roared to life.

Milo backed out of the driveway as his house, warping one way then another, bulged in the middle and imploded, collapsing into a cloud of dust.

17.

The target was minutes away.

They could hear Basque folk music coming up the route of the Fourth of July parade. A burly rodeo clown with bulbous red nose stepped up to the helium tank to inflate another balloon. The heat radiating from the pavement made Nico's eyes itch but he kept a watch on Jesse Walker anyway. He was so intent on fitting the lip of the balloon over the nozzle with his hook and one hand that he didn't notice the toddler wiping his snotty nose on his oversized rodeo clown shirt. He yanked the white clown gloves off and held up his Captain Hook. The toddler blinked as if struck by lightning, gaping in stunned silence, pudgy fingers sticky with cotton candy.

Nico questioned Jesse's motives for joining the PAST. Why would someone, apolitical his whole life, resisting enlistment in *any* cause, enlist in the Army in the first place, let alone join a bunch of injured warriors telling war stories. Jesse didn't tell stories, he was a character in everybody else's. His joining the Army came as a surprise. After a short career of flying choppers in Vietnam, he crashed and lost his arm. When he couldn't fly anymore, he became despondent, until he found flying on the ground in a Stinker Bomb.

Nico never pretended to be a hero, but he understood them more than most. He'd seen them come through the

Splendors of Bangkok. Walker wasn't the first one that couldn't take his foot off the gas. They affirmed Jack Kerouac's analogy of the comet streaking across the night sky. That's why they needed bouncers at the Splendors. Jesse was the model of a driven man, without any guarantee of longevity. Nico chose to conserve fuel for the fire by burning less brightly for much longer.

Two Basque dancers appeared, holding a banner waist-high. When they emerged from the shadows of the overpass, there were Basque musicians playing accordions, tambourines and flutes on a flatbed. Dancers revolved around a maypole lofted like a flag and carried by a thick-chested strongman. The traditional dance had been adapted for parades. Male dancers in traditional *gerriko* and *txapela* with white pants and shirt held onto multi-colored ribbons interwoven as they moved in opposing orbits around the tree of life, their ribbons tangled and untangled lines in moving dance. The dance ended when the dancers let go of the ribbons, releasing the binds that anchored them to this plane of existence. The dancers reversed and started all over again by picking up a ribbon.

The snot-nosed toddler's mother pulled the boy toward her bosom, glancing with mild distrust at the rodeo clown. Nico intervened. "Hey champ," he called to the boy, "how about a red balloon?"

The mother softened at Nico's hobo eyes. She released the boy's hand. The boy shuffled forward, his mother's hand on his shoulder. "Kay," he sniveled, wiping his nose with the back of his hand and transferring it to the front of his shirt.

Jesse leaned in, thumbing a bulbous nose. "Go ahead, kid. Pinch it."

Nico sensed an unease in the mother who watched carefully as snotty reached up and pinched the rubber nose.

Jesse honked.

The boy yanked the hand back. Then laughed.

Jesse crowed and the boy crowed.

It was great fun!

Nico tied the balloon off. The mother was a looker. Mexican, he guessed. Dark-complected with long shiny black hair.

"Here ya go, champ." Nico offered the red balloon, but Jesse clamped his pincers on the string before the boy could take it. With a wicked smile, he transferred the balloon to the boy, extending his hook. The hook brushed the boy's skin and his eyes puffed up like a blowfish. Drool rolled down the edges of his mouth. The red balloon slipped his grip and floated up, up and away.

Nico's blood boiled. What was Jesse trying to do? They were in *disguise*.

The PAST urged Jesse to drive the getaway car, but he insisted on being a chief operative in the hit. It should have been Doc there with Nico. Giving in may have compromised the mission.

The boy's lower lips trembled as his face pinched tight. He began to cry.

Jesse started to panic. He covered the kid's mouth with his good hand.

"Don't touch my baby!" the mother, who was watching every move, screamed.

Nico apologized and handed the mother another balloon. She tied it to her son's wrist. Jesse's eyes widened at the sight of modest brown breasts under her tank top. The fingers of his good hand twitched.

"*Rápidamente*, Carlos." The mother tugged her son's arm. "We'll miss the parade." She half-dragged Snotty away, unaware of Jesse's eyes feasting on her backside. Picking his nose, the boy glanced back at the rodeo clown and stumbled on.

"Jesus, Jesse." Nico punched his partner on the shoulder, shaking his head.

"What was that for?" Jesse asked. He thrust his left hand into the huge front pocket of the overalls where it obscenely fluttered. Under the overalls Jesse wore a long-sleeved red and black plaid shirt stained with honest sweat. The stiff hair in the red wig stood on end in mock fright. The filtered cigarette between his painted lips bobbed in his mouth as it worked like a cat watching a bird.

Nico slapped the cigarette away. "You're married, remember? Jesus, Jesse! Put your hook away."

Jesse's white bowtie fluttered on his Adam's apple as Jesse rolled loose a low guttural growl.

"My God." Nico suddenly realized. "We've turned into Laurel and Hardy."

Jesse worked the glove over the hook. As far as disguises go, his rodeo clown was a practical solution. The black Converse tennis shoes attracted far less attention than Nico's Brechtian hobo floppers. If you enrage a Brahma bull you have to be able to fly. Rodeo clowns got that.

As usual, Nico over-thought his disguise. He went for the Emmett Kelly metaphor as it fit a certain public perception—the unshaven Viet vet with sorrowful eyes, begging on a street corner.

"We didn't come for girl-watching," Nico reminded him.

Jesse blinked and saluted. "Keeping my mind on the mission, sir."

"Right."

The parade passed underneath. Nico twisted a long hot-dog-shaped balloon with sharp squeaking noises into ridiculous animals. This one's a Saigon tiger. What about a Laotian Tree Frog? Thai Stick Man. He could hire out for birthday parties.

The target was getting closer. A marching band was approaching. He leaned over the guardrail, marking the parade's slow progress. He felt the pressure, his brain fried.

He remembered marching in this parade in summer dress—white shorts, red t-shirts and white tennis shoes, swinging his dented Bundy brass trumpet along Capitol Boulevard, counting steps as he played "Maria" from memory.

The Boise High School Marching Band rolled over the rise in red and white lines. Two dignified drum majors—one male, one female—strutted in fringed buckskins and long feathered headdresses. They did an about-turn, walking backwards, arms folded over their chests. In unison, their hands shot up and tom-toms led the band into the trumpet fanfare on "Malaguena."

Big Skye kept up, walking alongside, hunched over a clipboard, exhorting guidons to watch their lines, the skin of his bald pate tight as a kettle drum.

The band marched on, playing the fight song, "On Wisconsin." Twenty deputies of the Ada County Sheriff's Mounted Posse thankfully followed the band. You can imagine what happens to the lines when you're dodging horseshit. In light tan shirts and dark brown riding pants, the deputies pranced their mounts in loose formation, reins in one hand, waving cowboy hats in the other. Every ten yards or so, a tail eased up and dropped a steaming load onto the hot pavement. The posse emerged on the bright-side of the overpass and three teens in coveralls trailed behind, scooping up turds and dumping them into a red wheelbarrow.

Deputy Jericho Sinclair rode a muscular Morgan. Jericho was a real war hero. He waved to the crowd like a politician. He'd fought in one of the first big battles in Vietnam. Nico suddenly felt paranoid. Like the deputy's eyes were on him. *Settle down*, he reasoned with himself, *we're just a couple of clowns working a parade*.

Under the helium cart, they'd hidden a plastic bucket of rank pig's blood and a bundle of leaflets. The leaflets read: SUPPORT OUR TROOPS: QUESTION THEIR LEADERS. Their objective: draw attention to the blood of American boys spilled at the hands of pig politicians.

They'd scouted out the overpass. It was a good strike zone.

Near the end of the parade was the Governor of Idaho, on an elevated platform built onto the Boise Cascade Freedom Day float. Twenty inert American flags waited to lift their skirts with any hint of wind. The scarlet letters of patriotic slogans on blue banners bled into the mid-day heat. Two elementary school kids—a boy decked out as Uncle Sam, and little Lady Liberty—brandished sparklers and squinted from the smoke in their eyes. They flanked the Governor in his immaculate white suit and red tie, waving to the crowd.

On the flatbed, five Fair Maids in pastel gowns rotated on flower heads. After ninety minutes in ninety degrees, their smiles were melting. Near the end of the parade route, a cool breeze off the river would restore their wilting spirits.

The PAST hadn't bargained on the Lollypop Kids. Nobody would get hurt, Nico told himself. It's only pig blood.

Idaho's executive was a staunch conservative, friend of loggers, miners and the ever-exclusive club of good ol' boys, surrogate for Nixon in the escalation of war. His white top shimmered like early snow in the Tetons. This good ol' boy, Nico told himself, could stand to be splattered with a little civil disobedience.

Nico removed the plastic bucket of congealed pig's blood and hurried across the street. He had only 10 seconds before the float emerged on the bright side. On Jesse's signal, Nico pulled off the elastic cover and lifted the bucket up onto the guardrail. Jesse snapped rubber bands from a bundle of leaflets and let fly. Spectators watched in bemusement, expecting maybe coupons from a local merchant. The leaflets fluttered down like ticker tape. The Governor snatched one out of the air, read it and scowled up at them just as Nico tipped the bucket. Warm blood with the consistency of gravy spread out in a graceful red arc right smack onto the Governor's uplifted face.

SPLOOSH!

The splatter effect was something grand. The Governor gasped, spitting pig's blood. Five Fair Maids recoiled into their flower heads. Unfortunately, the Lollypop Kids were in the strike zone, hugging the Governor's knees. The rank odor was so strong they started to heave. Barf and pig's blood mixed slicker than snot, and the Governor lost his footing. He plunged headfirst into the apricot lap of Fair Maid Emily Tillman. It knocked Emily backwards off her flower head where she landed on the flatbed, legs splayed, arms flapping like a goose. Her apricot gown flew up around her hips. The Governor's head planted face first in her lap.

The float driver veered left then right, then left again, vision impaired with streaking stains of congealed blood. Parade watchers scattered as the Freedom Day float bounced onto the sidewalk, crashing into a light pole. The jarring stop of steel against steel so frightened dear Emily that she nearly suffocated the Governor; pressing his face against her hips, he let go of the flyer.

* * *

Jesse raced down the overpass in his Mercury fliers. Nico lagged behind like a duck in galoshes. Doc waited on the side street in a blue '65 Mustang, Manny at the wheel of a car borrowed from an original owner and fitted with temporary plates. They switched plates with a '62 Studebaker Lark towed to the junkyard two weeks ago after dropping a transmission out on Highway 49. Jesse threw himself through an open door into the backseat.

Nico lost one of his clodhoppers in a dead run, one foot whacking the pavement and the other in a colored argyle sock. He dove headfirst through the door, Jesse grabbing hold of his collar and then his rope belt, Nico's feet dragging as Jesse yanked him into the car.

"Get us out of here, Manny," Jesse commanded from the backseat.

Manny drove like an old woman.

Jesse peered through the back window. "Are you stoned, Manny? Step on it!"

"We don't want to attract attention," Manny explained.

"Like having two clowns in the backseat?"

"Okay. Mellow out, man." Manny assured him, "We're cool."

The Mustang swerved.

"Look out!" Tires squealed. Manny nearly rolled the Mustang, jerking the wheel to avoid a head-on with a Meadowgold Dairy truck. The Mustang climbed the curb onto the sidewalk and just missed a hunched-over gray-haired black man by inches. The man shook his cane in the rear view mirror. "Keep your eyes on the road."

Nico caught a movement out of the corner of his eye. He turned to the back window. Jericho Sinclair was giving chase on his Morgan and gaining fast. "Wow," Nico was impressed, "it's Gene Autry!"

Manny cut the corner and accelerated. Jericho took a shortcut up and over a grassy embankment, across a ramp, and down the other side with the Morgan breathing hard behind the Mustang.

"C'mon, Manny," Jesse snorted.

Manny floored the Mustang. It fishtailed up Walnut with more horses under the hood than Jericho could squeeze between his legs. The Mustang screeched on two wheels around the corner on to SE 22nd. The chase was done.

By the time they heard any sirens, the Mustang was inside Manny's cousin's cool garage. Sitting in the darkness, Nico wondered whether to hold his breath or laugh in relief. He hadn't felt this alive in months.

The PAST carried out the bloody deed: they baptized the Governor into the brotherhood of those with blood on their hands. And they did it with nobody getting hurt or arrested. Now the Governor knew what they knew: *every* American had blood on their hands. Until they wore it every day, smelled it ripening in the sun, they would continue their daily consumption as if the war was only an inconvenience.

They looked at each other, self-satisfied.

Odds were they would never get caught. Even if they did, so what? It wasn't as if they'd killed anyone.

18.

Milo down-shifted as they fishtailed the steep drive toward the riverfront. Monica sat on her hands as the Naugahyde was hot with afternoon sun and burned the backs of her legs. Geo cuddled Gayleen in the backseat though her smile trembled to the edges of her mouth in the rear view. Milo turned west on to Marine Drive without stopping, heading into the stalled storm.

"Shouldn't we be heading inland?" Geo asked. "What if there's a tsunami?"

"We need to get out of town to a safe place," Milo answered. He watched Geo sneak a hand up Gayleen's jester shirt. She gripped his wrist.

"Maybe this isn't a good time to leave our families," she said.

"I think we should stick together," Geo said.

Gayleen groaned, "Oh, you wish."

"It's easy for you, Geo, you don't have any real family," Monica piped in, "unless you count your father."

Geo glared, stone-eyed.

"If something happens," Gayleen pointed out, "we may not make it home again."

"You wanna go home then?" Milo asked. Cherry sped past Bumble Bee Seafoods on Marine Drive then to the Mooring Basin with the Port coming up fast.

Gayleen pushed Geo's mouth from her neck. "My parents aren't home anyhow. They're opening a new bookstore in Seaview."

"What about you, Monica?"

She shrugged. "If something terrible happens, my parents will call Zelda and I won't be there."

"Should I take you home?"

"No, it's the other way."

Cars stalled on the side of the road made the way hazardous. People milled about as if they were waiting for the power to come back on. Cherry was the only car running. A mob clogged the intersection at Young's Bay Bridge. Milo laid on the horn. A tight gauntlet of desperate faces melted away as Cherry passed through. A long-faced emaciated man thumped Cherry's hood with the heel of his hand. Once they cleared the mob, Milo headed for the 4,200-foot bridge. The flashing green light on the vertical lift span changed to red. The gate dropped—*clang, clang, clang*— and Milo stomped on the gas pedal. The '56 Chevy crashed through the gate on to the 130-foot lift span as it started to rise. Cherry broke through a second gate on the other side, her bumper scraping concrete when Milo hit the brakes. He fought to hold the skid with Monica screaming under his arm. The 350-horse turbo engine rumbled over the bay into Warrenton.

"Wow!" Geo grinned in the back seat. "That was a real charge!"

Cloud shadow darkened the car's interior as late sun broke on the backs of clouds. Milo glanced at the rear view. No one was following. "We're going to the bunkers. It's the safest place."

"The Battery Russell?" Geo's tone was disappointment.

"No, no, the other bunkers."

"That's government property," Gayleen said. "Won't we be trespassing?"

"Afraid of a little trespass?" Geo asked.

Gayleen's face flushed, "No, but the fence is like eight feet high…with barbed wire on top. How you gettin' over it? Are you going to fly?"

"Don't worry," Milo said. "I know a way."

The long military history of Fort Stevens began with the Civil War. The Union army constructed earthworks with gun emplacements to protect the mouth of the Columbia River against Confederate attack. The Battery Russell was built before World War I and was fired upon by a Japanese sub early in WWII. The shells were fired in darkness and never landed close as the fort was totally blacked out. Now the battery was a tourist attraction: the only continental American military base attacked since Fort Sumter. Forts at the mouth of the Columbia, north and south of the jetty, were decommissioned after WWII, their guns disassembled. Several other bunkers remained the property of the federal government after Battery Russell was donated to Fort Stevens State Park.

In spite of No Trespassing signs and an eight-foot tall fence, a few undaunted locals found ways into these lesser-known fortifications. Once inside the perimeter, they scared up an interior landscape full of shadows and alien space. The bunkers opened layers of consciousness left dormant for generations.

Milo had never trespassed before Johnny and Monterey Jack guided him through the rite of passage. Life came with risk. Pioneers never followed road signs. A full year of college didn't match what he learned from those two. "There's some incredible bunkers in there."

Geo smirked in resentment of Johnny and Monterey Jack. He didn't like them much. A self-limiting script doomed him to repeat the same old story. In contrast, Johnny and Monterey Jack were blazing their own trail, even if through government property. Geo wasn't righteous, he just lacked imagination. Milo understood how it felt to be stuck. When he lost his father, a boundary between death and life began to fade in and out and he occasionally caught a glimpse of some other world.

Ahead of them Warrenton was empty of people. In his rear view, Geo's hands roved over Gayleen's hips. "Let's live in the moment," he said.

Geo virtually lived at Milo's place to avoid his old man. Sometimes he felt Monica and Geo were both too posses-sive of him. He needed more. He'd bonded with brother Geo over the absent father theme. Monica would never under-stand that kind of bond.

Milo took 104 through Hammond into the Fort Stevens Historic Area.

Rain forest darkened the interior as old growth pine, spruce and cedar leaned in over twisting black road. The day faded into dull grayness. Milo switched on the low beams and imagined Cherry was a pilot boat lost in the fog, caught in a current that swept it into uncharted territory.

When the radio found a signal, Chuck Berry was singing "No Particular Place to Go." The timing was perfect—Geo bouncing around in the backseat, wanting Gayleen to scratch his itch. "No, no, up a little, up a little. Under the shoulder blade. There. Yeah, yeah."

The station hissed in static through the car speakers. A voice cut in. *"Stay with me, buddy. Hold on."* The words melted into a hiss.

Milo thumped the speaker and it came back with:

> *This is KAST, Astoria, 98.6 on your AM dial. The time is 7:30. Now for the news. State officials reported today a strange red tide making its way toward the Oregon coast. Dispatched from its station in Astoria, the Coast Guard cutter, Yocona, confirmed the red tide (or spill) would reach beaches by 9 p.m. The Coast Guard has not determined the exact nature of the phenomenon but advised residents to stay indoors.*

"Well," Milo said, "we should have the beach to ourselves."

Geo leaned forward, bringing his head between Milo and Monica. "Jesus, find some music. You're killing the mood."

All the channels were broadcasting the same warning:

It is not known whether this red tide poses any threat to the environment...

In the rear view, Gayleen firmly pushed Geo's offending hand back onto her hip. Milo's eyes shifted back to the road where a hitchhiker stood in the middle of the road, skeins of fog unraveling from his shoulders. He held a cardboard sign. *Road to Freedom.* Milo slammed on the brakes. Monica braced herself. Geo bumped heads with Gayleen as he recoiled from the sudden stop. The car shuddered on the narrow shoulder. Milo shifted into reverse, throwing loose gravel until rubber found pavement.

"What the hell, Sunny?" Geo cried. Gayleen was holding her head.

Milo climbed out of the car. Lacy fog impeded his range of vision but an indistinct shape lay there in the road. A sign. Hand-lettered in black crayon. *Enchanted Forest.*

"You guys see that hitchhiker?"

"Hell, no." Geo's eyes were nickels.

The girls looked puzzled.

"Never mind," Milo said, holding up the sign. "Where's The Enchanted Forest?"

"Northern California, I think," Monica guessed.

Milo handed the sign to Geo and climbed back into the car.

"That's Trees of Mystery," Gayleen answered with certainty. "Never heard of the Enchanted Forest except in fairy tales."

"Should I drive, Milo?" Monica asked, scooting closer. Milo put the car into gear and plowed ahead through the fog.

* * *

Fort Stevens on the south jetty and Fort Canby on the north formed the Harbor Defense System to defend the mouth of the river. Fort Stevens was part of an American tradition of laying claim to the land then digging in to hold onto it.

Two rows of wood-framed Victorian officer and family houses surrounded an overgrown parade ground. The local historical society converted one of the officer quarters into a military museum. An old piece of ground artillery rested out front. Many of the houses were privately-owned now, many neglected and occupied by poor families.

Milo slowed and switched off the headlights. Cherry inched forward as he fought the impulse to turn them on again. They were off the paved road, still driving without lights. He navigated dirt ruts flanked by ghost fir and shadowy spruce.

Even in first gear, Cherry bottomed out in deep ruts until it turned to sand. The car wouldn't go any farther without getting stuck. He parked it.

"I hope you know where you're going," Monica whispered where the sand finally stopped them at twilight.

His last time at the bunkers with Johnny and Monterey Jack was a moonlit night; they found the way easily. With this weft of fog warping through mossy trees, good light was aborted and so was his sense of direction. Despite a record-setting drought, the dense multi-storied forest and its undergrowth captured moisture like a terrarium. Still, Milo's intuition pulled his inner compass to magnetic north. He would find the way.

Monterey Jack believed in change; that is, he believed in a revolution of human consciousness. "We all live in our minds," he said, like any good narcissist. Milo found it a little disappointing. But Monterey Jack didn't give up. "Reality's a movie and we're all directors. Step outside the movie house, you alter the script and the story changes."

Milo wished Johnny was with them as he knew the bunkers best. He snuck his hand across Naugahyde and pinched the back of Monica's leg. She jumped, slapping his hand. Her reputation was at stake. If they were arrested trespassing on federal property she would be a ruined woman. He squeezed her hand. "Trust me."

They abandoned the car. Milo opened the trunk and Geo tossed the empty wine bottle at a tree. The glass didn't break against the soft moss-covered bark. He shrugged and snatched his sports bag from the back seat.

They were interlopers here, Milo thought. They should tread lightly. He fetched the survival gear. Monica leaned against the back fender near the taillights and scratched her belly. Milo tugged her hands away and filled them with pillows and a marine radio.

"Aren't you the Boy Scout?" she said.

19.

Dark Bavarian beer spilled from the overly full pitcher as Nico set it down on the lacquered-wood table in the German Club beer tent. He pulled up a folding chair and sat down. Two pitchers down, one to go; Jesse up, two to one. "You know why you can't get laid, Little Engine?" His voice boomed louder the drunker he got. "You're too damn respectful. You gotta remember you're not asking them to do something they don't wanna do. Sex is a line you gotta cross to come out on top. We're talking battle of the sexes here, brother. Conquer or be conquered. Either go after what you want or hate yourself in the end."

"You make women sound like dogs."

"Like animals, Little Engine. Animals."

"Right. We're all animals. What about Coco?" Nico asked.

Jesse laughed. "She has her moments."

"You don't deserve her, you know that?"

"Now, you're changing the subject." Jesse took a long draft from the blue stein and inspected his Stinker shirt for spills. "As much as you wanna deny it, Little Engine, we're joined at the hip."

Nico had never looked at it quite that way. The July midday swelter inside the heavy canvas of the National Guard tent made the sweat flow. Jesse sniffed the air like a wolf and squinted, sweat darkening his eyebrows. "You and I, Little Engine, are sitting at opposite ends of the same boat. If I sink, so do you."

Jesse finished off a glass and poured another. "What Coco loves in you, man, is what she can't get from me—it's not sex. You're the civilized one, you see—so rational and under control. I'm her wild man. She can't control the wild man in me and she needs control. What she loves puts me out there on the edge all the time. I'm out of control. What she loves most in me is what she'd destroy unless she has somebody like you. Understand?"

Nico didn't understand.

"She never let you fuck her."

Nico's face tightened as if he'd been sucker-punched. "I never said she did."

Jesse's grin infuriated Nico. "I know. You got no wild man. Women want a wild man until they try to live with one. Guys like you settle for *friend*."

Nico resented the suggestion that he couldn't have been Coco's lover. Senior year he took her to the Ada Theater to see *Dr. Strangelove*. They necked in the balcony. Nico felt her up and after the movie, the conversation wasn't about a secret underground White House or NORAD. "Nicky," she said, "do you think friends should have sex?" The shock blew him backwards like a grenade. No, because then they'd be lovers, something more than friends. "Well, can you be both lovers and friends?" Nico didn't know what to say. Her Dutch blue eyes drew a line in their relationship he was afraid to cross over for fear of losing the friendship. He needed more time to make these fine distinctions. Whatever he said she would hold against him forever. He might have said something like "*Free love* doesn't mean something *cheap*." Didn't his resistance have more to do with his failure than hers?

Jesse burped loudly and poured another beer. "I'm no Mr. Nice Guy, but I want to give her what she needs." Jesse fixed Nico in an unblinking gaze. He wasn't sure what Jesse was asking of him. "And I won't give her up without a fight."

Nico wondered if that was a threat or just incredible drunken candor.

"Since we're in the same group," Jesse confided, "I think it would be safe to tell you we're gonna have a kid."

Nico's face flushed. "We are? How did we accomplish that?"

"She was supposed to be on the pill."

"So you don't want this kid?"

"C'mon. Can you see me with a kid?"

"Time to man up," Nico's voice was cold.

Jesse emptied the pitcher into his glass, sweat rolling out of him. He stood up, unbalanced, both hands flat on the table to steady himself. "Look, if something happens to me, Little Engine, promise me you'll watch over them, bring some normalcy into their lives."

For a second, Nico was actually touched, then he laughed. "Coco doesn't want *normalcy*."

Jesse straightened up, holding onto the back of Nico's chair. "She's a woman. She has the right to be of two minds. She wants a wild man to break the routine and she wants the routine. I can't give her both."

Nico swayed as the earth rolled under him. They swayed together, hands on each other's shoulders, pressed close, two shameless drunks shouting into each other's face. "Nothing's gonna happen to you, ya bastard. You're indestructible."

Jesse saluted with his hook. "To being indestructible!" Their glasses clinked together and dark beer slopped onto the sawdust floor.

The German band finished a Hofbrauhaus drinking song. Nico became aware of the din of voices as the tent filled with more people. Jesse sniffed the air so Nico sniffed it too. Yes, the animal could smell German sausage. Jesse put down his stein and yanked Nico by the back of the collar toward the food booth. "C'mon," he said, "and pay attention."

The folk dancer at the food booth flipped reddish blonde hair in long braids back over soft white shoulders as she leaned down, elbows resting on the counter. The low-necked, tight bodice of German Club dancers pushed her full breasts into eye-popping cleavage. A loose Cinderella skirt flared at her hips. She conjured visions of bawdy German milkmaids. "May I help you?"

Jesse licked his lips. The dancer steered her gaze wide of his bold stare. She hadn't imagined Jesse's staring at her breasts might be in the job description for volunteers.

"Gotta say this for the Krauts," Jesse confided to Nico, "they sure know how to dress *die frauleins*." Nico wavered behind Jesse's squared shoulders. Jesse pressed up against the booth and placed his good hand on the counter. She wasn't impressed. *"Sprechen Sie Deutsch, fraulein?"* Jesse asked, too loudly. The server nodded. *"Werden Sie mit mir nach Bet kommen?"*

The dancer's face reddened. She pulled the braid back over her shoulder to conceal her generous domain. Her eyes were polished filberts. She reminded Nico of an innocent Coco who ran to him a few years ago after one of Jesse's famous spontaneous combustions. That's when Nico got the nickname Little Engine.

"Can you help me, please?" Jesse asked the dancer, sounding wounded.

The girl took a deep breath and stepped up. "What do you want?"

Jesse resisted the opening. Instead he ordered without taking his eyes off her tits. "How about a hot sausage in a bun."

"Do you want sauerkraut with it?"

"How about a smile?"

After serving him, the dancer shuddered and tried to withdraw, but Jesse grabbed her wrist with his good hand. "Wait, don't I get anything on it?"

"The condiments are right there." Her eyes rolled towards bowls of mustard, ketchup and relish.

He let go and opened the bun, fingering the sausage.

"Does your friend need something?" The girl's eyes caught Nico looking on.

Jesse glanced over his shoulder. "Who said we were friends?"

"I...I thought you came together."

"Came together? Do I look like some fag, Gretel?"

"That's not what I meant." She blushed.

"What my friend here needs is to get laid. Can you help him with that?" Jesse laughed without lifting his bloodshot eyes from her cleavage. Nico ordered a sausage and bun. He couldn't stomach that rancid seaweed they called sauerkraut.

When Gretel returned, Jesse made a point of running his sausage back and forth through hot mustard in the bun, making lewd sounds. He yanked the meat out with his twin hooks and wagged it obscenely. Before Gretel could turn, Jesse grabbed her arm. Her eyes looked to Nico for help.

"C'mon, Jesse." Nico intervened. "The beer's getting warm."

Jesse loosened his hold on Gretel's arm. "So Gretel, you dance?" A rather stupid question considering she was in a dance group. "Dance on Saturday at The Enchanted Forest. You been there? Light shows. Good bands. Nico here's the manager. He'll let you in for free."

"I'm not Gretel," she said, twisting her arm out from under his.

"Well Not-Gretel, maybe we'll see you there."

Milo led Jesse back to their table.

"She has the hots for me," Jesse said, finishing his beer.

Jesse was always pushing the limits, riding that fine edge. The closest civilian equivalent for running a Huey nose-down through a gauntlet of fire was the race track. And where had it gotten him? To a place where Start and Finish were the same, where you won without getting anywhere.

* * *

Funny little Valentine. Should've seen it coming. Nico was falling into the same old role.

"They *all* want it," Jesse mumbled, dropping the GTO into third gear and gunning it. Nico caught himself at the sudden acceleration. "They act all offended because you remind them deep down they're still animals too." Jesse brought his square face into Nico's, swerving slightly into the other lane. "Coco most of all." His breath was heavy with sausage and beer. "You put her on such a pedestal. What can ya do with something on a pedestal?"

In the middle of their junior year Nico was dating Coco. He drove Jesse home one night after a party in Jesse's car. Jesse insisted they stop by Lillian Marshall's house. Jesse got into the backseat with her and used his drunkenness as an excuse to grope her. Nico pretended to be zonked behind the wheel. He was stone sober but went along with Jesse's little drama. He was always going along with Jesse, and feeling bad afterward.

"You had no such problem." Nico's jaw muscles ached from clenching his teeth.

"Damn right," Jesse admitted. He pulled into the Grand Central parking lot.

While Jesse went for beer, Nico found the music department and an 8-track tape of *Last Time Around* by Buffalo Springfield. He bought it at the department counter to avoid checkout and went looking for Jesse. He turned down an aisle and nearly ran into a razor-edged hunting arrow Jesse held leveled at his chest. Nico knocked several sleeping bags off a display shelf ducking back. "Jesus, Jesse!"

Jesse aimed up with the bow, drew back the arrow with his hook, and let it fly. The arrow tip lodged soundlessly in porous, lightweight ceiling tile. Nico's jaw dropped. Jesse nonchalantly returned the bow to the rack and walked on. Nico dropped a five spot at the sports counter and followed Jesse out.

Nico caught up with him in the parking lot. "Why'd you do that?"

"To see if I could."

"Scared the shit outta me."

"I had hold of it!" Jesse said.

"You're dangerous."

* * *

Next morning. Nico heard a knock on the front door. Harley's '67 Plymouth Fury idled in the driveway, the big hemi rumbling, its whole chassis rocking. It was a cloudless day, July sun already topping the neighbor's black walnut. Someone sat on the passenger side. Nico opened the door.

"What's up, Harley?" Nico asked.

"C'mon, we gotta go." Harley pressed with a sense of urgency.

"Where we going?"

"Jesse didn't come home last night."

Nico locked the door to the house and ducked into the backseat. "What? Did the wild man come out last night?"

"Coco's worried he's wrapped around a tree somewhere. We're dropping you at the house to babysit while we go look for him."

"Why me?"

"She asked."

"Why don't I just take my car then?"

"We'll come back for you. If you need it, Jesse's Goat is there. He must be with somebody."

Harley backed the Fury out of the driveway.

"Jesse dropped me off last night around 9 p.m.," Nico confessed. "If the GTO's at home, Manny's the likely suspect."

"Naw, Manny's driving a sugar beet truck in Nampa today. He ain't seen 'im." Harley drove up to Hill Road and turned toward the Walker home. "Sorry. This is my old buddy, Eddie—Eddie 'Too Fast' Buchanon. He's from North Carolina. Eddie, this here's *NeeKo*. He's an engine man."

Nico straddled the driveline hump and reached over the seat to shake Too Fast's hand. He had a good firm grip. His eyes were steady under thick prescription glasses. He wore a mustache like Yosemite Sam and the black NASCAR team jacket with his name stitched in red and white on his chest proudly displayed patches from major sponsors—Valvoline, Champion, Goodyear, Prestone and Moog. With all their experience and history, the two of them, Harley and Too Fast, acted like a teenager. Their roots went deeper than racing engines, deeper into the South, into a shared history in one place. Too Fast pushed his Daytona 500 baseball cap back on his forehead, brought up a big thermos from where he kept it on the floor between his feet. He poured some coffee in the metal cup and handed it over.

"Too Fast works for Junior Johnson's NASCAR crew," Harley said. "Under that Skin Bracer you'll pick up the subtle aroma of burnt rubber and hot asphalt." Harley elbowed his friend, who elbowed him back.

"Where're you gonna look for Jesse?" Nico asked, taking a small sip of the hot coffee.

"Track first," Harley answered. "Hopefully he's got his mind on Saturday's race." He tapped Too Fast on the shoulder with his fist. "Too Fast came up from Asheville for Margo's Hungarian goulash."

"And to find out what a gear head like Harley sees in Idaho." Too Fast said, looking around him as he drove down Hill Road, shaking his head. "Ain't seen much yet."

"What's that?" Harley leaned his deaf ear toward his friend.

"I say Boy-zee's full of hicks." Too Fast twirled the waxed ends of his handlebar between thumb and forefinger. "Just like home, huh?"

"Hick-deep in the Blue Ridge Mountains," Harley said. "Boiseans aren't hicks, they're mountain men. Too Fast used to drive, but it was a short career. He was always too fast in the turns." Harley winked in the rear view. "Now he's too sophisticated for mountain men."

The banter between old friends made Nico wistfully nostalgic.

Too Fast opened the window and shrugged at the urban sprawl. "Can't figure out why a guy with gasoline in his veins traded super speedways for *this*."

"Sure you can." Harley drove with one hand on the steering wheel, the other scratching his turkey neck.

"Things are changing." Too Fast tapped a Salem Menthol out of the pack and lit it. "Money's better. Cars are safer. The sport's more popular than ever. We got graduates from Stanford and MIT designing cars."

"Too many money men," Harley said. "They eat in the finest restaurants, stay in the finest hotels, dress in the finest clothes; they walk and talk about markets and take too much off the top. NASCAR used to be a bunch of pump jockeys in the stands hootin' and hollerin' and drinkin' beer. Now the sport's all about protecting somebody's brand. Used to be y'all could show up at a NASCAR banquet in a t-shirt and Levis. Drivers like Curtis Turner and Fireball Roberts don't fit the image anymore. Yeah, it's changed."

"If it hadn't," Too Fast pointed out, "the sport would've died."

"Who died?" Harley picked a Menthol out of the pack and held it up to Too Fast. "This is the only thing from North Carolina I can't live without." He took a long drag.

"Turn up your HEARING AID." Too Fast responded. "I said the SPORT would've died!"

"It is turned up." Harley fidgeted with his hearing aid. "You're just squawkin' like an old woman."

"So how long's your vacation?" Nico asked Too Fast.

"Depends. Harley says your man's got PO-TEN-CHAL." Too Fast's emphasis was for Harley's benefit. "So I wandered this way on a scouting trip. Ralph's thinking of expanding, maybe a second team."

"Pap still cookin' brainkiller back in the hills?" Harley's cigarette bobbed between his lips.

"Pap gave up brewin' after a whole Mason jar of his lightning helped Andy Winter walk right off a cliff. Andy's widder blamed Pap. He blew up the still a week later as something happened that made him believe that widder was a real witch. Andy was always saying 'My wife's a real witch.' But pappy never took him literally until that cliff." Too Fast nudged Harley with his elbow. "You remember that old '40 Ford sedan with the flathead V-8?" Too Fast turned halfway in the seat to narrate. "Harley pulled the seats of that sedan and blowtorched this porthole into the sidewall so you could lie down and follow the road. Then he rigged up the steering so it looked like nobody was behind the wheel. A driverless car goin' down mainstreet. Turned some heads, for sure. But it was a lot of work for one pass through town before the cops closed in."

Harley smiled at the memory. "The good old days when men were men and cops didn't have radios."

Being on the Stinker team meant a lot to Nico. It kept him looking ahead to the race. Yet here he was falling back into the old days, playing babysitter to Coco, because Jesse didn't come home again.

Harley pulled his Fury into the driveway and parked behind the GTO. Nico climbed out and exchanged courteous nods with the Blue Ridge boys as they backed out and turned up the Country. Coco Bird opened the screen door and stood barefooted on the porch holding a pale blue robe tight around her waist, hair wrapped in a towel.

"Heard from Jesse?" Nico asked.

"Not yet."

Coco Bird showed no signs of great stress, but she *was* angry.

"Did someone pick Jesse up last night?" he asked.

"How should I know? I *work*, remember?" she shrugged. "I hope he fell into the river and drowned."

"River's too low to drown in."

"You can drown in a glass of vodka, Nicky."

"Don't worry." Nico climbed onto the porch and encircled her shoulders with his arm. She smelled fresh from the shower. Naked under the robe. "Why haven't you learned to drive yet?"

"I tried to have Jesse teach me, but he makes me nervous. The first time I backed up in his GTO I backed right into the door of a parked car. Now I'm too afraid of making a mistake with his precious GTO." Coco went into the house. Nico followed.

"So get another car."

"Maybe you could teach me sometime?"

"Yeah sure," Nico replied, "I'm nothing if not patient."

Coco checked the clock in the kitchen. It was just after 7. "I got this doctor's appointment at 9, and I'm not ready yet." She unwrapped the towel from her head and dried her hair. Fresh coffee perked on the stove. "There's day-old donuts on top of the fridge. I gotta get dressed."

Nico poured a cup of coffee and opened the box of day-olds. He took out a maple bar and bit into it. The icing was hardening but good enough to eat. Coco hurried down the hallway to the bedroom.

Nico browsed their record collection, sorting in his mind if it was a clear Coco or obvious Jesse. With little else to spend money on while in the service, the PAST had the best record collections. The Walkers were no exception. Blood, Sweat and Tears (Coco), The Moody Blues (Coco), Savoy Brown (Jesse), The Paul Butterfield Blues Band (Jesse), Johnny Cash (Coco), Jimi Hendrix (Jesse), The Steve Miller Band (Jesse), Cream (Coco), John Mayall (Jesse). Nico pulled out one of the older albums. Roy Orbison. One of the few albums Jesse kept that preceded the British Invasion. Nico put it on and sat back on the couch, drinking coffee, eating a now two-day-old maple bar, as Orbison's rich tenor glided into falsetto.

Nico once necked with Coco on the couch at the Bird residence while listening to Orbison. He had been such a clumsy clown, walking on his hands into unknown territory. His mind again touched her, despite his best intentions. He could still taste her lips. Jesse was right. He had put her up on a pedestal. She needed a hands-on kind of guy. Nico had his chance. She was married now.

"Nicky," Coco called from the bedroom.

"Yeah?"

"Could you please play something else?" she called. "Orbison makes me wanna cry."

"What do you wanna listen to." Nico flipped through records in the box.

"Anything else."

"Okay." Nico placed Savoy Brown onto the turntable and dropped the needle on "Hellbound Train."

A minute later, Coco came bounding down the narrow gauge of their hallway and burst into the living room in a red-hot blouse and black stretch pants, brushing out her hair.

Nico looked up from liner notes. "Did you have a fight?"

"How? He was gone when I got home." Coco ran fingers through long tresses of reddish-brown hair and tossed it back over her shoulder.

Nico heard a knock and lowered the volume on the stereo. Coco peeked through the front window. Deputy Sheriff Jericho Sinclair stood on the porch, bare knuckle brushing a modest mustache, gray eyes peering out from under the shade of a brown Stetson. "Oh God," Coco covered her mouth with open hand. "Something terrible's happened. I know it!" The cold panic in her eyes forced Nico to open the door.

Sinclair looked past him to Coco. "Ma'am."

Coco clutched Nico's arm, looking faint. Sinclair's poker face revealed nothing. The war had not changed him in that respect.

Nico nodded, "Jerry. What brings you out today?"

"Is Jesse home?"

Coco's visible relief took Sinclair by surprise. Fear of the worst had passed. Her face relaxed. "He's not here."

"Okay. Do you have any idea where he is?"

"No." The answer was a short burst like a rifle shot. She turned away and Sinclair directed his gaze at Nico.

"Jesse wasn't here when she got home from work last night," Nico said. "Is something wrong?"

"Nothing life-threatening." Sinclair slouched into his easy carriage, reminding Nico of a tall Andy Griffith. "Can we talk? Outside?"

"Sure." Nico flashed an apologetic smile. "I'll be right back," he called to Coco who glared from the corner of the room. He followed Sinclair on to the porch, down the steps and to the deputy's squad car in the drive. Sinclair nodded for Nico to get in on the passenger side. "Am I being arrested?"

"Have you done something, Nico?" Sinclair removed the Stetson and tossed it onto the back seat. As the deputy ducked into the car, Nico noticed his hair was thinning on top. The hero was growing old, must be thirty by now. Behind the wheel, Sinclair's high forehead nearly touched the visor even with the seat pushed back. Sinclair reached over and pulled a grocery sack closer so Nico could get in.

"What's going on?" Nico wondered aloud.

"Heard you're managing The Enchanted Forest. Tomas is an old family friend."

"Yeah, same here."

"He caught a lot of flak at the city council meeting over opening this teen club. He assured everyone it would be alcohol and drug-free."

"It *is*," Nico said. "What's that have to do with Jesse?"

Sinclair deflected the question by asking Nico who worked the door at The Enchanted Forest.

"Good guys," Nico assured him. "Both vets. One checks ID. The other screens clientele. We deny admittance to anyone we suspect is drunk or stoned."

"What's their names?"

Nico felt a bit under the light on that. His chest tightened, his pulse quickened. "Mark Mayfield and Pat Parsons. Ex-Marines. Nobody fucks with them."

"Mayfield." Sinclair blinked as if calling him up with the roll of his eyes, running the flat of his hand through thinning hair. "Do I know him? They call him 'Doc,' right?"

"Yeah. Doc's a nickname. He's the leader of our group."

"So he's a musician?"

"No, our support group."

"Ahh. And this Parsons." Sinclair leveled his gaze. "I don't remember him."

"Friend of Mayfield's, come up from California. And Josh Brownton helps us find new talent."

"Judge Brownton's kid? That's one nut that fell a long way from the tree."

"Yeah, but he's a smart dresser," Nico cracked, meaning no disrespect. It came off a little flippant.

"So you guys got a group? Meet at the clinic?"

"We've been meeting lately at The Enchanted Forest, put a little music on and enjoy our time together. Do you play cribbage?"

"Cribbage? Nah. Sounds all too exciting for me." The deputy lifted the grocery bag onto his lap and opened it. "Do any of your cribbage players ever dress up as clowns?" He pulled a red wig from the grocery bag. "Jesse, maybe?"

Nico felt his breath catch. He shook his head. "Uh-uh. Jesse hates clowns. Clowns give him the jitters."

Sinclair's casual gaze made Nico wonder. Was he fishing for something?

"Jesse in some kind of trouble?"

"Now when is Jesse *not* in trouble, Nicolasa?" Sinclair twirled the wig on his fist. "We had a little incident at the Fourth of July Parade, maybe you read about it?"

"I only read the Sunday paper, sports and comics mostly. No news is good news."

"Right. Well, these two war protesters dumped a bucket of pig blood on the governor's head…"

Nico laughed out loud. "You're kidding me!"

"Nasty scene. Really rank pig blood."

"Was he hurt?"

"Noooo, the governor's fine. Got a hornet under the hood though." Sinclair reached into the bag, pulled out a leaflet, and smoothed it against his leg. *Support Our Troops: Question Their Leaders!* "You seen this?"

"Can't say as I disagree with the sentiment." Nico pinched his chin. "Make a good bumper sticker. So you're saying the governor's looking for these guys?"

"We're just talking to people."

"That's why you wanna talk to Jesse?"

Sinclair set the leaflet and wig aside, reached once more into the grocery bag of crime evidence and pulled out an oversized floppy shoe. "Reports are a different clown was wearing this."

"Want me to try it on?"

"Nah, that's okay, Nico. It's not a glass slipper."

"I'd better get back inside. Coco Bird's got an appointment at 9 with the doctor. She's pregnant."

"Congratulations," Sinclair said.

"No, it's Jesse's."

"Of course," Sinclair agreed. "Who else?"

Nico climbed out of the cruiser. "Hey Nico. One more thing." Sinclair ducked his head toward the passenger door. "When those clowns made their escape, the driver jumped a curb and damn near hit an old man on the sidewalk."

Nico stooped with forearms resting on the open door frame. "I hope he's okay."

"His name was Willy Sampson. He collapsed and died later in the hospital from heart failure." Sinclair's eyes widened. Nico blinked. "The old guy had a weak ticker. He was 82. Still, who knows? He might've lived for years."

Blood pounded in Nico's ears. All he could think to say was "Wow." The single syllable reverberated in the echo chamber of his skull. He closed the squad car door and watched Sinclair back out of the driveway. The PAST intended to have no more than pig blood on their hands. The drop was a well-planned act of guerrilla theater. No one was supposed to get hurt.

Coco appeared on the porch, awash in morning light. It always surprised Nico how much the light loved that woman. Her beauty made him close his eyes. "What's that about?" she asked.

"He asked about Doc and Pat Parsons."

"The Black Panther?"

"Pat Parsons? He's not a Black Panther."

Coco's eyelids fluttered. She offered the keys to the GTO. "We'd better get going."

They talked as he drove to the doctor's office. Jesse was the main subject.

"He's always going back there now," she said.

"Back where?"

"Vietnam."

"Did anything unusual happen around the time he started going back?"

Coco's eyes shifted to him. "He got locked in a duel at the track with Whitey O'Riley. Neither would give an inch. Jesse lost control. He said he didn't remember, but he started drinking too much and had these terrible dark moods…as if he's daring death to catch him. He'll just outrun it."

They both pushed their limits, Nico thought. Jesse in a racecar, Coco in her sanity. Jesse couldn't outrun death and Coco's Dutch heritage clung to an irrational faith in the power of the human mind to control unruly nature. One day Jesse's psychic landscape would be transformed much like the Dutch landscape. Dark waters inevitably break through dykes in natural disasters and Coco Bird might well get washed away.

A dry lump stuck in Nico's throat. He swallowed hard. "Sinclair wanted to warn me about concerns the public has with teens drinking and using drugs at the Enchanted Forest. I assured him our guys were policing it."

"Did he say why he was asking about *Jesse*?"

"He didn't say."

* * *

They took West Hill Road, heading downtown. A late-model black Impala convertible passed them going the other way with a woman driving. "Stop!" Coco yelled. Nico braked and pulled onto the shoulder. "Jesse was in that car."

"Did he see us?"

"How could he?" Coco hissed through tight lips. "His face was buried in her neck."

"So what do you wanna do?"

"I don't know."

Coco's face turned red. She made a series of disgusted grunting noises then said, "Turn around." Nico started to turn around. She changed her mind. "No, screw him! I'm not going to miss my prenatal appointment to chase him." She had second thoughts, sweeping her hair back and staring ahead. "No, I need to confront him." She let out a desperate yelp as if wounded. "Damn him," she said. "Turn around, Nico. Please."

"If that's what you want."

Before they got to the driveway, they met the sleek Impala coming back. Behind the wheel was this moon-faced blonde with short curly hair. She wore dark red lipstick. Her cheeks were flushed. Eyes sparkling. He couldn't be objective, but he thought she looked fresh from a good bang.

20.

Milo stopped to get his bearings. He peered down fern-congested trails. None of them seemed to match his memory of the terrain. Black branches shredded the luminous fog. The four of them came to where two vine-choked sections of eight-foot fence were spliced together at a steel post with a "no trespassing" sign. Milo recognized it. One section had come loose but they pushed it back into place to make the breach hard to find. Milo yanked the fence back so the others could crawl under. Inside, he led them down a narrow trail. The ground was spongy, the path obstructed with fallen logs. He held back limbs to save them from whiplash. This was his sacred ground. For them it would be alien space.

Monica slipped off a log and landed on a cushion of leaves. The emergency pillows helped break her fall. She heroically held the radio high, saved and unbroken. She turned her ankle and scratched an elbow. "I heard something big in the bushes," she said.

Milo couldn't hear anything. He set the blankets down on the log and pulled Monica up by the arms and sat her down on the blankets to take a look at her ankle. She fought back tears as he kissed her trembling mouth. He probed the ankle and she winced, bravely, bearing the pain. "I'm okay," she insisted, pulling herself up by Milo's arm.

Milo rolled the blankets up, tucked them under his arm and Monica leaned against him all the way up the trail to the bunkers. Wet fingers of fern tickled his legs and the sodden cuffs of pegged Levis rubbed his shinbones. A Steller's Jay renounced their intrusion. Cold silence closed around them like a change in the weather. This could be the last place on earth.

In an unlikely show of chivalry, Geo draped his letterman's jacket around Gayleen's shoulders. Then he jacked up the Budweiser under his arm as Gayleen walked barefooted beside him through sand, one arm encircling Geo's waist, the other swinging his sports bag.

Their party of four crossed a stream on rotting timbers that once formed a railroad trestle during the Second World War. Army engineers needed the rail to transport large basalt boulders on flatcars to reinforce the south jetty. Gayleen was the lightest among them so she crossed first and the decayed wood did not collapse. The others followed, crossing to another trail through dense vegetation toward hard-edged masses of dark concrete rising like ruins, their lightless passageways promising more somber interiors.

Milo felt like an Egyptian living in the shadow of the pyramids. Any trespass on this land was justified by right of local imagination. He would not be denied access to his own history by government fences and a few posted signs. The bunkers belonged to the people. Stained from decades of leaching iron rust, the underground complexes stood as mute testament to the threat of invasion. Gun emplacements overgrown with tangles of blackberry and vine maple saplings fell into black holes.

This could be their last stand.

"This one's called Battery Pratt," he announced with certainty. "Just beyond is West Battery." Milo led them through blackberry brambles and sword fern toward a longer concrete emplacement with empty gun pits ringed with rusted iron. Across the way was the Battery Mishler, the command post, its guns removed at the end of the war. Unlike the other bunkers, Mishler was largely underground.

Milo directed Monica up a steep, cracked stairway to an observation room. The tower looked out over the mouth of the Columbia River. Geo unzipped the sports bag and unrolled the recovered sign, *The Enchanted Forest*. He propped it up on the lower level before following Gayleen up the stairs. The battery tower stood on square concrete pillars above the rest of the emplacement. The tower was a long pillbox-style window that permitted a 180-degree view of the jetties. At the narrowest point, the great river was four miles wide. On the river side, the battery's thick concrete apron angled down to deflect enemy shells. West Battery had been built and backed up by an embankment of sand called the Parados, protecting the rear.

Humus, rust, and decay mixed with salt air. Milo gazed northwest to where cargo ships queued up in a line of lights blinking on the horizon. Battery Russell covered the ocean side and was open to the public. Even though Milo couldn't see the ocean from the tower, the eternal sound of surf pounding rock and sand echoed through him into the muted forest.

The tower was dry and out of the wind. Milo swept aside some dried pine needles and crumbling leaves, and arranged blankets on the floor. He set the lantern on the pillbox window ledge and switched the radio on, rolling the tuner until it picked up KAST's signal. The Tokens' popular refrain warbled into the twilight forest, sucked down in an undertow of waves and softened by a mosaic of firs, red maple and spruce.

Geo dropped onto the blanket, propping a pillow behind his back. He coaxed Gayleen to join him with a tug of her shirt. She shrugged him off at first to stare at the river mouth where storm clouds brewed over the bar. Undeterred, Geo grabbed hold of her ankle. "Hey, c'mon," he begged. He punched two holes in the top of a Bud, chugging half in frustration. Geo polished off the can, opened another and offered it to Gayleen. She accepted without a word and sat down beside him on the blanket. She took a sip and made a face.

"You'll acquire a taste for it," Geo assured her.

Again Milo heard something big in the bush—some animal perhaps. No one else heard it as the crashing coincided with a sudden gust of wind. The bunkers yielded to slow decay. In the onslaught of foul weather and vegetation spreading like a virus, creeping through every crack, even the thick concrete broke down. Violet light broke through dark clouds on the horizon. The sky torched in an apocalypse of scotch broom around the bunker's apron. Milo watched the light show enthralled as Monica took him under the blanket. It was a precious moment in the pandemonium of time, such elemental forces huddled in each other's arms.

The old fort was a conjunction point, a door between worlds. These points historically occurred at edge places like land's end. In glimmer and gloam where light's withdrawal opened the possibility of curious visitations and night journeys, some twisted physics prevailed. Maybe tonight they'd find that doorway, Milo thought. Conditions were perfect for magical thinking.

Geo ducked into a green army blanket and pulled it up over himself and Gayleen. Lumps moved around under the blankets like feral cats bumping heads in a gunnysack. Gayleen baffled Milo as one minute she fiercely defended her virtue, finding Geo to be vile and small-minded, then the next she hunkered down with him panting like a wild cat. A splinter of jealousy pricked his brain. He shook it out. What rights did he have in this matter? If Geo made it with her, why should he care? "Now that we've set up camp," he blurted, "let's check the place out."

The lantern's beam dissolved in curtains of thin fog. It illuminated a shadowy hole in the concrete on the level below. The weedy pit spanned eight to ten feet. "That was a gun emplacement," he said. "They were disappearing carriages."

Monica looked at him with disbelief.

"They folded up so they couldn't be seen by ships on the river."

Geo poked his head out from under the blanket. "Maybe you should go on without us, Sunny," he winked.

Monica's eyes rolled. "My ankle still hurts. Maybe we should stay here a while longer. Those black holes look dangerous." She kissed his neck, placed her warm hand on his chest.

Milo brought her hand to his lips, kissed the fingers, then lifted her to her feet and nudged her toward the stairs. "Stay close."

"Wait for us," Gayleen said, popping out from under the blanket.

"Ah, c'mon." Geo reached for her. She lifted his hands off of her hips and pulled him to his feet.

Milo held the lantern high. Monica held onto his hand. Gayleen followed with Geo in tow.

"Do we have to?" Monica whined, eyes dropping. "I think there's something big in the bushes."

They entered a tunnel on the lower level. The tunnel tunneled back into the hill behind the bunker. The temperature dropped. Milo soaked up the chill. "This was once a powder room."

"Powder room?" Monica asked.

"Like gunpowder. Back here was the shell room. And see these?" Milo lifted the lantern to a deeper, darker room with parallel rusty rails running along a cracked and brown-stained ceiling. "These rails moved ammo and powder to here." Milo cast the lantern's beam on to a wood and iron cradle in the middle of the room.

The air smelled of mold and must. Monica clutched his hand, afraid of falling into an open pit. In the silence, he could hear her heart beating.

Geo jerked the rusted rail. A chunk broke free.

Furious wings erupted around them. Monica cried, "Bats!" She ran outside with arms covering her head. Outside, in the velvet light, black silhouettes crisscrossed in front of her face.

Gayleen laughed. "They're just swallows!"

Milo guided Monica back into the tunnel, arm around her waist. She gripped his shirt, eyes wide with terror. A sudden flash cracked the tunnel with ambiguous light. Monica's nails dug into his arm. "Only lightning, babe."

Another flash. The sky outside lit up casting trees into sharp relief. In the flash, Milo saw a silhouette up in the tower. Before the afterimage dissolved on the backs of his eyelids, he went charging up the stairs with second vision, the lantern's beam bobbing with each step.

"Wait!" Geo called from behind.

Another dry flash. No thunder. Milo reached the tower. There, back to him, gazing out over the dark river was the Hammer Man. He turned, belching loudly and turning into Johnny Evenfall, Budweiser in hand. "Thank God it's *you*, Milo."

Once the adrenalin rush abated, Milo sagged, knees buckling. If Geo hadn't come up behind him, he might have toppled backward down the stairs.

PART THREE

Paradoxes as they appear in our
three-dimensional world
are in part the result of our attempt
to describe reality with limited analogies.
Many of our paradoxes are resolved
when our view is broadened
to include other orders.

—NORMAN FRIEDMAN, *Bridging Science and Spirit*

21.

The GTO attacked the turns on the road to Lucky Peak Dam, throwing Nico's shoulder against the passenger door every time Jesse accelerated. They followed the Boise River up the canyon, sunlight streaming through willows and cottonwoods. The motion sickness caught up to Nico halfway. Jericho stirred up a hornet's nest. The group needed an emergency meeting, somewhere public, somewhere they could keep a low profile. Willy Sampson's heart might have given out any time, but Nico couldn't avoid the feeling of culpability. He was in the backseat of the wild Mustang that sent Willy by close call to an early grave. They executed the hit on the governor flawlessly and congratulated each other with slaps on the back in the beer tent as a bald, bespectacled, 82-year-old black man, Willy Sampson, died in the back of an ambulance.

Jesse pulled off the road. He needed a Coors from the cooler. Wispy cirrus clouds were painted on a lavender sky like eyebrows; a jet pierced the blue like an arrow through time. Sun burned through the windshield. Even with four windows down, they boiled behind the V-8.

"Package is for you," Jesse nodded toward the backseat.

"For me?" Nico brightened in surprise, stretching over the seat to retrieve the shirt box.

"Go ahead, Little Engine. Open it."

Inside the shirt box was not surprisingly a shirt, a Stinker Station racing shirt with "Little Engine" stitched in white above the pocket.

"You're now official. Harley's man."

Dr. Neumann's idea was for Nico to reconnect with the past, get involved with the Enchanted Forest and the Stinker team. He was building social skills and re-engaging with the world. Wasn't that what he wanted Nico to do? Nico squirmed out of his paisley shirt and donned the racing silk. It felt good—really cool.

Jesse gunned the GTO through the narrow canyon, taking turns posted for 35 mph at more like 50 and what felt like 70. He dodged a fallen rock, throwing Nico's shoulder against the door, spilling his beer.

"Jesus, Jesse, take it easy. This isn't the racetrack!"

Jesse swerved into the other lane and took two cars in a straight stretch. He tossed a dead soldier and reached for another. The car swerved. Nico grabbed the wheel. For a second they tugged against each other. Nico finally let go. Jesse guided the GTO back into an easy glide.

For a short case, the count totaled three for Nico and nine for Jesse, but Nico paid half. Jesse's tolerance for alcohol was legendary. He never staggered or slurred his words. The Goat could end up in a ditch before Nico would even know Jesse was impaired.

Nico relaxed his grip on the door handle, leaned back and sang along with the Steve Miller Band. By the time "Space Cowboy" ended, Jesse slowed, driving leisurely, ready to talk.

"I think it's the myth of our time: Frankenstein. The righteous put so much energy into playing God and creating new life, instead they create monsters."

Now this was heady stuff coming from Jesse. It went against his whole grain. Nico was confused. Was Jesse suggesting the fruit of his loins might be a monster? Or maybe that marriage had become his monster?

The familiar and unwanted role "along for the ride" that Nico was entangled in a love-hate triangle. Jesse's need for acceleration couldn't find enough gears. Winning wasn't enough. The victor's cloak was shrugged off in a horrible hangover. It made him an unlikely *dad* candidate. Poor kid, Nico thought. He doesn't get to pick his parents.

Out of sun glare in a tight turn, a shudder of movement caught Nico's eye. "Watch out!"

The alarm in Nico's voice awakened Jesse's instincts. He jerked the wheel. The Goat swerved, brakes squealing. They came to a stop on the gravel shoulder in a cloud of dust. Both men sat silently in settling dust, breathing fast, hearts in their throats.

Out of a luminous blur in the middle of the dam road walked the wounded soldier carrying an M-60 on his back. Nico noticed the fatigues oozed a dark crude around the chest. The soldier from Kon Barr rolled the machine gun off his shoulder and opened fire. Nico ducked as bullets shattered the GTO's windows.

Nico cowered and covered his head with his arms.

"What the fuck?" Jesse said.

Nico straightened up then and squinted. No bullets had ripped the GTO; leaves of gold rained down in a summer breeze beside the dreamy river.

The soldier from Kon Barr pulled the trigger and the machine gun lurched soundlessly in his arms. Jesse opened his mouth and burped bullets. The windshield wasn't shattered, but Jesse rubbed his ears as if they were ringing.

"I feel dizzy," he said, then retched out the open door into the ditch. Within minutes, Jesse regained color and pulled out again. "Are you having a fucking meltdown, Little Engine?"

"Sorry," Nico said. "I thought I saw something. Maybe it was just a glare."

Black rimrock sketched a bold contrast to the yellow bunchgrass and blue sky, the silver bellies of cottonwood leaves dancing in the breeze.

Jesse inhaled deeply. "You okay then?"

"Yeah." Nico felt a slight surge of blood in his brain.

* * *

The GTO arrived at Sandy Point, a horseshoe-shaped beach below an earth-filled dam and reservoir. In big green crushed-rock letters *KEEP YOUR FORESTS GREEN* was spelled out on the ogee, an amusing description for drought-dry hills and black rimrock with sparse vegetation. When they created the park, they transplanted shade trees and gave them plenty of water, turning the picnic area into an oasis of sorts, a haven from the scorching sun. Jesse pulled into the parking lot and parked. A large plume of water released through discharge gates in the dam shot upwards in a great arc Boiseans called the Rooster Tail. Outdoor enthusiasts congregated on the beach and around the swimming hole. Jesse and Nico staked out a picnic table under the shade ten yards from the Goat. Nico docked the new 8-track, cranked up the volume, left the front doors open and went to fire up the grill. By the time Buffalo Springfield was "Four Days Gone," the grill was smoking hot.

Donny Sunderman showed up with Manny Hernandez. Manny lifted an ice-packed cooler out of his '55 Studebaker pickup's bed. The cooler was filled with brews, burgers and hotdogs. Donny hugged a grocery bag stocked with chips and condiments. He dropped them at the table and went back for his acoustic guitar.

Double Barrel took the local scene in an electrical storm with dual-lead blues that dimmed lights all over the Treasure Valley. Nico had asked them to open for The Bards.

Doc idled up on a black '56 Harley. Right behind him Pat Parsons rode in on a white '66 Electra Glide, wearing Josh Brownton like a backpack. It was always a spectacle seeing a white brother climb off a black bike and a black brother climb off a white one.

Josh retrieved his brownies from the pickup. A long-limbed scarecrow at six-four and 150 pounds, he made Nico's five-seven and 146 look solid by comparison. He lifted the foil on a plate of brownies. "Hey, who's been eating my porridge, Manny?"

The PAST sometimes met for blow-outs: meat on the grill, bottles of brew in crushed ice, two picnic tables of cafeteria-style sugars and salty carbs, and the holy grail of a fat doobie and a platter of brownies. Thanks to the news of Willy Sampson, the foundation for a blow-out was eroded by solemnity.

Doc laid out the cribbage board and started up with Parsons. "Sinclair's got nothing," he said. This was something of a signal that group could begin. "He's just dangling bait. I feel bad about Mr. Sampson. It was unfortunate his heart gave out, but Manny didn't kill him—his heart did."

Tradition taught the military to take kids from all walks of life and shave their heads, stuff them into drab green bags and declare them a *team*. Much more goes into making a team than throwing recruits together in a war zone. Soldiers, like those in the PAST, never blended into an easy chain of command. Good men paid the price for poor leaders. As a result, the PAST seemed to always require a little something extra to take the edge off: sex, pot, alcohol, flights of fancy. One fossil who keeled over at a bad time would not sever the bonds of brothers against the war.

While Manny rolled the doobies and saved the seeds in 35mm film canisters, Donny flipped charred burgers and rolled hot dogs sizzling on the grill. "What about Jericho, Doc?"

"What *about* Jericho, Donny? Nothing to worry about. You weren't even there."

Doc had this keen sense for sniffing out an ambush. He and Pat had squatted in mud on point enough times to develop something like instinct. They could tell the deputy was setting an ambush, looking to break up the PAST. "If Sinclair had anything on us, he'd have arrested somebody by now."

"You're singin' the blues like a white boy, white boy!" Parsons looked up from the cribbage board with a friendly grin.

"What worries me," Nico contributed, "is that Sinclair has Jesse's wig."

Jesse defended himself. "My wig and your shoe, Cinderella."

Nico slipped a dying roach into an alligator clip. "What about snot-nose and his mom? You forget about them? You showed them your hook."

Donny switched 8-tracks in the GTO to the Moody Blues *In Search of a Lost Chord.* He started playing along with the lead guitar. Palaver barely permeated the shutters of Nico's mind when the music took him into this ancient forest. Light filtered down through black branches. "House with Four Doors" drummed like a shaman inside his skull, opening doors to the sound of rotors carrying him back to the road from Kon Barr.

Jeep headlights fused into a single beam, cutting through jungle. Nico's numb butt stuck to the humid, hard seat. Tires punching potholes splashed red mud from a heavy rain, as wheels slipped in and out of ruts in the dim light. The road twisted and dropped away. After the sudden flash and when he blinked awake, a disfigured face leaned over him. He felt the wind ripping through the Huey's open door. Sweat poured off his blow-torched face. Bloody hands wrapped his head with battle dressings. "Ghost," the crew chief called over the whine of rotors. And the co-pilot shouted Mayday over the radio. The Huey crabbed sidewise, diving, pulling up and peeling off as machine gun fire hacked the fuselage. Loud voices in the cabin twisted with rending steel. Plexiglas shattered. The co-pilot was hit and slumped forward. The pilot strained to keep the rotors turning. The chopper plummeted.

Nico blinked, as if coming out of a reverie. As a product of escapist culture, he much preferred the fantastic voyage of Greek-heroes like Jason and the Argonauts, or H.G. Wells' *Time Machine* or Jules Verne's *Twenty Thousand Leagues under the Sea* to the daily routines of blue collar extinction. The crew of the starship *Enterprise* captured Nico's imagination with a utopian fantasy of alliances that transcended geopolitical differences to explore the farthest reaches of space. Bad faith and wrongful action tainted everything and everyone associated with Vietnam. Without the PAST, Nico didn't think he'd be able to cope with his distrust of government. One lesson that shaped his feelings about America: *no nation in the world could ever defeat America in America if Americans choose not to be defeated.* He came to this conclusion when America couldn't defeat the Vietnamese in Vietnam. The NVA would fight to the last man defending their country, weren't Americans just as strong? What fear did we have of invasion? Who could occupy us for long? We didn't need nuclear arms to defend our country. Americans loved their country no less than the Vietnamese loved theirs.

Instead of America changing Vietnam, Vietnam changed America. The war split the country in two—red and blue. Yet Nico felt a sense of renewal in defining what it meant to be an American; it should never involve blind faith, which is why Nico's slogan was *Support our troops: question their leaders.*

Doc said the burden of change fell on an awakened minority. They must break the hypnosis of consensus constraining the commoner to his commonness, in the silent majority that slept through change like Rip Van Winkle. By the time everybody was awakened, the revolution would be over. It left him in that luminous fog of gray everybody else saw as black or white.

"We need to follow up with another action," Doc said.

"Out of respect to Willy Sampson, shouldn't we hold up for a while?" Nico asked.

"That's exactly why we can't." Doc took his turn and waited for Parsons to counter. Donny and Jesse sat on the fence—both against the war but unsure what form dissent should take.

"We need to make sure we don't endanger the lives of innocent people just to make a point," Nico warned.

"I agree," Doc said, "but we *can* endanger our own lives

to make a point. How passionate are you about this? Bud-dhist monks torched themselves in the streets of Saigon, American protestors doused themselves with gasoline and burned to death."

"Could we agree on something a little less *dramatic*?" Donny strummed a full chord.

"Look, we engaged in an anti-war action, a free speech demonstration against the governor with unintended con-sequences. So now what? Do we sponsor a peace rally and sing Country Joe and the Fish or do we make an even bigger media splash? It's difficult to imagine the sacrifice and self-lessness involved in self-immolation. Though at this point it wouldn't be very original."

Jesse looked surprised, wondering if Doc was advocating self-immolation. "Not to mention the spectacle of making an *ash* of yourself," he said.

"You first," Nico dared.

"No, *you* first," Jesse dared back.

"Look, Ghost, you remember Tawnee Phillips?" Nico chuckled at the memory.

The gulf between Jesse's eyebrows narrowed. "Did you call me *Ghost*?"

"I don't know. I must have meant beer-swilling tanker."

"No," Doc clarified. "He said *ghost*."

"Don't you remember? The blackout?" Nico pressed. "The panties you ran up the flagpole?"

Distrust flickered into Jesse's eyes. "Why'd you call me *Ghost*?"

Nico shook his head. "Because I'm blasted."

Jesse's level gaze peered through a grim face. "We had this Lakota gunner on our crew, name of Stunted Horse—he named our ship Ghost Horse. I was its pilot."

A weak spasm ticked the edge of Nico's mouth. "You must have mentioned it."

"Not until now. Not even to Coco," Jesse insisted. "No one outside the crew ever called me Ghost. Don't anybody here call me that, okay?"

The PAST honored Jesse's demand. "Whatever you say, *Casper*."

* * *

Half-asleep, afternoon sun baking his brain, Nico listened to Donny's acoustic guitar. Jesse and Manny hiked downstream with fishing poles. Pat and Doc sat in the shade at the picnic table playing cribbage. Josh had apparently wandered off.

Nico decided it was high time he had a talk with God. He lifted his head and talked through the tops of trees to empty blue sky. "So You're the One with all the plans; what's Your plan for me?"

God answered in the form of an opalescent face, leaning through leafy branches, hovering above Nico's upraised eyes, features hidden by a glowing halo. Not-Gretel's brown eyes emerged from shadow, her lips mere inches away. Unbraided, long strawberry-blonde hair cascaded over sunburnt shoulders framing a generous smile and rosy cheeks. "Where's your friend?" she asked.

"Who said we're friends?"

She tossed her head. "I came over because I recognized you."

"Are you going to hit me?" Nico lifted his arm to shield himself.

"I should."

"I apologize for my 'friend'," he said. "He's not all there."

Under a thin oversized men's button-up shirt, Not-Gretel wore an orange bikini. Her brown eyes were flecked with jade. "Do you have a car?"

"Yeah, but not here. I came with Jesse. Do you need a ride?"

"No," she responded. "Do you need one?"

It was not a hard decision. Nico opted to catch a ride home. He glanced at Donny who understood without interrupting his finger-picking exercise.

"I'd love to catch a ride," Nico answered.

Not-Gretel's name was Idun Fiske. The creamy white skin at the Basque booth had been burned red in a single day. Nico flinched when she slid across the bench seat of her car, but he felt like something good was about to happen.

22.

Johnny Evenfall collapsed cross-legged onto the concrete floor. He looked exhausted. "Something got Jack."

By the time they all climbed to the observation room, Milo was shaking his head. "What? Are you drunk?"

"In Mishler." Johnny's eyes popped white as popcorn.

"Hey man," Geo glared at the Bud in Johnny's hands, "this is a *private* party." Geo counted cans like white sturgeon. His baleful eyes surveyed the plunder. "Six down already, and it's not even dark."

"Someone took Jack?" Milo asked.

Johnny nodded. He could have passed for one of *The Wild Ones* with long sideburns, black T-shirt inside a Levi's jacket, jeans rolled up in a cuff over his motorcycle boots.

Geo scratched his shoulder then wiped dead skin onto his pant leg.

"What happened?" Milo prompted Johnny.

"I don't know, man." He finished the can of Bud, his eyes glazed. "It's pitch black in there. We couldn't see our hands in front of our faces."

"What were you doing in Mishler? They always keep it locked."

"Someone left the padlock open. So we went in. It's a maze of dark tunnels. We heard a scream."

Monica yanked impatiently on Milo's shirttail.

Johnny shrugged his shoulders. "I turned around and he was gone. I believe something got him."

Milo reached down and pulled Johnny to his feet. His clothes smelled of driftwood smoke from a beach fire. "Show me." Milo steered him toward the stairs.

"I ain't goin' in," Johnny said.

"Just take me there." Milo's lantern beam found the stairs. Monica and Gayleen tried to follow, but Milo confronted them. "Wait here."

Monica stood her ground. "No way you're leaving us alone." She grabbed hold of Milo's shirttail.

"I'll just stay and guard the beer," Geo volunteered.

"Forget the beer," Milo said, a scornful frown following him to his feet. The girls stuck close behind Milo with Johnny in the lead.

Geo lagged behind, muttering, "I don't believe this." They made their way in twilight behind the bouncing ball of lantern light that splintered into spidery threads along the concrete walls as they moved from the West Battery across to Mishler.

"I thought you were in Portland," Milo said.

"Decided not to go," Johnny answered, pushing through brambles. Mishler's double door cracked. The padlock lay on the ground with the chain. Johnny pulled open the gate, iron scraping concrete. The entrance reminded him of an old mine shaft.

"The heart of Mishler is the old command post," Johnny said. "We think someone's living in there." He handed Milo the lantern. Monica tugged Milo's shirttail as they stepped into the dank and dark that immediately penetrated their bones. He directed the beam down the tunnel where black niches set into stained concrete once held gas lanterns. The darkness was thick as crude oil with the beam failing at every junction. It made their advance seem timid and uncertain. Monica clung to Milo and Gayleen clung to Monica's hips. Geo brought up the rear.

Each passageway faded ahead at another junction. He never imagined facing the unknown with a whimpering majorette riding his shirttail. He should've made them all wait outside, even Geo. "Jack!" he called. "You in here?"

"I can't believe this shit," Geo mumbled and the complaint rolled through the tunnel.

Monica tugged Milo's shirttail. "Can we go back now?" Suddenly the lantern dropped, light flashing across a water-stained ceiling like a meteor. Milo had stumbled into a small trench that intersected the passage. The lantern struck the concrete floor and blinked out. Monica screamed.

Gayleen called from behind, "You okay?"

"It's fucking dangerous in here," Milo answered, his calf scraped from the edge of the concrete. He ignored the pain and felt around for the lantern. He picked it up and whacked it with the heel of his hand. The lantern came on. Monica and Gayleen helped him to his feet.

"Geo, why don't you just take them back?" Milo suggested.

"This is such *bullshit*," Geo said. "He's playing us, your friend. He's running off with the beer right now."

A death rattle from deep inside the tunnel reached them in grim horror. "What's that?" Milo held the lantern higher. On the stained wall a cartoon with large bulbous nose and moon-shaped eyes peered down at them: *Kilroy was here*. On a whim, Milo switched the lantern off, whacked it good and switched it on again. Instead of Kilroy, there was crudely-drawn male genitalia with the caption: *Jane sucks Dick*.

"Look, cave art." Geo noted, inspecting the drawing.

Milo's lantern raced down the tunnel to the next junction. Again they heard the sound, coming from the command post. Around the next corner, he spotted a body crumpled on the floor in a heap. Milo kneeled to turn the body but nausea welled up in his throat instantly. The body broke apart with a sickening thud.

"Oh God!" Monica covered her mouth, backing away, retching. The skull wasn't human. The jaw protruded like a cow. An eerie light appeared in the wall around this floating disembodied face. The face moaned, then blinked out. Monica turned and ran smack into Gayleen who fell over backward against Geo who caught her in his arms.

A shadow crept up from behind them, howling.

Geo turned and tackled the shadow. He drove the body into the concrete wall. Monica and Gayleen screamed. A twisted face appeared directly in front of them—Monterey Jack with a flashlight tucked under the chin.

"Christ, it's me," the shadow protested, "we were just messin' with ya." MJ shined the flashlight on them. Johnny's mouth gulped air. Monica and Gayleen helped him up.

"We sure got ya," MJ sniggered.

Johnny hugged his soft middle. "Yeah, that was fun. Ha. Ha." Geo had driven his skull into Johnny's soft middle as if he were a tackling dummy.

"Dammit, you guys!" Milo kicked the corpse on the floor. "So what's this?"

MJ collected himself. "Deer carcass. What's left anyway. Pretty ripe, eh?" MJ picked up a bone from the heap and shoved it toward Monica.

She screamed, pushing his arm away. "Oh puke!"

"We could hear ya coming for a mile," MJ admitted. He mimicked the girls, *"It's dark in here. I'm afraid. Let's go back."* MJ made ghost sounds in Monica's ear.

Monica punched him on the bicep. "Shut up!"

"I told you," Geo said.

"No joke. There is a hobo camp in the command post," Johnny confided. "We found old clothes, a tattered mattress, empty cans and stuff. Wanna see?"

"Somebody's living here?" Gayleen snorted, eyes wide. She gazed over Geo's shoulder into the deeper dark ahead. "Who would live *here*?"

"Vampires," Geo said.

"Let's just go back," Monica urged.

Johnny and MJ shrugged and headed back out into the dry lightning. Milo sent the others back and stayed behind. "I'll be along in a minute."

"They brought beer," Johnny informed MJ.

"No kidding."

"It's a *private* party," Geo moaned.

* * *

Alone inside Mishler, Milo switched off the lantern and let the darkness seep into his brain. He relaxed. Walls and boundaries melted away. He floated bodiless, aware of himself as something more than flesh and bone. That's when he felt a presence. A suppressed clamor reached his ears from the command post. Poor acoustics defeated his sense of direction. He switched the lantern on and stood face to face with a drawing of Alfred E. Neuman wearing a conical hat with the caption: *Passage to freedom.*

Then Milo's lantern lit up another face in the wall. "C'mon, you guys. I asked for a moment." A shrouded figure ten yards away stood with back to the wall. The Hammer Man. He looked a little older, more material. He did not shrink or fade from the light but remained hunched, one leg bent back with his foot up against the wall as if waiting.

Milo inched forward, squinting. He uttered in a faltering voice, "Why do I keep seeing you?"

The Hammer Man replied. "It's easier for you to see me than for me to see you." His eyes shifted with wild intensity. "Put out the light. You're blinding me."

Milo lowered the light. The Hammer Man reached out suddenly, his bony fingers latching onto Milo's arm.

"Let go!" Milo reacted by striking the Hammer Man's arm. He let go.

Milo heard a roar followed by a sudden radiance. He ran blindly into walls, scraping his arms and elbows, scrambling out of the tunnel in a mad panic.

Outside, he kneeled in the tall grass with geometric patterns swimming in his eyes. As his vision cleared, he looked upon the clearing with ground fog, trees in silhouette against leaden sky. Milo wrestled with dread. Whoever or whatever The Hammer Man was, he was no apparition.

* * *

Monica and Gayleen huddled under blankets in the observation room. The temperature had dropped twenty degrees. Geo hovered over the girls like a guard dog. With arms around each other's shoulders the intruders, Johnny and MJ, gazed out over the darkening river mouth, drinking beers and having a smoke, their faces lit up with a lighter as Freddie Cannon's "Palisades Park" played on the marine radio. Geo's bad humor deteriorated into a black mood. He pulled Milo aside. "Those guys are queer, man. Look at 'em. They're hugging each other."

Milo put his hand on his friend's shoulder and smiled. Circumstances weren't favoring Geo's great moves on Gayleen and Milo felt strangely elated. The redhead was not as beautiful as Monica but more alluring.

"She's ready to put out," Geo scolded. "Those fags are ruining everything!"

Milo just shook his head, sympathetically.

"And they're drinking our beer..." Geo muttered.

"*My* beer," Milo corrected.

Geo grabbed another Bud and sat down in the corner brooding.

Storm clouds over the bar divided as they streamed over the river mouth in the shape of an eye. In the pupil of the blinking eye was clear night sky full of stars. Johnny and MJ studied the eye as dense clouds swirled.

"It's the Ghost Hole," MJ announced.

"What crap!" Geo spat. He'd polished off a beer with a belch, tossed the can from the tower down into undergrowth, and chunked holes into another with a church key.

Milo chastised him. "Don't litter. Leave no proof we were here."

Geo nodded and went to retrieve the can. He came back and pulled another Bud from the case for good measure. He set it on the floor between his feet.

MJ played middle-class beach boy to Johnny's brooding biker. Absorbed in Ghost Hole lore he was the perfect portrait of a surfer boy, a native Californian in snug white cords, button-down shirt and mohair sweater two sizes too big. He kept a small notebook in his shirt pocket on which he jotted down song lyrics. His focal point was all things esoteric. MJ loved talking about things like an advanced race of parallel and invisible beings who occupied the same space but were as far advanced from us as we were from apes. He was a goldmine of cool ideas. His cool was cracked when his girlfriend committed suicide. He believed her troubled spirit possessed his Chevy Monza.

Johnny turned to the girls like a tour guide. "The Ghost Hole's like the Bermuda Triangle," he explained. "It's why the bar is called the Pacific Graveyard. A strange force is centered there that churns up the wave action. I've never actually seen it until now."

Gayleen unknotted the hair at the back of her head and let it fall. She was an ugly duckling a few years ago, but now her face blossomed and her red hair twinkled with stardust.

Through the Ghost Hole, two or three streaks of light came wobbling west to east, in slow motion, moving inland over the river, parallel to the ground. "You see that?" Johnny cried. Gayleen and Monica flanked Milo, one on each arm. They gazed through the slotted window to the winking eye of heaven. The radio broke into static. The UFO resembled something like a swarm of fireflies in close formation crossing the sky in a continuous line, near enough to appear right over the river, just a mile away. A slipstream of orange and white controlled explosions erupted in a field of uniform sparks, as if the sparks were light particles in a glass jar, but the jar kept changing its shape.

The general motion of this sky light seemed unremarkable—no sudden turns or direction changes—but it moved steadily inland in "controlled flight" not "falling to earth." As it progressed slowly across the sky like a blimp, they watched until it grew dim in the east. The music came back on. Skeeter Davis was singing, "The End of the World."

"Now that's weird," Milo observed.

"It might be one of ours." Gayleen said, with stars spar-kling in her green eyes.

"One of *ours?*" Milo wanted to know more.

"We may possess technology far beyond what we know. The Russians have already sent a woman into space."

"Didn't we shoot up a monkey?" Geo responded, as if pointing out America was not without its own achievements in space.

Gayleen laughed and touched Milo's arm. "You know, like what's his name? The man who invented AC—Tesla?" She swept a wisp of hair away from her eyes. "He died like twenty years ago and had all these blueprints for gadgets and all these weird schematics for anti-gravity machines and high-voltage towers to control the climate. After he died the government confiscated everything. So what if it's our own government?"

"How does climate make a car stall?" Milo wondered. Johnny and MJ were huddled together, talking excitedly about possibilities and exciting new worlds.

"Our government wouldn't experiment on us," Geo as-serted. He snuck his arm around Gayleen's waist.

Milo exchanged glances with Gayleen. God, he thought, why doesn't Geo get the message?

Then came the newscast:

> *This is KAST, Astoria, 98.6 on your AM dial. The time is 8:18. We interrupt this program for an announce-ment from the emergency broadcasting network. The United States Geological Survey and National Oceanic and Atmospheric Administration have put the north Oregon coast and south Washington coast under a tidal wave warning. An earthquake with a preliminary mag-nitude of 7.2 was reported at 8:01 p.m. in the Cascadia subduction zone 180 miles/290 kilometers northwest of Eugene, Oregon. Roads to the beaches are closed and residents are advised to stay tuned to this channel until the warning expires at 9:00 p.m.*

23.

Nico rocked on the front porch with the *Idaho Statesman* spread on his lap. His bare feet on the green painted concrete felt cool. He decided to let Idun sleep. He sipped coffee and read an article on Senator Frank Church. Nico respected the senator's stance on the war and student protest.

The screen door closed behind him. "Good morning," Idun said, her warm lips brushing his ear. She was wearing one of his shirts. She straddled him, hands on his chest. The crumpled newspaper fell off his knees. The suddenness of her intimacy threw him off, and turned him on. They burst into flame nearly sucking all the oxygen out of the air. Church. State. War or peace. Who cares as long as he was blessed with another kiss from Idun. She dropped her head onto his shoulder. He kissed the sunburned back of her neck. The scent of French lavender in her hair skidded onto his olfactories like crippled Phantoms on the deck of an aircraft carrier.

Laughter erupted in bubbles from the community pool across the street. A small group of children with rolled towels under their arms avoided a spot on the blacktop where just yesterday they played four-square. They walked around it as they would an open manhole.

When Idun went back inside to take a shower, Nico strolled across the street to check it out. Blinking in the sunlight, he heard the children frolicking in the pool. He'd never learned to swim, in spite of nearly drowning once. He wondered how he'd become a dense rock that sunk to the bottom of everything. He tried to recall his first day of school. All he could conjure was a mirage of echoing halls and moon-waxed floors. He sensed a voyeur standing outside the window of his mind looking in.

Nico remembered when he and Jesse were twelve and took a shortcut home after school. It was a spring day with a light snow of apple blossoms in the air, adrift in the alleyway behind the No-Tel Motel. The sound of music drew their attention to an open window. Thin white curtains danced like petticoats. A compulsion to peek seized both of them simultaneously. The curtains billowed out. In the room, an attractive brunette dressed like a stewardess started stripping out of her uniform in semi-dark. The curtains sucked back in. Fixed to the spot by a splinter of afternoon light, they held their breath, mouths gaping. The sails billowed out again. She removed her bra. The man-shadow in bed was also watching her, the cigarette end brightening as he puffed steadily, smoke rising. Nico and Jesse gawked, unable to look away, their fascination rising as the naked stewardess moved to the bed. The couple made love to Conway Twitty, "It's Only Make Believe." The scent of sex reached into their imaginations. They would both swear the stewardess rolled in rhythm and came up on top, facing the window, her whole body aglow. She nailed them both in a bold stare as she rode to climax. That stewardess became Nico's dream lover, the epitome of earth-goddess magic and witch spell yielding in slow passion, her fragrance blowing blossoms off apple trees.

She might be his Idun. Idun greeted him with a hug after her shower. She had brought a change of clothes in her beach bag, a simple white cotton mini, black blouse with flapping sleeves, sandals the color of sunburnt feet.

The necklace she wore had a pendant with some insect frozen inside a chunk of amber. She apologized as she had to leave.

"Will I see you again?" he asked.

She kissed him lightly on the lips then skipped to her car. "Save me a dance."

* * *

The owner of the Belly Buster, a drive-in on the corner where Nico often went for brunch after night shifts at The Castalia, rested his tattooed forearms on the order window. His white shirt was ablaze with midday sun. His name was Mack and his quarter-pounder was a local legend. Mack handed Nico a bag with the burger, an order of curly fries and his special sauce. Add one strawberry milkshake and Nico had two meals in one.

"You okay, son?" Mack asked. "You look a little down in the mouth."

Mack was a rehabilitated truck driver with thick chest and bulging arms. He told stories of bar fights, road sex and highway killers to a select audience on the corner by the elementary school.

"The woman of my dreams left me this morning," Nico confessed.

"We used to call those wet dreams," Mack winked, "and they evaporate too quickly."

"She didn't even leave me her phone number." Nico counted out three dollars.

"Know her name?"

"Yeah."

"Then you can find her."

"But I'm already lonely."

Nico nearly dropped his shake when he heard a voice from behind him. "Want some company?" Nico turned and two men in black suits, white shirts, thin black ties, polished black dress shoes and black fedoras flanked him. Both wore dark sunglasses. Their rubber faces reminded Nico of Smith and Gannon in "Dragnet." They were like bad attempts to assimilate human feeling in robots.

"Nicolasa Enrique Bilbao, right?"

Tall and Lean peered at Nico intently, his sharp jaw sawing on his teeth.

"My friends call me Nico."

Short and Broad crowded Nico. "We know about your friends, Nicolasa." His voice sounded ominous, chilling the warm July air by several degrees. Nico felt some hostility from the man.

"Then why can't you pronounce my name?" Nico sat down at the picnic table, refusing to be intimidated.

"Dossiers don't come with a pronunciation guide," Tall & Lean answered. He reached into an inside pocket and whipped out a black billfold. Nico glimpsed the sun-sparked badge. Tall and Lean flipped it shut and returned it to his pocket. "I'm Agent Frank Hightower." His voice seemed comparatively soft, almost friendly, "and this is Agent Jon Lowman."

"How can I help you guys?" Nico asked, pushing a curly fry with too much special sauce through his lips.

"We've had you under surveillance. We've determined you're a pacifist; therefore, we need to consider you a potential threat to National Security." The edges of Lowman's mouth were flat and showed no hint of humor. Lowman placed his shiny black loafer on the picnic bench. He dropped his elbow onto his knee, doughboy face mere inches from Nico. His smoked sardine breath made Nico's eyes water as he calmly pulled tissue paper away from the cheeseburger and took a big bite, leaving special sauce on his chin.

"You're a Vietnam veteran, right?" Hightower towered over Nico, a stream of smoke from his cigarette gyrating into cloudless blue sky.

Good cop/bad cop, Nico decided. "You seem to know a lot about me."

"Your country thanks you for your service, Nicolasa." Hightower's brief smile felt mocking.

Nico wasn't surprised. "So the government's sending the FBI personally to thank our veterans now?"

"We talked with your Colonel," Hightower confided. "He sends his regards. Says you're a pretty resourceful guy, a good team player. Nico, your team needs you."

"So you're recruiting me for the FBI?" Nico picked up the milkshake and took a long draw on the striped plastic straw, squinting through a sharp brain freeze.

"Not exactly recruiting," Hightower said, pinching the cigarette from between his lips and flicking the ash. "We need you to tell us about the PAST."

Nico thought for a moment. "I can't remember much earlier than first grade."

"Not *your* past, smart ass, *the* PAST," Lowman hissed.

Nico shrugged.

"Your therapy group. The Peace Action Strike Team."

"Never heard of it," Nico lied, looking Lowman straight in the eye.

"We've talked to your doctors." Lowman came down astride the bench and scooted closer, fat hand on Nico's shoulder, his jacket open to show the holstered gun under his arm. He pulled some photos and spread them out like playing cards on the picnic table.

They had *photos*.

Nico picked one up that looked like it was taken at a topless bar.

"Not that one." Lowman snatched it back. "That's a different case." There were plenty of other pictures: surveillance shots of the PAST, individually and together, taken at Lucky Peak Dam.

Nico fingered one of them. "We were having a picnic. Is there a law against therapeutic picnics for vets now?"

Hightower sat opposite Nico and Lowman. "Laws were broken at your therapeutic picnic. Look, Nicolasa. You're a patriot, you can see this." He cracked his knuckles.

"Sure." Nico wondered what he meant by *patriot*? Someone who loved his country? Then hell, yeah, he loved his country. But he wasn't going to buy that bit: *my country right or wrong*. Citizens had a responsibility to hold their country to a higher standard. He'd heard that somewhere.

Lowman laid a photo under Nico's nose. "Mark Mayfield, alias 'Doc'." Then another. "Pat Parsons."

"Do you know these men?" Hightower knitted his stern brows.

"If you're who you say you are, you must know I do," Nico answered.

Lowman pressed him further. "These two are wanted for questioning in the firebombing of a recruitment center in Oakland."

A spasm of emotion flickered across Nico's face. Then he laughed as if it were a joke.

"Look, Nicolasa, you answered your country's call," Hightower removed his sunglasses. Their eyes locked.

"Yeah, so I wouldn't get drafted," Nico clarified.

"Well, at least you didn't run off to Canada, right? You even earned a Purple Heart, right? We're not looking to put heroes in jail here, right?" This time he looked at Lowman.

Lowman's eyes narrowed. "Cooperation would go a long way."

"Toward what? I never firebombed anything but a few ants on the sidewalk," Nico replied.

Lowman pinched a muscle in Nico's shoulder that made Nico feel uneasy. Hightower placed another photo in front of him: a close up of a Sad-Sack clown on the overpass. "A young man's career path can be cut short."

Panic rumbled up Nico's throat. His tongue thickened like wet leather. He swallowed too hard. "That was an *accident*." Suddenly the agents' initial impression of ineptitude turned to nasty guile. "We weren't even after *him*."

The FBI wasn't buying it.

"Who *were* you after then?" Lowman squinted, dazed with disbelief. "The Fair Maids?"

"Don't worry, Nicolasa. We're not here about the governor," Hightower assured him. "We don't like him either."

"Then what is it you want?" Nico wondered.

"Mayfield and Parsons."

* * *

Next morning, rocking on the front porch, Nico pondered his situation. How did two bumbling FBI agents bait him into spying on his friends? "Just keep your ears open," Hightower had instructed him. Only the government would send two clowns to catch two clowns. If they had photos of Nico up to his neck in pig blood, then it stood to reason they had photos of Jesse too. But Nico felt they were reaching when it came to the firebombing in Oakland. Nico went to the library and looked it up on microfiche. The bombing happened at night after the recruiting center was closed. No one was hurt. The action still qualified as an attack on America by the left-wing. The only reports putting Mayfield and Parsons in Oakland that night were speculative at best. They could well have been on the road to Idaho. The Feds had dossiers, photos and copies of Mayfield's writings published in a G.I. underground newspaper. If he were to believe them, Mayfield and Parsons concealed conspiracies of nothing less than the violent overthrow of the U.S. government. Nico simply didn't believe them. It was the job of the FBI to create dossiers on everyone. Nico and Doc reached common ground in the need for social change. They were both radical, but they disagreed on actions one might take to achieve radical change. Doc's intelligence and commitment were self-evident. Nico didn't question that. He admired Doc and Pat's bond of loyalty and, even if they were in Oakland, so were a million others.

Later that morning, Nico was listening to children frolic in the community pool. A black shade had been drawn over his life before war. His childhood phased into some mythic past, beyond a rising mist with blasted trees and twisted bodies. He felt the loss of his own aborted adolescence. It was a loss that isolated him from old friends and classmates. Even when he engaged in conversation with a neighbor,

Nico drifted off on some internal tide, shouting across the imagined distance. What was once home had been profaned by whatever hitched a ride home on his back.

Nico didn't know how to contact Idun. He looked forward to Saturday night. "Save a dance for me," she'd said. Idun only contributed to Nico's confused state. He knew next to nothing about her. Where did she live? Did she have her own place? Did she work a job? Did she have feelings for him, or was the other night an experiment in free love?

Nico wandered over to the Belly Buster. Mack wasn't there. Instead, a woman who must have been his wife took Nico's order. The burger wasn't as good, but good enough. She redeemed herself with an extra-thick strawberry shake. Nico thanked her and told her to keep the change. As far as he knew the federal agents could have been monitoring him since he was a boy playing war with a spring-loaded molded-plastic Mattel machine gun, tossing pinecone grenades into garbage-can tanks, or mounting a frontal assault on a doghouse pillbox. They died in such dramatic fashion, spinning mid-stride, struck by a ghost-bullet, falling, rolling, jerking in mock agony. These Watchers waited for the right time to lead him off to defend a promise nobody intended to keep.

The universe, Nico decided, was like a glass paperweight with someone's breath on it. The thumbprint of a dispassionate God smudged his awakening with shadows that grew longer, darkening recent memory. Nico straddled the picnic table bench much like Lowman did and listened to the kids splashing in the pool. The lifeguard blew on her shrill whistle. He felt for the children. Hoped they might enjoy a future without unintended victims, without all the good memories being annulled by wrong choices. Then the splashing stopped. Lesson was over.

Children melted into early evening. A cloud blocked the sun. Nico was suddenly overcome by a cold, opaque presence. His tired eyes fell on a suspended bridge of light breaking through summer leaves making a soft dapple splash on the blacktop across the street on the playground. Time held its breath. That same old tune came from a distance, growing louder around the same spot the children had been avoiding. The Kon Barr soldier materialized.

Other than that odd vision of light in the lobby of the V.A. Hospital, Nico hadn't been having visions so much as strange thoughts. Now, after one visit to a psychiatrist, he couldn't *stop* seeing things. If the Kon Barr soldier was imaginary, how come he appeared in the same spot those children had avoided? This time he wore a dress uniform with ribbons and medals. The soldier did not look injured. His blond hair whipped a bright face, fair as Baldur. Until he turned and Nico saw the other side: face shrunken and discolored, one red-rimmed and fogged-over eye roving uncontrollably. Nico should have expected him, but still he wasn't surprised. The wounded soldier would always be there, unseen by the children in the pool. More felt than seen, tucked away behind a veil in his mind. Nico's vision personified *all* the soldiers who died in 'Nam—many still in their teens—virgin spirits attaching themselves to his survivor's guilt. He stepped over that thin line between living and dead, this world and the next, where the Kon Barr soldier still fought the war.

* * *

The air was stagnant on the morning of the trophy dash. Nico stepped out onto the porch and found a square lavender envelope inside the screen door. The classic laid-weave of the folded card could have been a wedding invitation, but wasn't. Inside, the note read: *Time to talk.* The address wasn't the V.A. hospital, rather the old Skating King roller rink in the warehouse district, not far from The Castalia Lounge. The rink had been closed for five years.

At the Skating King, Nico pushed hard against the boarded-up double-doors. They didn't budge. Cracked-up blacktop girded the building and in the side lot ripped-out tongue-and-groove, strips of splintered lathe and rotted plywood filled dumpsters. He pulled a chunk of rusted iron loose and wheezed as white gypsum wafted up his nose. He picked a path through broken glass and boards with protruding nails and put his shoulder to the metal door at the back. The door broke inward, opening with a creak.

The rink stood dim and empty. Dust motes swam in waves of light that broke around the cracked door. Nico's footfalls echoed as in a deep cavern. "Hello," he called.

> You do the Hokey Pokey
> and you turn yourself around—
> *that's what it's all about.*

The sudden sound of an organ made Nico's head jerk. He heard a sharp whistle in his ear. All motion on the floor stopped. There she was mid-stride, frozen like a still photograph. The whistle in her hands. Colored lights rolled across the ceiling and skaters started up in a ghostly rewind.

Back in the ninth grade, Nico went skating because he knew Coco was patrolling the polished wooden floor in a short skirt with a silver whistle. Just watching her spin center-rink inspired fantasies. She filled out the tight-knit costume, well-formed limbs inviting the eyes of clumsy clowns who crashed in her wake. Coco Bird leaned back into the spin, her ponytail lashing. Nico could barely stand on skates. His stiff robotic steps while clinging to the rail left him vulnerable to crazy kamikazes like Jesse, come round that tight turn sweeping by nip-and-tuck, missing the wall by mere inches. Then down the straightaway he went, weaving in and out of more cautious striders, heroic in his black shoe skates reflecting the lights like sleek Porsches. Nico lost his balance and fell, dusting the floor with his backside, a sharp pain shooting up the tailbone and shocking his brain.

The whistle blew and blew again. Speedsters changed direction. Nico now found himself chugging against the current. His feet flew out from under him once, twice.

Coco skated over, red pom-poms on her toes bouncing in rhythm, perfume entrancing him like witch's brew. Once satisfied nothing was hurt except Nico's pride, she skated off across the floor with graceful ease.

Lady's Choice.

Nico held his breath while Coco skated the dim rink over in search of a reckless clown that outclassed him on skates—in most everything.

When they skated by, hand in hand, Nico couldn't take his eyes off them. It was all so perfect, the king and the queen waltzing together in this bubble of light filled with organ music, step by step, swaying hip to hip.

When the dance ended, the bubble burst. The house lights came on. Jesse raced to get out in front. Perfect was only a dream and Coco couldn't live in it. Nico faced awkwardly inward, blisters popping in sweat socks. He let go of the rail and stepped out on toe stops to start, hitting stride in the straightaway, holding a nervous lane in heavy traffic. He was just getting the knack when Jesse whizzed by, crouching low to the floor, swinging wide, then cutting in close to the rail, missing Nico by a spider's breath. Nico locked his arm around the waist of a middle-aged woman, who shrieked with surprise as he dragged her down. They sprawled, arms and legs in a glorious tangle and Nico swore he heard Jesse laughing. The laughter resounded off the walls. Coco blew her whistle, but Jesse didn't slow down. Nico clambered to his knees, hands pushing off the pillow-soft bosom of the fallen woman. He helped her up and apologized. Someone pulled him away by the arm. He turned and stood nose-to-nose with the two-faced soldier of Kon Barr.

The house lights came on in the Skating King.

The floor of the rink was stripped to rough subflooring. The bones of the remodel were laid bare in reinforced ceiling, new joists and walls. Nico's nose burned with turpentine and adhesive. Where the snack bar used to be, there was now an office cubicle with wooden half-walls and no ceiling. Nico found his way through the scatter of tools, stacks of tiles, plasterboard and plywood to a walnut door. On the door, a black plaque with white letters read: *Captain Karl Neumann, M.D., Psychoanalysis.*

The brass door handle clicked. He opened it. Behind a Royal typewriter in the reception area sat the same humorless secretary he'd encountered before. She glared through horn-rimmed glasses, twisting gouache red lips. "You again?"

At least she remembered him.

The office mirrored the V.A. hospital office to the smallest detail: bookcases filled with esoteric titles, two straight-backed armchairs with reading lamps, receptionist's desk guarding the inner mysterium of Dr. Neumann. The only visible change was the wall-sized painting was now a bold abstract that looked like the inside of someone's brain.

Nico handed the receptionist the folded lavender card. She opened and read it with a frown. She checked her appointment book, and shook her head. "I don't see a scheduled appointment, Mr. Balboa. Didn't you check with me before you left after the last visit?"

"I'm sorry." Nico's face flushed, too tired to correct her persistent mispronunciation of his name. "I forgot."

He didn't know why he came here. The thought of seeing Dr. Neumann made his stomach uneasy. Did the doctor's interest in him stem from an honest wish to help or some fascination with personality disorders? This was possibly his last earthly opportunity to convince a reasonable man of his sanity.

"Captain Neumann," the secretary keyed the intercom, "Mr. Balboa is here for an appointment?"

No answer.

"Captain?" she called again.

Neumann's voice crackled over the speaker, garbled as if crossing time and space. "Send...him...in."

The established façade of Neumann, the psychoanalyst, struck Nico as a bit incongruent considering the good doctor's penchant for working the lunatic fringe. Such a maverick persona granted dancing room for the unorthodox. One might have expected spirit masks, potions and voodoo dolls.

Nico relaxed into a black leather couch, massaged by the musical fingers of a string quartet. Mozart? Maybe a fugue? As a trumpet player, Nico hated fugues—too many rests. They always put him to sleep.

Neumann listened as Nico in unprompted reverie related the recovered memory of the chopper crash and the pilot *Ghost*. Nico talked about Jesse's panty theft and how baffled he was that Jesse didn't remember it. "So I checked my yearbook," Nico confided. "There was no Tawnee Phillips."

Neumann set aside his notebook, poured a glass of ice water into a crystal tumbler and held it up to the floor lamp. "Clear water can still be polluted."

Was Neumann suggesting Nico's mind was polluted?

"I thought maybe she'd transferred in," Nico continued his story.

The doctor sipped the ice water, washing it around in his cheeks before swallowing. "What do *you* believe, Nicolasa?"

Nico wondered what difference it would make. Neumann suggested an analog for Nico's experience in Vietnam might be a prolonged "altered state of consciousness." Re-creating such a state could lead Nico to "the numinous reintegration" of his "fractured psyche." Or some psychobabble like that. Nico thumbed his chin. It wasn't like he hadn't experienced an altered state since leaving Vietnam. Did Neumann want to make him feel stupid?

Neumann next suggested a few sessions of hypnotherapy. Nico should be assured the method was proven for recovering repressed memories. "You may recover those memories on your own. As a tool, hypnotherapy tries to release water from behind the dam. It takes pressure off without the dam breaking."

"Isn't there anything quicker?" Nico wondered.

Neumann stroked his beard and chuckled. "Quick answers aren't always *right* answers. We Americans want instant gratification. Happiness on the installment plan. You and I right now are partners in an archeological dig and I look forward to talking about the artifacts we will recover."

Neumann sat down on the leather chair beside the couch and picked up his notebook. Inside the cover was a small flat leather case etched with symbols. At first the symbols were something like Celtic runes, then Mayan glyphs. Neumann rubbed the leather. The case rippled like living skin. The symbols were now Buddhist or Hindu. Neumann opened the case. Inside lay dog tags on a silver chain. "I'm giving you back what you lost."

Nico pulled the dog tags out of the case. They swung pendulous, clinking together on his chest. He stilled one of the two between his thumb and forefinger. They were his, right down to the NP for *no religious preference*. "My dog tags?"

"No," Neumann corrected, "your *identity*."

"Are you going to use these to hypnotize me?"

Neumann laughed. "No. I use this." The doctor leaned forward and wagged a forefinger. On the tip of the forefinger, he placed a silver thimble. "Follow the thimble with your eyes. I want you to relax now. *Gooood.* Take a deep breath, in through the nose, out through the mouth. As you exhale, release all the tension in your body. Feel that cold tight tension melt from the center of your being, dissolving, absorbed by the cushions of the couch. That's right. Breathe in to the count of four: one, two, three, four. Now hold: one, two, three, four. Release slowly to the count of seven. *Gooood.* Follow the thimble. Do you feel your body?"

A pleasant warmth spread through Nico's body at the mention of it. It felt like he was floating in a hot bath. He'd fallen into the Escher print where up and down meant nothing. Neumann's voice reached him from a distance. He felt lighter than air, drifting into blue, blue sky.

* * *

The sky darkened. Clouds gathered. The jeep pushed through tough terrain to beat the storm. Tires shimmied in and out of ruts and bumped over small ravines bisecting the road with runoff. The road cut through thick jungle and narrowed into perilous corkscrews. Reports of attacks by the NVA on the pipeline run-

ning parallel to Highway 19 underscored their exposure, the foolishness of the errand. If they made it to Camp Radcliffe they could join the gun trucks with mobile firepower and roll with the convoy over Mang Yang Pass.

In the front seat Chu Len's lowered eyes stole side glances. Lu Bien sat in the back. Both girls were seventeen or eighteen, innocents with bright teeth and supple breasts. Nico could see the Colonel's eyes peeling their green skins and finding exotic fruit inside. He didn't notice the soldier in the road until the jeep was on top of him. He cranked the wheel, braking hard. The jeep skidded sideways and stuttered to a stall. The soldier dropped to his knees.

A sudden light blinded Nico. He regained consciousness in a muddy hole beside a mangled hulk of smoking steel. He was lifted onto the deck of a chopper, felt hot rotor wash pressing down on him, chopper blades in a blur. They lifted off and Nico wavered on the edge of consciousness. A voice in the cabin shouted,"Go, go, go."

Phosphorescent flares popped and died in dark sky. Sudden burst of red and green tracers. .50 caliber bullets penetrating steel. "Get us out of here, Ghost." The crew chief's sweaty face leaned over Nico, battle dressings clutched in his hands, fighting to stanch the flow of blood. Nico's stomach contracted. His mouth moved soundlessly.

When the sun came crashing through the windows at the field hospital, the man next to him stared back stonily. Nico felt sour acid climb in his throat. The man was the crew chief who moments earlier fought to save his life. This recognition sent a jolt of searing white pain through Nico's skull. He slipped back into darkness, the light receding to a distant point as if he were sinking in a deep dark sea.

* * *

"Hypnosis," Dr. Neumann explained, "helps purge negative psychic residue." Nico's mind felt uncluttered for the first time in months. Everything in life was a metaphor, the doctor said. Nico shouldn't fret about negative images. A negative image, after all, was only an image unexplored. Subjective reality, he said, is a tool for creating your life-script, a mind-movie in which one imagines a more balanced whole, a more integrated Self. The soul then works like an alchemist to perfect the power of transformation. Nico represented an anomaly which was why Neumann reached out with a personal invitation. Nico was a curious amalgam of head injury, trauma, coma, survivor guilt, sexual repression, drug use, excessive drinking, and hopeless worship of the unattainable. He presented a challenge. One day maybe Nico might have his own classification in the growing compendium of psychiatric disorders. Neumann offered a means of re-entering the "dream" to confront feelings and fears that manifested in Nico's mind as the Kon Barr soldier.

Neumann did not mind talking about his own war experience. It was part of the method for getting patients to be more open. He'd been a surgeon in 'Nam in '65, before the war escalated, before the Tet Offensive. Neumann explained that many combat vets presented the same general affect as that of lobotomized patients. Psychology's view of lobotomy sprung from this false premise that thought and emotion were separate. If emotion, the cause of pain, could be severed without changing a patient's personality, they would have a cure. The theorists got it wrong, of course. The cure turned patients into virtual stereotypes for open-mouthed, drooling zombies—the walking dead. Viet vets, Neumann believed, suffered a sense of isolation and numbness, cut-off from the social norm. The effect could be mitigated by strong bonds formed in combat or intense identification with one's unit. Dropping a green soldier into the bush for on-the-job training then plucking him out of his unit after a year of desperate hypervigilance and shipping him home on a commercial airliner added up to a figurative lobotomy. "We cut away the bad emotion," Neumann explained, "leaving a will to survive, at the expense of virtues like altruism and self-sacrifice, the ability to experience something larger than the self. Survival without attachment kills the soul. We have to go through hell, sometimes, to find heaven."

Neumann's job was to guide Nico in the rediscovery of the trauma of psychic lobotomy. Then he'd find his own path to heaven.

Neumann believed what happened on the road from Kon Barr had formed some connection with the unknown wounded soldier. His memory of the connection got lost in the lobotomy. Perhaps these visions presaged a re-linking through which he might recover the connection. Such a theory would never wash with Neumann's more behavioral colleagues who denied the reality of such phantoms. Nico's case wouldn't convince them otherwise, as Neumann's method could not be separated from his madness.

As a study group, Vietnam veterans offered Neumann a general analog for the whole culture edging closer to breakdown. If we could understand what happened to them, we could understand how to restore balance in a more open society.

"You and Jesse represent the yin and yang here, don't you think?" Neumann ventured. "Lama Anagarika Govinda named four dimensions of consciousness as point, line, plane and space. Your friend occupies the dimension of line—an inability to comprehend more than a series of points following each other. You have experienced the higher dimension Govinda calls *space*: three-dimensional consciousness that 'consists in the co-ordinated and simultaneous perception of several systems of relationships or directions of movement, in a wider, more comprehensive unity without destroying the individual characteristics of the integrated lower dimensions.'"

"Yeah, that's me." Nico's blank expression forced Neumann to redirect.

"Think of it this way: our task is to integrate the sleepwalker of your prior existence with a new dimension of your personality that was involuntarily formed in a foreign land. You may not have set out on a vision quest, but that's what you got. Now we need to build upon the older, underlying strata of adolescence and early identity formations without destroying any foundations or natural resiliency. A lot of things get stretched anytime something new is born. The goal here is to achieve a sense of unity where you can let go of the fear of losing yourself if you break out of the chrysalis like a butterfly."

Neumann advocated for better scientific knowledge while drawing upon myths, stories, poems and art for models of subjective realities, archetypes from the dim margins of human existence that have personal meanings. Many Vietnam veterans still walked around like zombies at the edge of a cliff, lost and uncertain, trying to get home. Others readapted and fell into the flow of community living as if they had been on vacation. Neumann studied such strange phenomena as reports of combat veterans being able to tell who would die in the next engagement. He described how those marked by death might lose any distinguishing features even before the fire squad went out on patrol. Witnesses have said they could see nothing behind their eyes. Survivors told Neumann how they steered clear of the walking dead for fear of being taken out with them. Neumann didn't know if these survivors foresaw the death of comrades or if fear of them as combat pariahs created the very condition that kept them from being saved. Nico couldn't avoid these questions when considering the Kon Barr soldier.

Neumann didn't discount anything. Keep an open mind, he encouraged. Ernest Hemingway, George Patton, Charles Lindbergh, all had inexplicable experiences in war. Accounts of the first gas attack in France during the First World War reported unprotected allied troops facing a rolling cloud of lethal gas. A figure in a Royal Medical Corps uniform appeared with a bucket of liquid and small cups in his belt. Speaking English with a French accent, the corpsman offered an antidote. Those who drank the bitter brew suffered no ill-effects.

Then there was the "Angels of Mons" incident where soldiers on the battlefield reported being rallied to victory by an illusory white cavalry.

If Nico had the internal resilience to withstand what Govinda called an "ecstatic breakthrough," then he would likely survive anything. Jesse, whose lifestyle charged in high gear toward the promise of breakthrough, lived inside a speeding vehicle going around in circles, where start and finish were the same. Nico felt, for once, a small advantage.

* * *

After the appointment, Nico thought of buying flowers for Willy Sampson. The old guy wasn't even in the ground yet. Didn't matter. He couldn't take flowers to the hospital. Jericho Sinclair might trace them back to him. He'd have to wait to pay his respects.

His phone rang. Coco. Nico could tell from the half-whine, half-rant. Jesse didn't come home.

* * *

She met him at the door in a yellow housecoat, throwing arms around his shoulders and kissing him on the cheek. "Thanks for coming," she said.

"Well, you're in better spirits than when you called," Nico observed. "You must have heard from him."

Coco pulled him into the living room. The local rock station was playing an old standard, "Palisades Park." It brought back good and not-so-good times. Yes, Jesse had called. He was already at the track. He and Harley wrestled all night with a steering problem. She was embarrassed that she called Nico in such a panic. "Now that you're here," she suggested, "you can take me to the track."

"I was going early to help the crew," Nico pinched his mouth into fish lips between thumb and forefinger, as though squeezing out the words. "He didn't mention any steering problem."

"They just found it last night." Coco twirled on her heels and marched down the hallway toward the bedroom. "You can help me decide what to wear."

"It's only the racetrack, Coco." Nico poured a cup of luke-warm coffee and checked the top of the fridge. No donuts.

When Coco returned, she laid out several outfits over kitchen chairs. She tucked a bi-color polka-dotted dress under her chin, opened the arms as if dancing with a doll. "With black stockings..." Coco held up large coin-shaped earrings, "...and these." Then a lovely short smock dress with horizontal wavy lines and yellow stockings. Next she flourished a pair of flared tangerine genie-style pants with a rose-colored ribbed stretch shirt. "How about this?"

He shrugged.

She glared. "Maybe you need to see me in it."

He nodded.

She spun on bare heels and trotted back to the bedroom.

Nico took the smock dress and draped it over the pol-ka-dots so he could have a chair at the kitchen table. He sat down his coffee cup and absently thumbed the dog tags around his neck. Neumann said he'd given Nico back his identity. His eyes fixed on a cactus in the window. "Suite: Judy Blue Eyes" was on the radio. Coco called his name. He took tentative steps down the hallway. It was a gauntlet of family portraits: Jesse behind the wheel of his metallic green '57 Chevy, with Coco practically in his lap.

Coco got a thrill out of Jesse peeling rubber in the parking lot after school. She loved dragging the gut downtown in the middle between them, Jesse driving and Nico as co-pilot, arm out the open window. She stretched over Nico to wave her red silk scarf; he was already two beers down. Nico's mind switched on in proximity to her scent. The young brothers at the No-Tel Motel stood slack-jawed and blinking. Coco's cheerleader skirt rode up the backs of her thighs and the heart shape of her perfect ass made him sick with want.

Jesse went places with her Nico would never go—Table Rock, rafting on the Boise River—did things with her Nico was afraid to do. In his scrambled brain he wanted to be in the driver's seat, gazing over city lights at night, feeling her warmth against him. He remembered the night Jesse asked him to take a walk. It was late autumn and when he got back to the car the windows were all fogged up. He didn't want to be the one shining the flashlight into their backseat sauna so walked home. She stroked the tuck-and-roll, biting her lip for piston pulse and high octane, clutching the straight hot stick and ramming it into gear. Need for speed pressed against the seat by the g-force of sudden exhilaration. Just once he wanted to be in the driver's seat. And here he was again: the guy Coco called to fix things.

Nico inched along the portrait gallery, feeling uncertain. Jesse was an exhibitionist—twisted face, tongue sticking out, eyes crossed—except in this one Nico shot on the steps of the First Presbyterian Church after Chad Summers' funeral. It was unposed. Jesse was wearing a black suit, his eyes were cold against the stone. Coco said it was her favorite. Jesse hated it. Just before the bedroom was a small self-portrait of Vincent Vandermeer. The portrait was about twelve by twelve and hung next to Nico's photo of Jesse. It was an oil painting in neutral, subdued tones, with soft light and long shadows. Next to that was a framed, grainy black and white photo of Caroline and Lenny. The contrast was so stark between Vincent and Lenny. He associated the shadows in their eyes with the Depression. The details fractured every façade. The graduation picture was taken against warm white brick at Boise High School with Coco flanked by her boys, Jesse's arm around her waist, hand on her hip flagging the middle finger at the photographer.

The bedroom door was ajar.

He came to a stop. "Did you call me?"

"I'll be right there, Nico."

He glimpsed her reflection in the dressing table mirror through the cracked door. A surge of adrenalin made him step back. Like a bashful boy, he stepped up to the crack and gazed at the reflection. She was standing in front of the mirror in black panties, patting body powder onto her skin with a puff. Her breasts white as skinned pears took his breath away. Coco was no longer a lanky teenager but a mature woman in possession of herself, whose every breath blew on the coals of his long-suppressed desire. Moral paralysis held him back, but his mind pushed on into the bedroom.

Coco sat on the edge of the bed pulling on knee-high stockings. She smoothed the wrinkles along sleek calves. With her bra dangling from one hand, she stood up and gazed at her own reflection. The pregnancy did not show yet. She slowly slipped her arms into the straps of the bra and adjusted the cups over her nipples. When she lifted her arms, Nico noticed nasty bruises that looked like finger marks.

Nico's jaw tightened, his anger at Jesse rising. Coco pulled on the rosy stretch shirt which emphasized her breasts and still-flat tummy.

"Jesse was so wiped out last night," Nico said through the door, "How did Harley get ahold of him?"

"Maybe he stopped by the station?" she answered. Her reflection stepped away from the mirror. A second later she pulled open the door and stood in front of him. "Well?" She tilted her head to brush out her long sorrel hair. She was a knockout in the genie pants and tight red ribbed shirt. She threw an orange scarf around her neck, held out her arms and twirled like a model. "How do I look?"

Nico wondered if she knew he'd been watching. "Like you're going to prom."

24.

The storm broke with wild fury. Black sky split open and began to pour. Milo expected the radio station to announce gale warnings. Instead, strange oriental music surged over the airwaves, breaking through static.

Gayleen and Geo huddled in a tight ball on the floor of the observation room, covered with a blanket. Monica invited Milo into hers, thin smile wilting into spurned woman. Milo stood aloof, staring off into the rain. He reached his hand out the narrow window, palm up. Rainwater rolled down his arm. The rain was black. When he turned around, Geo's hands were moving under the blanket.

"Do something," he heard the Hammer Man say. He looked at Monica who shivered in the corner wrapped in a blanket. Johnny and Monterey Jack were croaking along with the strange music. The rain fell harder. Gayleen struggled with Geo under the blanket.

A lone seagull fought against wind-driven black rain then broke off, riding inland over a soft blur of stunted trees, its white body turning black until the bird suddenly vanished. Milo looked down at his hands. It was only rainwater.

Johnny and Monterey Jack stood nose-to-nose at the observation window, passing a hand-rolled cigarette back and forth, inhaling deeply, holding it in until they gagged up puffs of smoke and giggled. Milo was watching skeins of fog ripped away by wind when he noticed his friends change before his eyes.

MJ combed a scraggly beard with open fingers. His long hair tangled in a gust that blew in through the window making him push wire-rimmed glasses up the bridge of his nose. He wore flowery pants that flared at the bottom, and long strings of beads.

Milo was wearing pants with flaring legs too, and a fringed leather vest over a loose flowery blouse; low black boots made a growl when he moved. He laughed at the funny clothes.

Thunder cracked over the river mouth. The wind chilled; the temperature dropped. Geo's aggression re-doubled and Gayleen struggled.

"Stop this," the Hammer Man's low voice again warned Milo.

Milo didn't know what to do. Geo was out of control. Gayleen's legs thrashed under him as he pinned her shoulders back. "STOP!" she cried.

"C'mon," Geo huffed, "you want it as much as me."

MJ popped the lid off a small film canister and handed it to Johnny. "Save the roach, man."

Monica sat in her corner, hugging her knees. "I wanna go home."

Milo collared Geo round the neck, yanking him off Gayleen. She sat up, eyes red and puffy. Geo spun Milo around by the shoulder and punched him square in the face. He took Milo into an armlock and forced his head between his knees. "Go on, Sunny. Suck yourself."

Gayleen threw off the blanket and emerged like a butterfly in tie-dyed mini skirt and white pantyhose. Big curls of auburn hair were held back with a headband. She flat-handed Geo alongside the head. When he turned on her, Milo got to his feet. MJ and Johnny watched as if they'd been transported into someone's dream. Monica kept hugging her knees.

Together, Milo and Gayleen wrestled Geo to the ground and pinned his arms and legs. He looked betrayed. "Milo, let me up."

The way Gayleen handled herself surprised Milo. He had underestimated her.

From the corner, Monica cried, "Take me home *now*." She dropped her blanket and arose in a black vinyl mini, fishnet stockings, arms in long black gloves crossed over a black blouse with a white crocheted vest.

Everyone was wearing beads.

"Let me up," Geo protested. He looked out-of-date in a plaid button-down, white cords and be-bops. "They're coming."

"Who's coming?" Milo asked.

Geo's face paled in a lightning flash. He peered intently through stunted pine in front of the bunker. "It's too late."

MJ caught Geo's shocked expression. "What? Is my lipstick smeared?"

Johnny whipped around with a Zippo. *"War. What is it good for?"* he asked, then pulled out a big fat doobie, flicked the lighter and took a long toke. "Peace, brother."

Thunder shook the tower followed by another lightning flash. Cause and effect had reversed.

Geo screeched at him, "You'd better fight, you hippie bastard!"

Johnny howled looking out over the river mouth. "Look. Far out!"

Milo let Geo up and followed Johnny's pointing finger to the sky over Astoria. It glowed like the northern lights. The whole town was ablaze. So this is how the world ends, Milo thought, with a drowned man picking up sledgehammers and his best friend attempting rape.

Geo and Gayleen stood in stunned silence.

Raindrops fell so hard they knocked seagulls out of the sky. One bright flash after another walked step by step toward the bunkers in quick succession. Thunder grew louder and louder. Monica ducked into Milo's arms.

"It's okay," he assured her. A shuddering rumble rolled over their common ground. The tower rocked on its concrete supports. Their hearts pounded; their breaths caught in their throats.

Johnny and MJ gasped in unison. "Righteous, man. Unreal!"

"It's an earthquake," Gayleen shouted, her voice ruffled by rolling thunder.

"It's the Big One!" MJ shouted above her, rubbing red eyes.

With thunder and flash in reverse, silhouetted figures swarmed up from the river, crawling on their bellies over the Parados, weapons cradled in their arms. They were being shelled, Milo decided. That's what the flashes were. Had they slipped into the past? Back to World War Two with a Japanese invasion of the Oregon coast? Strange voices sounded in the dark. Milo recognized the strange music was George Harrison's song from *Sgt. Pepper's*. They were being attacked. With the next flash, the invading force had vanished. Tendrils of yellow fog curled through blasted trees. The landscape transformed into an eerie dreamscape. Milo kept thinking he was causing it—whatever *it* was.

Johnny and MJ gazed over the river. Flashes pulsed on and off like a strobe light. Johnny pointed into the dark. "There. See it?"

In the next flash, Milo glimpsed a dark figure mounting the concrete parapet, dragging a sledgehammer. The figure rose to his feet and hefted the hammer, rolling it up and around behind his head. He pulled it over with brute force, his whole body shivering as the hammer came down cracking with thunder.

25.

The Meridian Speedway was a half-mile asphalt oval track that ran jalopies, sprints and stock cars. The course banked in the curves. A concrete wall with a heavy screen fronted the wooden grandstands on the north side. The south wall was a wooden façade covered in ads. The green infield grass was kept groomed. The pit area and viewing platform lay at the west end. Mostly volunteer crews worked for beer and bragging rights. Sponsors barely kept races from turning into destruction derbies. The longest race ran 100 laps so the primary role of the pit crews was loading and unloading the cars.

Nico climbed into the grandstands with Coco on his arm. She spotted the Stinkers working below on the Bomb. She waved frantically. Harley and Too Fast were knocking heads under the hood while Manny and Joe were jawing and not looking up. Coco's tight smile collapsed into chagrin. "Where's Jesse?"

Nico shrugged. "How should I know? I've been with you."

"He said he was here."

Nico checked his watch—12:30. Time trials started at 1. The sprint cars were done. Two jalopy races and a Powder Puff finished last laps. The Fireworks trophy dash started at 2. "Maybe he's in the bathroom."

Annabelle stood mid-section waving her scarf so Nico could find them in the stands. His detour to fetch Coco made him late. His mom was wearing a mid-calf polka-dotted dress with wide white lapels, quite trendy in the '50s. Maury sat in his trademark faded green E-Z Flush coveralls and re-born red NASCAR cap from Harley. Uncle Frosty was there too, sulking behind sunglasses, in a knit shirt exposing way too much beer belly. Beside him was a young woman. At first Nico thought Uncle Frosty must have robbed the cradle again but as he and Coco sidled up the aisle, Nico saw his favorite kissing cousin and the mouth he'd never forget. She was prettier than before. What were they? Sixteen? Fifteen? Her lips awakened some relative taboo.

Shelly Bilbao squeezed Coco's limp hand. Coco's eyes looked around her while Shelly's held steady and bold. Nico introduced Coco as Jesse's wife. "Oh, the driver," Shelly said. She swept back a knot of chestnut hair. His cousin in green short shorts and white halter top raised a caution flag for Nico. *Cousin; remember.* He glanced guiltily at Uncle Frosty. She must have taken after her mother. Nico didn't see his uncle in her much. She wasn't wearing a ring.

Nico spread the blanket on the wooden bench next to Shelly. Coco pecked Maury on the cheek and gave Annabelle a hug. His parents lavished attention on Coco in sympathy after Vincent died and puritanical Lenny had locked her into an emotional strait-jacket. Whenever Coco had another hit-and-run incident with Jesse, she came to see them—at least until she got married. Going to the races would be something Coco would never do with Lenny Bird. Coco was happy to claim the Bilbaos as a second family.

Annabelle could charm the most intimate details out of anyone. She had the mother thing down. She was a strong woman in spite of looking like Vivian Vance. Whatever quality it was that opened communication, Annabelle possessed it. Nico learned Shelly was visiting Frosty on summer break. Nico already knew she was a junior at Reed College in Portland, where she still lived with her mom. She was getting her degree as an art teacher and painted beautiful abstracts her father didn't understand. Annabelle also shared Nico's status with Shelly.

"Your mother says you're going to work for NASCAR?" Shelley said.

Nico shook his head and glared at his mother. "I don't have any plans. I like what I'm doing." He found it hard not to stare at his cousin.

"That figures." Frosty butted in.

"Daddy!" Shelly's voice cracked with rebuke. She turned back to him apologetically. "You look good, Nico."

"You look good too, Shelly. How's school?" She did look good. He remembered being zipped up in a sleeping bag with her. Now he sat sandwiched between Coco on the right and Shelly on the left, their breasts pressing against his Little Stinker elbows.

"One year left," Shelly said.

Nico looked around her. "Thanks for coming, Uncle Frosty."

Uncle Frosty scowled. Nico was already rehearsing in his mind how to invite Shelly to The Enchanted Forest.

Coco untied the orange scarf from around her neck and held it out to Nico.

"What's that for?" he asked.

"For Jesse, of course."

"Oh, right, the driver." Nico answered. "Of course."

"To wrap around his arm for good luck."

"Yeah, right, for good luck." Nico wrapped the scarf around his wrist and went to find Jesse. Coco's sense of decorum forbade an intrusion into the den of a greasy bunch of speed jocks. He couldn't imagine her shouting over revved-up engines. It wasn't the proper setting to showcase her finer features.

Fifteen minutes before time trials, still no Jesse. Nico was leaning up against the front fender of the Stinker Bomb when he came around the corner wolfing down a hotdog. "Look," Nico announced to the crew, "it's Casper come home." The pre-race curl of Jesse's lip went from sneer to snarl. "Coco wanted me to bring you her scarf for good luck." Nico untwisted the orange scarf from his wrist.

Jesse stared at it in disbelief. "Her knight in shining armor."

"She's up there. Wave." Nico tied the scarf on Jesse's good arm.

Jesse lifted his limp hand holding up an empty bottle which Coco could see from the stands. He plucked a Coke out of a cooler, placed the top of the bottle against the edge of the Stinker's bumper and gave it a good whack with his hook. The bottle cap flew off. He handed the bottle to Nico and opened another.

Nico chugged down several gulps and wiped his mouth. "You drunk or just hung over?" he asked.

"I don't get hung over," Jesse said.

The track temperature must have been ninety. Manny sloughed his team jacket. Across his chest, Godzilla rose out of the sea backed by a mushroom cloud. The caption read: *Godzilla's Children.* "Like it? I designed it myself."

Nico grimaced. "That's really depressing, man."

"We're all born under a bad sign," Manny claimed.

Now Nico knew for sure; everyone was a philosopher.

If Jesse raced hungover, it wouldn't be the first time. He felt it gave him an edge if he loaded up on caffeine, planted his foot on the gas and went all out. Harley gave him hell for it; Joe Sample wouldn't tinker with success; Jesse was in the running every race. As far as he was concerned, Jesse could wear women's lingerie behind the wheel of the Stinker Bomb.

Too Fast surveyed the track. "Good God, Harley," he complained, "you couldn't have gotten farther away from NASCAR unless you took up horse racing."

"That's on alternate weekends," Harley joked. He made final adjustments to the carburetor while Jesse revved the engine. As the stocks started firing engines, Harley brightened: the old excitement tingled back into his limbs in spite of the bush league.

Jesse won pole position alongside Whitey Riley in Sizzling Shamrock #90, a '57 Pontiac with Rosie as crew chief, sponsored by Capitol Transmissions. No surprise there. They'd been battling all season.

"How's she handlin'?" Harley asked Jesse when he pulled into the pit.

"Felt a little loose." Jesse climbed out through the window.

Nico checked the steering linkage. "Good here," Nico reported.

"Yer driftin' in the turn," Harley noted. "Doan get on it so hard. Ya'll are runnin' on that corner like a dog on linoleum."

"Like Bambi on ice," Too Fast added, turning a Daytona ball cap backwards so he could shimmy up onto the fender and poke his head into the engine well.

Jesse leaned through the driver's window and inspected the front seat.

"Lose something?" Nico queried, following the gaze.

"Naww."

Nico glanced up into the grandstands. Fans were milling about, coming and going, veering left or right of this spot behind the screen. Within seconds, the soldier from Kon Barr materialized. He unshouldered an M-60, leveled and sighted in Nico's direction. Nico wasn't sure if Kon Barr was targeting him or Jesse. Jungle fatigues sagged on the soldier's bony frame. He looked like he'd crawled on his belly through a monsoon. But his weapon sparkled clean and ready for duty.

"Maybe you shouldn't race today," Nico offered.

"What? Hell, it's nothing, Little Engine." Jesse climbed back into the Bomb and poked his elbow out the window. "We won pole, didn't we?"

Nico gazed back toward the stands. Kon Barr had vanished.

Jesse cranked the ignition on the Bomb. He needed to take position. Harley popped the hood. Jesse tried again. The Stinker Bomb wouldn't fire.

"What's wrong?" Nico asked Harley.

Harley shrugged. "It was fine a minute ago." He pulled on the battery cables and checked the carburetor.

"We gonna scratch?" Nico checked back to the starting line. They were waiting on Jesse. Harley grabbed a crescent wrench and rapped the battery terminals.

Jesse tried again. The Stinker Bomb roared to life. Harley dropped the hood, and the crew jumped back. Jesse peeled out and moved into pole position beside Whitey Riley. Sitting next to Jesse in the front seat was Kon Barr, M-60 between his feet. The drivers revved their engines, waiting for the starting flag. Twelve cars lined up for the trophy dash. Other cars in the running were Darrell Harper's #9 '58 Ford, Bill Tremblay's #33 '56 Buick Special, and Gene Whitlock's #50 '57 Plymouth.

Jesse and Whitey Riley entered turn one knocking doors. Nico headed back into the stands. 100 laps. No pit stops. Jesse was on his own. As he mounted the stairs, high clouds feathered a blue sky. The temperature had dropped to a comfortable eighty-five. Shelly and Coco made room on the wooden bench.

Annabelle leaned forward to talk around Maury. She wondered if Coco wanted a boy or a girl?

"A girl, I guess," Coco answered with some hesitation. "Imagine raising two Jesses?"

Annabelle chuckled. "So you're moving South?"

"I'd prefer Jesse went back to school."

Nico felt obligated to inject some reality. "Jesse's lookin' at Daytona."

Coco flipped her hair back, exposing white neck. "I'd be so much happier if I had someone more stable and dependable," she said, hooking her arm around Maury's bicep, "like your dad."

"You should have married a plumber," Maury said, patting her hand.

"Nothing wrong with plumbers," Coco said.

"And you can't put a number on having someone who can clean your pipes regularly," Annabelle said. Nico laughed out loud. Annabelle didn't get the joke. "That's worth re-membering," she added.

Shelly leaned into Nico, talking at Coco about Reed College. Her skin exuded peaches and cream. Nico felt giddy as she placed her hand on his thigh. He wondered how Idun would fit into this fantasy.

Jesse and Whitey moved out in front. On the tenth lap, #19 hit the concrete wall in front of the stands, bounced off, sideswiped Tremblay's #33 Buick Special, spun out and rolled to a stop on the grass infield. The driver was shaken up, but not injured. A smashed bumper forced Tremblay on to the infield. Tire scraped bumper and burned acrid in the still July air. Tremblay's crew pulled the bumper out so he could return to the track. The caution flag came out. Drivers held position for two laps. Then Jesse and Whitey separated from the pack. Jesse drifted high toward the wall in turn two, losing time each lap until he was two car-lengths behind Whitey.

Frosty lifted his binoculars. "That turn's giving him trouble."

"Can I see those?" Nico asked. Frosty handed him the field glasses.

Nico tracked the stock cars with the binoculars as if passing from #33 to #9 to #50, until he found #8, the Stinker Bomb with bright orange scarf streaming out the open window. Frosty was right. Jesse drifted high in the second turn every time.

"I'll be right back." He apologized and got up. He worked his way down the aisle back to the track and rejoined the Stinker crew. "What gives?" he asked. Next lap Jesse drifted high again.

"Our lap leader will receive a $20 credit at K-Mart," the P.A. announced. Whitey flew by in first place.

The team stood by the low concrete retaining wall. "I've been telling him to back off the turns." Harley said.

Jesse again lost time in turn two.

"Why's he drifting on just that turn?" Too Fast wondered.

Through the binoculars, Nico had seen Jesse fighting for control of the steering wheel. Kon Barr kept grabbing at it each time around turn two.

"You see an oil slick?" Manny strained for a better view.

"The other drivers ain't goin' high." Too Fast pointed out.

"Should we call him in?" Nico wondered.

"With fifteen laps to go?" Joe shook his head. "He can pull it out."

"Wait, look!" Harley climbed a mounted tire for a better view of the track. Jesse was getting on it now, barely holding the Stinker Bomb to the track in the other turns, gaining ground on the leader until four more laps had the Bomb dogging Whitey, bumper to bumper. The two fought for position, Jesse losing ground in turn two, making it up in the other turns. Jesse and Whitey streaked by, door handle to door handle, in the straightaway in front of the stands.

"Oh yeah," Harley shouted over the crowd, "now that's a race!"

"Our lap leader will receive two cases of Pabst Blue Ribbon Beer from Albertson's on State Street."

"At least he's mastered the left turn," Too Fast joked.

In the backstretch, Jesse hooked Whitey's rear bumper, spun him onto the infield grass, but Whitey recovered, fishtailing onto the track half a lap behind, just ahead of Darrell Harper. The rest of the pack was four or five car-lengths behind Darrell. The crowd stood hooting and howling.

"Sure thing." Joe gave Harley a high five.

Two laps from victory, Coco's orange scarf came undone, flew off Jesse's arm, out the window. The Bomb shot high and careened off the wall. It ricocheted into the infield like a smoking meteor plowing up the grass. Jesse Walker would not finish today.

Whitey Riley took the checkered flag.

The Stinker crew rushed on to the infield. The ambulance streaked past, lights flashing. It reached Jesse just as he crawled out of the Bomb with only cuts and bruises. A cloud of steam rose from the broken radiator. One tire had burst.

The wheel rim had been twisted, hot to the touch, resting at the head of an ugly gash in the infield sod. By the time the Stinker crew got out to him, Jesse was sitting in the back end of the ambulance with medics checking him out.

"You okay?" Nico held out the recovered orange scarf he'd picked up off the track.

Jesse nodded, taking the scarf. "Good luck." He wiped his eyes with the scarf, leaving streaks of grit.

"What was going on in turn two?" Harley asked.

Nico helped pull Jesse's arms free of the racing suit.

Jess sat in the ambulance with four arms, two limp and boneless, lying in his lap like a sloughed skin. He scratched his chin with his hook. "Told you she was running loose."

Harley shook his head.

"JESSE! Oh, baby!" Coco shouted as she hurried across the infield in peep-toe black pumps, her genie pants fluttering against her legs. Jesse waved the soiled scarf. Coco hugged him, kissing his face. "Thank God, you're okay. You *are* okay, right?" Coco looked over at the medics. They nodded. "Thank God."

"I won two cases of beer," Jesse offered as a consolation.

"Maybe you should skip the dance tonight," Nico suggested, "and have a few more beers."

"Don't race. Don't dance. I wanna celebrate coming through this with little more than a scratch." Jesse took Coco's hand. "We're gonna be here for awhile, babe. Gotta get the Bomb towed and trailered back to the barn."

"I can help with that," Nico volunteered.

Jesse spoke to Coco. "Why don't you just go with Nico's folks? I'll pick you up around 8, okay?"

Red, white and blue streamers popped outside Whitey's window as he took the winner's lap. The pace car shuttled Jesse and Coco back to the pit. Nico walked back to the grandstands, humming unconsciously along with "America the Beautiful" coming through the loudspeakers.

* * *

The crew loaded the Bomb on to its trailer and Coco left with Nico's parents. Nico squatted North Carolina-style with Harley and Too Fast, their backs against the concrete wall. Harley offered a Salem to Too Fast. "Where's Jesse?"

"Ain't seen hide nor hair of that boy since his woman left."

"Maybe he went off alone to collect himself," Joe suggested. "He's pretty much avoided the crash stage 'til now."

Harley placed the filtered menthol on his lower lips and sucked as he lit it. "I never saw such a thing as what happened in turn two before."

Too Fast twirled the ends of his mustache. "Maybe too much drink in the kid."

"Naww. He can handle that. It's something else."

"That boy's all pedal to the metal." Too Fast sniffed and wiped his nose with the back of his hand.

"He'll learn," Joe said.

"If he doesn't kill himself first," Nico said.

Nico noticed Manny casting a worried glance at the tunnel out to the parking lot. Nico raised an eyebrow, inviting Manny to confession, but the big guy looked down instead.

"Can we fix her?" Nico asked Harley, thinking the Stinker Bomb was just one more thing Jesse had broken.

"With time and money. Ain't much of either." Harley flicked ash from the cigarette. He mopped his sweaty forehead with a handkerchief.

"We'll miss a coupla races," Joe answered, voice trailing off with lack of conviction. "The season's not over. We'll be back."

"What's that?" Harley cupped a hand to his ear.

"We'll be back," Joe repeated, bolder this time.

"Yeah, right," Harley agreed. "We'll put tight pants on her. Maybe he'll finesse her a bit more."

"Ha!" Nico's cynical snort caught the irony right between the eyes.

"Lot of cats out there." Too Fast balanced a Coke on his knee. "Cats who've been running short tracks all their lives, cats with lots of talent. They ain't ever gonna see a super-speedway." Too Fast pressed up against the wall and exhaled a stream of smoke. "But if y'all come back to NA-SCAR, Harley, I'll set up a practice run at Charlotte. Junior might go for it. We need a bold new driver."

"Jesse's bold. Gotta say that for him." Harley stubbed the cigarette out. "Takes some bold to shoot through a smoke screen wide open, not knowing what may be wrecked on the other side. Reckless has a lot of luck surviving in someone with good instincts."

"Instincts without experience." Too Fast noted.

"What's experience without instinct?" Harley wiped trickles of sweat from his forehead. "Where the hell is that boy? We gotta shake a leg. Margo's goulash is in the pot as we speak."

"I'll see what's keeping him," Nico volunteered and walked under the grandstands to the ticket booth across from the public restrooms. He found Jesse at the turnstile outside the front gate talking with Jericho Sinclair. The deputy sheriff leaned over Jesse like a heron over a beaver. Jericho's eyes were red and watery, fixed and angry. Nico had never seen the man lose it like that. Jesse looked un-ruffled. Nico felt the sweat thick on his brow. He wondered if the FBI agents told Jericho about the pig blood baptism of the governor? Would they be arrested for involuntary manslaughter?

Jericho lumbered to his cruiser. Jesse headed in Nico's direction, so he ducked back into the shadows, observing as Jesse entered a small office. Nico waited behind a grand-stand support column for several minutes. Jesse came out with a woman on his arm—the moon-faced blonde with short curly hair, snowy white complexion, smeared dark red lips. Full breasts swelled inside a low-cut red dress. She was wearing no stockings. Jesse kissed her on the lips and patted her ass, turning her toward the exit. The blonde turned in the parking lot and blew Jesse a kiss.

Jesse came trotting around the corner toward the pit and wound up face-to-face with Nico.

"Who was that?" Nico probed.

"Junel," Jesse answered. He lifted the first two fingers of his good hand to Nico's nose. "I tell ya, that girl could swallow a sword."

"Jesus, Casper." Nico pushed his hand away in disgust. "You're fucking *married*."

"Yeah." Jesse licked his fingers. "So's she."

"Someone could tell Coco."

"Go ahead, Little Engine."

Nico's anger reached a dizzying pitch. "You're not good enough for her."

"So I hear."

"You hurt her and I swear…"

Jesse's tongue rolled around his cheek, eyes wide. "Swear what? She's *my* wife."

"You know what I mean."

"No, tell me."

By the time reason caught up with Nico's loose tongue, he'd backed into a tight corner. The thought of Jesse screwing around on Coco made him tremble with rage. Even as Jesse stripped the dignity of the only woman he ever loved, Nico realized he couldn't call attention to Coco's abuse or he might turn on her. What was he to do? Confess to watching Jesse's wife getting dressed? "I'm just saying *if* you ever treat her the way you just treated that woman, I hope somebody kicks your ass."

Jesse headed straight for the GTO with the intention of getting to Coco first. Nico's neck muscles ached by the time he got back to the crew. He told them Jesse would meet up with them later. Harley hung back, gripping Nico's hand too long, pulling him eye to eye in a manly way. "Yer running a mite loose yourself, aren't ya, champ? The caution flag's out."

Nico let his shoulders drop. "The caution flag is always out. Is car racing the only metaphor you have?"

"Can't be plainer." Harley let go of Nico's hand. "I admire your virtue in sticking with old friends, Nico, but those two belong in a kennel."

"I need to know she's okay," Nico assured him. "She's having a baby."

"*His* baby. Don't get between them or you'll catch it from both sides. Put a few car-lengths between you."

With a slight nod, Nico mumbled. "You're right. Couldn't be plainer."

"What's that?" Harley got up into Nico's face. "I didn't hear ya. You okay?"

Nico discharged a quick salute, "Okay, sir."

"Good." Harley climbed into the passenger side of the Bronco. They drove off and Nico wondered what sort of crazy lay ahead.

* * *

The Enchanted Forest occupied the whole upper story of a converted warehouse. The ceiling and inside walls had been painted black. Mote-filled beams from three 16mm projectors crisscrossed in a pattern. On the west wall an un-focused Bogart and Bacall played backwards, the north wall, behind the bandstand, erupted in fireworks, and the east wall chased Road Runner to the edge of a cliff where Coyote went on over. Overhead projections augmented the running films with swirling amoebae in agitated plastic bags filled with food-coloring and vegetable oil. Palpitating red, white and blue spots entranced the head trippers.

Blended in visceral harmony, two electric blues guitars circled each other. Distorted dual leads ripped the wings off angels: Donny Sunderman and prodigy Terry Clancy, on the bridge of "Summertime Blues." It got the whole place stomping. With top hat perched on a red crown, wearing a black vest without a shirt, Donny's magic Telecaster trans-formed the Mad Hatter into minor deity.

Nico waited near the lady's room for Shelly to return. Volunteer go-go dancers shook their booties on a raised platform. As manager, Nico bore witness to the sad orbits of lonely people, gyrating to the beat, on the sidelines, vic-tims of a messy business: love. And yet sex was meaningless without it. Nico had fallen in love with every woman he'd ever been with. His heart was always broken. He was an anachronism, trying to find meaning in a meaningless plot.

On the floor Manny danced with a pudgy, big-breasted white girl with shoulder-length dishwater-blonde hair. Her name was Paula Rhinehart. Paula hung all over him like the smell of garlic. Nico could smell the marijuana on Doc's clothes. Nico flashed on Agents Lowman and Hightower. Fireworks were exploding in Doc's glassy eyes. He shouted into Nico's ear, his words shredded by deafening decibels. Nico shrugged, shaking his head, hands over his ears.

Double Barrel finished their encore.

When the applause died down, Doc pointed to the fireworks display. "Now that's what I'm sayin', man. I'm that guy in the fire pit torching those rockets." Projectiles burst on the wall in chrysanthemums of light. Screamers wilted into weeping willows. One rocket detonated right over the heads of the hunkered down pyrotechnicians.

"Yeah, Doc," Nico agreed. "You'd be perfect."

Doc's true element involved this choreography where he danced under a rain of fire. He felt most alive with the reek of sulfur in his hair, eyes stinging from smoke. The civilian equivalent for the ex-Marine was firebomber. Vietnam would always be on fire inside the man—inside all of them—but it didn't make them criminals. They all had problems. Take Jericho for instance. What made Junel look for love from someone like Jesse, someone incapable of it? They were all broken in countless ways.

Shelly returned from the restroom, her eyes soft and glistening. She'd changed into a long India-styled wrap-around skirt. Only a few articles of clothing stood between them. He took her hand, her palm dry and warm between his hot and sticky clams. "We've got 15 minutes between bands."

The Basque Dancers' booth was set into an alcove, separated from the dance floor by a partial wall, six feet high. The partial wall was plastered with black-light posters of Jefferson Airplane, Quicksilver Messenger Service, Big

Brother & the Holding Company, Mothers of Invention, Jimi Hendrix, Country Joe and the Fish. The scent of spicy cooked Iberian chorizos made Nico salivate involuntarily. Chorizos in sourdough buns complemented with soft drinks and coffee was a good business decision, but difficult to police. They had to clean the floor after every dance and field complaints when someone slipped on mashed chorizos and mustard doing the Watusi. But no one had sued.

Shelly passed the steaming chorizo on sourdough under her nose, sniffing the spicy aroma. She brushed hot mustard on the bun, pressed the sourdough tight around the sausage and stuffed the end into her mouth.

"Hi, Nico," a voice called from behind him. Nico turned around and, sure enough, it was Idun eyeing Shelly with keen interest. "Did you save me that dance?" she said. She looked incredibly hot in a loose puff-sleeved red blouse with white bell-bottoms, white crocheted vest and multi-colored beads around her neck. Her strawberry blonde hair spilled over her shoulders and, even in the dimness of The Enchanted Forest, she emanated radiant health and good nature. Nico hadn't heard from her since their night together.

"Idun," he burped, giving her a timid hug. He introduced Shelly as his cousin and said she was visiting Boise on summer break.

"Cool." Idun shook Shelly's hand. "Nico's been raving about this group."

"Double Barrel or The Bards?" Nico asked. "I've raved about them both." Just then the road manager for The Bards pranced onto stage and raised his arms. The crowd cheered. Donny and crew came back out to set the stage.

The age limit for The Enchanted Forest was 25. Older patrons paid at the door, got stamped, and ducked downstairs to the Castalia Lounge to suck a couple brews during the opening act. It was a necessary revenue stream. Pat Parsons managed the door. He decided who got back in, which was something like Friar Tuck enforcing temperance among the Merry Men.

What Nico knew about dance he'd learned from the Basque Dancers when he was fourteen. It taught him enough ways to move that he could improvise to anything. He joined the club because of a girl. Dance says a lot about culture and tradition. Popular dances mirror their societies. The dancers at The Enchanted Forest were doing their own thing, hardly ever in unison. But everyone could do it. Folk dancing knits together a community, much like those bright ribbons tied to the tree of life in a long parade.

So many in The Enchanted Forest struck Nico as alone in their heads, unable to communicate except physically, aggressively, sexually. The dance floor was that kind of space. Nico felt the impulse to do his own thing yet didn't want to give up his sense of belonging in the place he called home.

Donny heard The Bards in Walla Walla back in November and again in Centralia a couple of weeks later. They played a long piece he claimed was the future of rock. A rock symphony, he called it. It wasn't just a dragged-out jam. "The Creation" was a well-structured composition in movements of poetry and music, with accomplished musicianship, good lyrics, melodic vocals, and sound effects all fused into one big head trip. "These guys are the real deal. Not just a garage band," he said.

Nico felt awkward as The Bards struck into their hit song, "Never Too Much Love." Who should he take for a spin? Since he'd invited Shelly, he danced with her first. A slow dance. Manny and Paula danced near them, his hands under her blouse flat on her bare back. Nico closed his eyes and inhaled the scent of Shelly's hair and skin. She gently inserted her leg between his, so he could feel the back of her hip against his crotch. Her hands stroked the back of his neck. Nico's body melted into hers. When he opened his eyes, his gaze fell on Coco dancing in a spotlight with Jesse. They clung to each other in a habitual grind. The way Jesse gripped her ass made Nico shake his head. From Jesse's customary inebriation, they must have pre-functioned. Coco met Nico's gaze, her eyes tense with fatigue. Her coldness infected his mood. She was unhappy.

Nico swung Shelly around to change his mood. And there he saw poor Idun sitting on the edge of the band-stand, watching a film run backwards. He blinked and swung Shelly again; this time he picked up Junel watching Jesse from the sidelines, her eyes shadowed, looking a little bewitched. She rose to her feet, cat-balanced and poised ready to spring. Nico didn't want any scenes. He looked around for his crew.

Swaying under virtual fire in a world of his own, Doc was not to be disturbed in his attraction to a strobe light. Nico decided he must intervene. The Bards finished the song. Nico quickly excused himself and left Shelly and Idun staring stonily after him. He caught his glittering gadfly, Josh Brownton, and cornered him, cupping his hand around Josh's ear. "I need you to keep an eye on someone."

"Sure, Nicky. Who?"

Nico nodded toward Junel, whose glare was locking on Jesse like a heat-seeking missile.

Josh nodded back. "You need an intercept?"

"Just watch her."

Josh made a quick study of the body in tight sweater and short skirt. "No problem," he said.

But problems set in. Coco broke away from Jesse and headed for the ladies' room. Junel saw her window of op-portunity and leaped across the floor. She moved so fast Nico couldn't cut her off and she grabbed Jesse's good arm. Jesse yanked it free. Nico overheard him say "Look, we had fun. Just let it go."

"Three times," Junel pleaded for tender mercy. "And you *liked* it."

"I must confess, Junel," Jesse ducked under her arms, "the second and third times were more out of pity."

Nico didn't need to hear any more. He cut an angle through the crowd to waylay Coco. Near the ladies' room, a crowd had gathered, leaving a small clearing. Nico thought they'd made a clearing for him, being manager and all, so stepped into the clearing only to slip and drop in a heap in someone's vomit. "Aww, shit," he uttered. "Why didn't anyone warn me?" Greasy chorizo and sourdough soaked in beer stuck to his bell bottoms.

The people standing around the clearing winced. A hippie with long brown hair responded with a shrug, "We thought you were coming to clean it up, man. Aren't you the manager?"

Coco came out of the lady's room with a fistful of paper towels, dabbing at a big wet spot on the front of her shirt.

"She did it," the hippie said.

Coco saw Nico climbing to his feet. She covered her mouth and ran back into the restroom. A minute later she returned with paper towels in one hand, covering her nose with the other. "God, Nicky, I'm so sorry."

Nico ran to the men's room and came back with a big wet spot on his crotch and butt. Coco made fish faces, trying not to laugh. He took her hand as the lights blacked out. "What now?" he moaned, thinking it was a power outage, but The Bards opened their 20-minute rock symphony in total darkness, with a strange sound like an alien spaceship hurtling through outer space. The first words of "The Creation" cracked through darkness and the Enchanted Forest's black ceiling and walls lit up with galaxial light, creating a rolling virtual firmament. Nico and Coco danced, hands avoiding each other's wet spots, watching the stars.

Junel came rushing by to the lady's room, unable to stanch the flow of her waterworks, throwing the door back on its hinges. Coco didn't notice. Josh stationed himself outside the door. He gestured to Nico.

Mid-movement in the making of man, Kon Barr appeared, his sunken eye rolling like a white marble in his ruined side. Nico scanned the crowd for Jesse. He was dancing in ecstasy, flanked by Shelly and Idun. Humphrey Bogart retreated into war and Doc's eyes were ablaze with apocalypse. Kon Barr hobbled right on past an unseeing Josh through the closed door into the ladies' room.

The sensory overload of music and light show encapsulated Nico in a sound cushion. Before he reached the restroom door, Paula came crashing out, seizing him by the arm. "We need you in here."

Half-listening to The Bards' haunting new song and trying to do his job, Nico felt insulated from events unfolding around him, as if it were orchestrated by something bigger than him. He hurried past Paula into the lady's room and found no Kon Barr, no inferno engulfing the firetrap warehouse, no wildcat women pulling hair. He found instead a wounded blonde in a stall, standing on a toilet seat. Junel's pupils were dilated, her jaws clenched. "Call an ambulance!" Nico shouted to Josh. "She's having a bad trip."

> *This is the way the world ends*
> *This is the way the world ends*

26.

Over the bunker's sloping parapet a web of fine cracks formed. Tubers like small periscopes broke through and leaves unfurled. Sinewy vines crawled in slick profusion, opening profane flowers with poisonous tongues. Pithy middles split their skins, steaming into pot smoke and yellow fingers swirling over the battle ground. The sledgehammer fell and fell, shattering the concrete.

Johnny and MJ jabbered away, heads cocked, eyes wide with wonder, plugged into their own music. Monica clung to Milo's arm. He practically dragged her to get within earshot.

"That dude's got a mighty swing," MJ marveled.

"Casey and his hammer, man," Johnny added.

"Hammer Man? Do you *see* him?" Milo interjected, looking for corroboration.

Monica trembled under Milo's wing. "What are they talking about?"

Milo shook his head.

"Yeah, man. Big hammer." Johnny squinted, sweeping his ponytail back over his shoulder.

"I thought I was going bonkers," Milo slumped in relief.

The observation room quaked, cracks branching out in all directions. Wormlike tubers wriggled free, ran along the ground. Bright poisonous petals opened with tongues lolling.

"That's *monster* weed," MJ held up the doobie.

"Didn't need *any* weed for this," Milo pointed out.

"Then you're on a natural high, buddy," Johnny said.

The image of the Hammer Man blurred into falling rain.

"We gotta go *now!*" Monica tugged Milo's arm. He didn't budge. She left him and marched towards the stairs as a sudden rupture climbed the observation tower. The grudge of her go-go boots descended the stairs with Geo behind her. The crack widened. The tower began to crumble.

Gayleen sent the alarm. "They're gonna overrun us!"

Milo blinked as if awakened from a trance. He helped Gayleen over to the stairs. "C'mon, guys," he called back to Johnny and MJ. They stood transfixed in lightning flash, numb with fascination. An outbreak of wild vines choked the grounds between the Parados and the battery. Geo and Monica lost their bearings, ripping at each other, scratching each other's backs. Monica's eyes were black holes of mascara. She whimpered, afraid to look, as twisted tendrils wrapped her ankles pulling her down. Menace overtook them like a puppet show with shadows acting out the thunder that boomed even louder.

"Get down!" Gayleen screamed, covering her head. Milo grabbed her by the collar and dragged her, kicking, toward the Battery Mishler. "We can't go in there," she pleaded. "We'll be killed."

Milo grabbed her shoulders. "We'll be killed if we don't."

"You're hurting me. Let me go!"

He let her go. She stood up dazed and off-balance, tears streaking her cheeks. "We have to get into the bunker." Milo touched her shoulder. She ran away but there was no escape from the hungry tendrils. The storm passed, its fury spent, sweeping inland like a wave. With terrible awe, Milo searched for the Hammer Man who had shattered the world. Unseen vines, ferns and creepers still insinuated Milo's skull. The ground writhed with living vengeance. Rain turned to blood.

An animal roar punctuated thickets of blackberry and rose.

Milo jumped at the sound, blinking blood from his eyes. Geo had gone berserk. He wrestled Monica to the ground. She fought back but unable to free herself. Geo pinned her down by the shoulders, tearing at her clothes. Monica slapped him to no avail. "You know you want it."

Milo left Gayleen blubbering on her knees, falling to hostile vines, to free Monica from Geo. He pulled Geo by the collar to get him off. Geo punched Milo in the groin. He collapsed in agony.

"She's a collaborator," Geo hissed.

Angry voices shouted through bullhorns. *Kill G.I. I say again. Kill G.I.* Geo climbed to his feet and kicked Monica in the stomach. "I'm gonna kill me some gooners."

Monica sat on the wet ground stuffing grass into her mouth. As Milo entered the Battery Mishler, he glanced back. In the next flash Geo slashed at angry vines with a fighting knife. Again some animal penetrated the tempest with its roar. Yellow eyes burned through withering branches.

An Asian tiger pounced on Geo. It's jaws closed around Geo's throat, leaving his last cries in the wind. "Fucking cow! Fucking gooks." He struggled up to his knees, life pulsing from his body, the tiger on his back ripping loose an arm. The shock wave knocked Milo backwards as a fireball erupted where the observation tower had stood. High in the sky, a dark object arced in twilight and dropped in slow motion. Milo stepped back and it landed upright a few feet away—a motorcycle boot with leg severed below the knee. Vines came up and surrounded it, dragging it into the ground. The tiger leaped into the forest with Geo's left arm. Geo's body lay in a rash that blistered and cracked into open sores.

Even with its guts ripped out, the marine radio spewed music: The Doors.

Gayleen and Monica rolled in the mud, scratching and tearing at each other. Their mouths convulsed as panic filled their eyes with tears. Monica's flesh was flaking off polished bone as she broke free of the vines and made a mad dash. Her voice sounded like a dry cough. "**CHA!** CHA! Cha." Distant thunder boomed as the storm passed and the rain stopped.

Milo called to a beckoning Ahab waiting at the entrance to Mishler. "Who are you?" he asked. The chemical smoke in his lungs triggered a spasm. He stumbled in a daze, tripping over barbed wire and falling into a foxhole. When he stuck his head out, he found himself on a battlefield. He was using the mushy head of a Japanese samurai as a stepstool. The decapitated body slumped against the foxhole wall on the other side. Milo climbed out by stepping on his shoulder for a boost. Nearby a Roman soldier in body armor was hung up like a doll in razor wire. A severed arm less than ten feet away from a bloated carcass still clutched a sword. An armless man foundered in mud wearing Confederate gray. Uncounted casualties from different wars from different times lay with holes in their heads, arms or legs blown off, gashes in their chests, hacked and disemboweled by Berserkers in battle rage, their bloody stumps burned and quartered. The stink of war made Milo retch on an empty stomach. Paralyzed by numbness, he crawled over a dead Austrian with the steel erection of a bayonet run through his middle. An Indian boy scalped and staked out, spread-eagled. A slab of intestines in the clenched hand of an S.S. officer, his own body separated into parts, feet from ankles, legs from hips. Milo skidded through gore to the entrance of Mishler. He stumbled inside.

27.

Deputy Sheriff Jericho Sinclair's cruiser pulled up in front of The Castalia Lounge as his sedated wife was being lifted into the back of an ambulance. He spilled out, unknotting his legs, cantered to the ambulance and climbed in beside her. Her eyes were twitching with hallucination, as if overwhelmed with flashes. He held her hand, his own red-rimmed eyes locking on Nico.

Kon Barr looked on unaffected as the ambulance pulled away. The Boise Police shut down the club. Sergeant Ames called Tomas, but he was out of town. The Bards loaded up their equipment, accepted the check, expressed the hope that the music wasn't the cause of anything, and drove off in their Bardmobile. Nico closed The Enchanted Forest. After this, Tomas wouldn't defend the teen dance club with the city council. This spelled the beginning of the end. How could they prevent someone popping a tab in the restroom? The moralists who believed rock 'n' roll incited revolution would have the edge.

* * *

The veterans of the PAST weren't very different from the bargirls at The Splendors. Believers fight to resist the temptation of a corrupted self. *Just trying to survive* became their mantra. They sacrificed their bodies and their minds. The consequences of their actions rippled out into the wider world. They profaned a sacred space, and were banished and dispossessed and predisposed to walking in their sleep at the edge of a cliff. Nico could sympathize with all victims of war, with the hostesses withholding true intimacy for the promise of a Kon Barr farm boy flying them to an all-electric home on Main Street middle-America. The PAST had been forsaken by country and community after they fought and died for them on no-name ridges in a strange land to preserve an economic caste system. They would be silenced with the threat of dishonor for speaking truth: they died for politicians and corporations wanting a home field advantage without yard lines or end zones. The game scored in body counts. And the count kept going up even after they came home, crashing into trees and drowning in shallow water. With their brains fried from failed coups in the most extreme states, they were walking casualties. Social indifference drove them together like street gangs with G.I. jackets. Outcasts christened with sardonic nicknames that separated the killing self from the guy in love with the girl next door. There could be no "after" Vietnam for Nico, or Doc, or any of them. No matter which way they turned they bumped into ghosts. The PAST surrounded them. Their whole lives had been distilled into it. Escape was a temporary illusion.

Nico had eaten dead dust in enough crawlspaces to learn how to fall asleep curled up in a corner, his head under a lead pipe. Maury had dragged him underground more times than Nico cared to remember. After his dad brushed and sealed the new couplings, he would come looking for Nico to gather the tools. Nico couldn't be found. Maury got so agitated he started banging the pipes. That's where Nico was now, caught up in this web of the PAST, unable to move forward, his head aching from the mere effort of planning dinner, waiting for Kon Barr to start banging on the pipes.

* * *

Nico sent the bartender home and closed early. A bubbling lava lamp at the end of the bar cast molten light onto the ceiling and candle lamps flickered in the booths. Another light show. The only lightbulb was hanging over the pool table. The joint had a small grill in the back where Nico played short-order cook. Donny leaned over the Wurlitzer punching songs into the jukebox. His first play was the Righteous Brothers. Donny knew how to warm up the girls.

"Sure dark in here," Shelly noted. Shadows flickered on her skin. The cool climate of western Oregon had conditioned her to perspire even in the dark interior of the lounge. She dabbed her forehead with a napkin. "Can't see who's groping me."

Nico glared at Josh. He and Nico both showed their hands above the table.

Shelly's eyes twinkled with tease.

"If they aren't doin' it, then they're thinkin' it," Coco Bird declared. She picked up the juicy burger and took a bite, condiments spilling around the bun. She laid it down on the plate and licked her fingers.

His group had gone home, but Donny stayed with the team. He scooted into the booth next to Josh. Without a prompt he launched into a narrative of his recent mescaline trip. "I looked down at my feet and toes and they were those of an alien. I could feel my body afloat in space like anti-gravity, but I'm not sure if it was all in my mind. I don't know how to describe it."

"Mescaline isn't a new drug, Donny," Nico said. "It's purified peyote."

"I know what mescaline is," Donny scolded. All things mystical had become his new religion. "I switched to organics after a bad trip on acid."

Josh offered Shelly a brownie and said with a wink. "Nothin' more gentle than grandma's recipe."

Shelly declined. "You make it sound like laxative."

"That too," he replied.

"Anyone seen Jesse?" Coco asked. No one answered. She tugged on Nico's arm.

"I've been too occupied to keep an eye on him." Nico knew it sounded patronizing. In spite of how the dance ended, there was still the evening left and he had both Coco and Shelly on an arm. He didn't know where Idun had gone, but hoped to catch up with her later.

"We should find him," Coco suggested.

"If he's not back in half an hour." Nico chewed a brownie. "I promise."

"Watch out now," Josh warned, "you'll get really stoned on those brownies."

In the booth, Coco's warm body pressed against his right side and Shelly's against his left.

"You remember Peak Experience out of Seattle?" Donny asked Nico.

"Spokane, not Seattle." Nico corrected him. He remembered the lead singer swaying in front of the mic, dancing with the strobes.

"I was on mescaline that night. I remember dancing with this girl when I realized the whole thing was this big mating ritual. I could see most of the couples weren't really dancing together. This poor slob's got no idea his girl's mind-fucking the lead singer. What's worse is the singer knows it. Everyone on the floor's competing for sex. I danced up a storm, I'll tell ya, and these women gravitated toward me. I started waving my arm in front of my face like this," he demonstrated with a limp arm like an elephant's trunk, "and soon everybody's swinging lame arms in front of their face. It's a kick. I couldn't stop laughing. We're animals, man."

"So did you get laid?" Josh asked.

"Fuck, no," Donny answered. "It was a *mystical* experience."

"Probably because your trunk wasn't long enough." Josh flapped his arm between his legs. Donny flipped him off. "Age of Aquarius" dropped in the Wurlitzer. Paula finished off a chocolate milkshake and pulled Manny up from the booth to slow dance. Coco and Shelly sang to each other in stereo.

Doc's girlfriend, Veronica Toms, rested her chin on a cue stick. She had been struck by some insight. "If the Piscean Age is the age of Christ, is the Age of Aquarius the age of the anti-Christ?"

"Oh, that's heav-*vee*," Paula replied, resting her head on Manny's shoulder. "Isn't that heavy, Manny?"

Donny sang protest songs in their booth at Oktoberfest. The PAST wanted to raise consciousness, maybe sell some *Make Love Not War* posters, counsel potential draft resisters, hand-out some anti-war literature. You know, like a regular club on campus.

"You guys!" Doc chalked the blue tip of his pool cue. "Revolution isn't a party with drugs and free love."

"No such thing as *free* love," Pat said, lining up a straight-on shot but missing the corner pocket. He poured a glass of Pabst. "Ain't that right, Veronica?"

"Free love doesn't require us to give up our feelings," Veronica clarified. "What fun is sex without feeling?"

Doc took off his bush jacket and dropped it onto a chair. "So these hippie protesters burn up draft cards along with the flag. They have student deferments, smoke dope, get laid and play an instrument. That's free, right? They're not paying for it. What would they do if they got drafted tomorrow? I'll tell you. Half of 'em would run for Canada—and I can respect that—but the other half would report for duty. In exchange for a GI Bill, VA home loan, medical care and a small death benefit, Uncle Sam asks for little in return, only that you give back the uniform, cut your hair, go back to school or find a job. You can be done with war. Your duty now is to blend in, contribute to society. If I had it to do again, I'd fight like hell to avoid the draft. You can't decide you're against the war in a combat zone. By then the debate's over, the rights and wrongs of killing are weighed by the brass. You can't quit and go home."

"Yeah, but how can we trust someone who's gotten out then goes back in again?" Pat cracked a smile in reference to Doc's second tour of duty.

"A guy who re-ups," Doc explained, "will always justify it. I was helping to get my unit back in one piece. That's the real burden of leadership. Either way, your choices define you, so you live with them."

"Give me free brownies," Paula noted, "and enough milkshakes to keep them going down so smoothly."

Nico, the milkshake aficionado, concurred. "Hear, hear."

The Wurlitzer lit up with Canned Heat's "On the Road Again" and Paula shimmied to the middle of the room. The graceful sweep of her hand down the line of her throat pressed between full breasts in a silk blouse. She didn't talk a lot but she knew how to make a bold statement. Her vocabulary revolved around *"Heavy"* which she uttered with breathy emphasis on the second syllable and *"Bum*mer" with emphasis on the first.

Pat banked the two-ball into the side pocket. "Maybe we should break into the high school ROTC Armory. Steal those M-1 carbines and old BARs," he suggested. Nico couldn't believe what he was hearing. Such an action, he warned, goes well beyond guerrilla theater. Maybe agents Lowman and Hightower were right. Maybe they were militants. Then he laughed. How better for the government to describe two ex-combat Marines with an attitude than as *militant?*

"The Bill of Rights protects free speech," Doc squinted through the smoke to eye the eight-ball for the corner pocket, "until it interferes with business-as-usual. Then it's restricted by some law-and-order candidate to designated areas. No one must be inconvenienced by this little dissent, this unhappy minority. Money interests are tied up in property. If demonstrations of free speech cannot restrict themselves to designated areas, chances are they will be trespassing on private property. How far do we go in disrupting business-as-usual?"

"I won't be part of any plans to vandalize or hurt anybody," Nico set his mark.

Doc said sit-ins and shut-downs were part of the revolution, but so were sabotage, disruption and manipulation of the media. "Why bother protesting to those who work for business-as-usual? This government is a handmaiden to capitalism." Doc formed a bridge on the green felt with his fingers, cue stick gliding back and forth inside a raised thumb. "We need to go after the money interests that make war their business-as-usual."

Shelly looked on in calm bewilderment. Veronica looked on with adoring eyes. Paula looked on, blinking, trying to process it. Veronica Toms was a wanna-be-cool-like-a-socialist-folk-rocker from the Bench. Her infatuation with Doc squared with the intensity of her local uprising—against her parents.

"So tell me, Trotsky," Shelly weighed in, "how will we limit business-as-usual? Who decides how much is too much?"

"I'm for *small* government," Doc corrected with a whack of the cue against the cue ball.

Nico began to worry. "Isn't small government *weak* government? I mean some corporations are bigger than government on any scale."

"It doesn't matter, if the People depend on corporations for their jobs. Companies are bought and sold every day." Doc sat down with a pool cue between his legs while Veronica stepped up for her shot.

"So small business is okay, unless we have weak leaders who cannot protect them." Shelly sipped on a daiquiri. "So what do you see, Doc, as the outcome of this revolution?"

Doc regarded Shelly with fairness. "Freedom, of course. Power to the People. That's the only worthwhile end."

Shelly pressed her lips together. "Ain't nothin' free in this world, darlin'."

The PAST had often argued about the finer points of freedom, rights and responsibilities. They generally agreed more often than not. It was important in group to keep a good perspective. Nico's dad always told him defending freedom was a responsibility, but as far as Nico could tell, he did not owe the government or the corporations. He'd already given up years of his life to their service. Taking responsibility for one's actions suggested freedom of choice, yet The Man was all about social conditioning and taking away choices. The Man didn't honor the sacrifice. Wars would end when politicians and judges entered their names in the lottery, when their sons were drafted and sent away to fight for their convenience.

Coco blew lightly on the flickering candle, held her fingers spread over the flame, moving them as if to warm them, seeing how close she could come to the flame without getting burned. Her eyes reflected the flicker like Doc's reflected fireworks.

Manny pulled Paula into a booth, her legs wrapped around his waist, nearly knocking over the table.

"What do ya think, Nico? Do ya wanna hit the armory with us?" Doc incited.

"What?" Nico responded, not understanding.

Doc laughed.

Without warning, the front door to The Castalia flew open. A swarm of federal agents—ATF, FBI, DEA, NSA, NBC, CBS—poured into the lounge behind oiled blue barrels of shiny new guns. Among the vicious faces holding them in their crosshairs were Lowman and Hightower.

"FREEZE!" Lowman shouted. Their hands shot into the air. Doc and Pat dropped cue sticks and dashed out the back only to be met by armed agents coming in through the alleyway.

"*Bummer.*" Paula untangled herself from Manny and exited the booth hands up.

"ON THE FLOOR! FACE DOWN! HANDS BEHIND YOUR HEAD! **NOW!**" Lowman ordered.

Nico flashed on senior year. The time he and Jesse were driving around after curfew and stopped at a car lot on Fairview Avenue. They were just browsing when three police cruisers pulled up, lights flashing, night-duty cops surrounding them with their guns drawn. Nico assured the police they weren't looking to steal anything, just looking. "At 2 a.m.?" the cop asked. Jesse explained, "It's the only time to avoid salesmen." The cops let them go with a stern warning.

This was a bit more serious. The agents frisked him, twisted his arms and his hands behind his back. Doors would need to be replaced. How would Nico explain this to Tomas? On his belly, Nico demanded, "Do you have a search warrant?"

"Okay," Hightower said, "you can let him up."

Nico sat on the floor, the shiny barrel of a DEA agent's gun inches from his head.

Hightower dropped a warrant onto his lap. "Did you lose my card?"

Two other agents dragged Pat and Doc back into the middle of the room, hands cuffed behind their backs. The ex-Marines weren't resisting, but Lowman clubbed Pat in the head for good measure.

"He wasn't resisting," Nico observed.

"He was thinking about it," Lowman jerked Pat to his feet.

"What are you arresting them for?"

"Making plans," Lowman accused.

"What plans?"

"Take your pick." Lowman nodded to fellow agents and they shook down the ex-Marines. Plans flew out of pockets, out of shirts, from the cuffs of pants. The Castalia was a snowball blizzard of impossible papers: blueprints, notes jotted on the backs of napkins, phone numbers on match-book covers. Doc and Pat possessed plans for breaking into the ROTC Armory at Boise High School, plans to blow up Columbia River dams, plans to derail Amtrak, plans for vacations in Hawaii, plans for an antigravity device, plans for a manned mission to Mars, how to build treehouses, de-velop fiber optic lines and communication satellites. One agent punched Doc in the belly and knocked the stuffing out of him: unpaid parking tickets, books not returned to the library, centerfolds ripped from *Playboy* magazines. Agents chased evidence dancing away in little whirligigs, fluttering against windows. They swept the hardwood floor and bundled them into folders. The plans were locked in a briefcase and cuffed to the arm of an NSA agent. Doc and Pat were forced into a black limousine which drove off with an escort.

Nico watched without expression. He felt tired of being *opposed* to everything anyway. Opposition to everything depleted the good energy. The PAST should begin *rebuilding* America, not tearing it down. We should have plans and plenty of them or we'll keep reliving the past. We must find common ground and make it sacred. Otherwise we will be consigned to designated areas.

* * *

After the raid, Shelly sat in the booth half-asleep, one elbow on the table, eyelids growing heavier by the minute, her chin slipping off her hand, jolting her awake. Coco had called home. No one answered. Just the four of them were left: Nico, Coco, Josh and Shelly. Nico and Josh placed the busted doors back into their busted frames but couldn't lock them.

"I need to find Jesse," Coco said, eyes misty with worry.

"Go ahead, Nico," Josh said. "We'll wait here."

Nico retrieved a cup of coffee for Shelly and wrapped his G.I. jacket around her shoulders to ward off the predawn chill. "Is that okay?" he asked. She nodded, accepting the coffee with gratitude, steam rising into her face.

Nico and Coco searched up and down streets in the warehouse district. Coco's heels echoed into cool air. Thin high clouds parted giving way to lower clouds pushing through the valley, their bellies black. The temperature dropped into the 70s. The morning breeze off the Boise River woke Nico up. "Maybe it'll rain," he said in weak conversation. Feeling awkward, he tagged on, "The mountains are stone dry."

Coco's silence felt almost punitive. The low clouds streamed around the moon like a fast-running stream. Kon Barr popped into Nico's head whistling that old tune.

Kon Barr waited for him on a dirt road fronting the river. He stood bathed in soft moonlight. Cheeks sunken, gaunt from starvation, eyes bulging, Kon Barr nodded down the road. Nico started that direction and Kon Barr fell in beside them. By the time they reached a thick copse of cottonwood, only Coco walked with him. "Why're we going this way?" she asked. "Jesse wouldn't bring his precious GTO down this road."

Nico touched her elbow. "Just a little farther."

A winged grasshopper caught a gust of wind and clung to Nico's pant leg. He swiped it away. At the river's edge, he picked up a round flat stone and skipped it three times in the backwater. The stone shattered the moon's still reflection. In a few weeks a man might walk on the moon. Would the moon be the same afterwards? All the great adventures of the human mind spoiled one mystery after another. Nico couldn't imagine a world without mystery.

Coco stepped carefully around dark roots at the crumbling edge of the bank, bending low to hurl a rock. It didn't go very far. Nico laughed. She punched him in the shoulder. "Don't make fun of me."

Nico took her by the arm.

"I was lost without you and Jesse," she confessed. "So I dropped acid at this party. I remember walking Warm Springs Avenue with Chuck Woller. Do you remember Chuck?" Nico rolled his eyes. "Yeah, you remember him. He was strange but nice." Chuck was a lucky four-leaf clover, remaking his undraftable status into a symbol of peace and love, tending the home fires while the heroes brought democracy to those who didn't want it. "It was a Kodachrome fall day," she went on, "and I hear this brass band right behind me. I check Chuck. He checks me. 'You hear that?' we both say simultaneously. We turn around and there's nothing there. We both hear this loud, brassy band playing John Phillip Sousa and skip off down the Yellow Brick Road. Seriously. In each other's trip."

"Maybe there was a brass band."

Coco thought this over. "I hope not."

Nico nodded, knowingly. He pointed ahead to a vague outline in the high grass next to the river. "There."

"What am I seeing?" she asked. A few more steps answered her question. The GTO emerged from the shadow of a granddaddy cottonwood. Nico inched up to the rear of the car. Coco waited two paces back. Soft moonlight illuminated the backseat. Inside, two round white balloons on a string floated up and down. When Nico's eyes adjusted, the balloons became Jesse's bare ass. He laughed, thinking Jesse was mooning them. Then he picked up on the woman's knees, shapely calves, slim ankles locked around Jesse's hipbones. Jesse's artificial hand pressed so hard against the side window that a crack formed in Idun's moonstruck face.

By the time the paralysis of sudden shock released him, Coco was hurrying up the road the way they came. "Wait!" he called after her.

"Just leave me alone, Nicky."

He caught up to her. "It's not *my* fault. I didn't know. Shouldn't you be mad at *Jesse*?" Nico didn't know if he was in love with Idun, but the pain he felt was certainly real. His joints felt weak. Why did Coco's pain mean more than his? He couldn't protect her anymore. "Why do you let him treat you that way?" Nico gestured in helplessness.

"What would you have me do?" Coco's voice quavered.

"Leave him."

"I can't. I…"

"You're going to get burned," Nico interrupted her in a low voice.

"Is that what you think?"

Nico's frustration grew. His lips trembled. "I can't do this anymore."

"Can't do *what*?" Hurt displaced rage in Coco's eyes.

Dr. Neumann was wrong. Nico didn't need to reconnect; he needed to disconnect. Boise wasn't home anymore; it was hostile territory. Nico walked the same streets he walked before the war, but they were different now. "I need a change."

"Why are you telling me this now?" Coco blinked.

"My God, Coco, think of the baby." Nico hugged her and felt her face on his neck.

"I *want* the baby to have a good life," she whispered in his ear.

Nico held onto her, afraid to let go. "I could give you both a good life."

"I know." She kissed his neck. "I'm afraid of what he might do."

Nico held her tight, hands on her shoulders. "I won't let him hurt you."

"What?" She pulled back, rubbing black holes. "No, I mean—to himself. Jesse'd never hurt the *baby*." She rubbed her stomach. She didn't even show yet, but the pregnancy had already changed her. She was thinking about the future—something neither Jesse nor Nico could do.

"You plan on staying pregnant forever?"

"I know he loves me."

Nico wasn't angry with Jesse so much as Idun. He felt disrespected somehow. "Why defend *him*? You don't owe him anything."

"Yes, I do. We *all* do. He lost his arm."

"Men lost their *lives*. You're just afraid—like the rest of us."

"Yes, I'm afraid…"

"Not a very good reason."

"Jesse may be damaged, but at least he knows it. You're *all* damaged. Your sacred brotherhood of wounded warriors all lined up in parade dress with purple hearts—and I can only help one. I choose him."

"You don't need to come with *me*." Nico choked on the words. Reason didn't kick in until after his heart had failed. "Just start over, you and the baby."

Coco kissed him lightly on the lips, touching his cheek. "You know what burns me up about your brotherhood, Nicky?"

He shook his head.

"You think you're the only ones wounded by the war."

28.

As Milo entered the Battery Mishler, a wet chill cut into his veins. He felt his way along the concrete wall, his heartbeat on the surface of his skin. The Hammer Man's face lit up behind the shuddering flame of a lighter. He stopped. The lighter flared out but left an ember burning in a cigarette.

"Ain't this a trip?" The Hammer Man said. Each draw on his cigarette illuminated his head as it bobbled bodiless down the dark tunnel, a twisted trail of smoke fading into total gloom.

Milo stood still, petrified, not wanting to go deeper into the battery.

"Let me show you around," the Hammer Man volunteered. Milo lurched ahead through the passage and found a junction. He went down and around trying to catch up to the head as it flared briefly from puff to puff. The Hammer Man urged him on. "It's a real maze in here." The Hammer Man stepped through a curtain and held it open for Nico. "Watch your step."

Milo stumbled over the threshold and tumbled onto a stack of rugs that broke his fall—Persian rugs, throw rugs, braided rugs, shaggy rugs, rugs on rugs. He rolled into a sitting position propped up by pillows in a wide concrete bunker command post awash in candlelight. Wood paneling lined the interior of the room and on the panels a mural had been painted. Silhouetted trees in moonlight turned the bunker into a forest. Sheer fabrics draped through rings filtered low light into an interior twilight. They were not alone. Couples swayed together in hammocks and writhed in beds of pillows. Patchouli incense burned in a dish, a fragrance enhanced with pot smoke and warm bodies.

"Welcome to The Enchanted Forest," The Hammer Man said, his arm sweeping in a grand gesture, his dark eyes set like blueberries into pasta-pale skin. A leather headband kept the copious black hair from tumbling into his face. His thick eyebrows and round shoulders were made all the more distinctive by the hook nose and bird-like features. The sledgehammer was now an axe, an acoustic guitar that rested in his lap. He sat cross-legged on a plush pillow, wearing ragged cut-offs and a tie-dyed shirt. He strummed the guitar and started describing this musical he'd composed based on *The Hobbit*. He smiled through his fillings as several adoring girls clung to his every word. Milo cringed at the thought of some pervert preying on young girls. Should he warn them? *Save yourselves. The croon's a vampire.*

Beside the Hammer Man was this short, wiry dude with coal-black beard and a pockmarked face. He knelt down to a low table and separated dried reddish-brown leaves from seeds, then filled a hookah bowl with weed. The stereophonic sounds of passion in the command post left Milo feeling alone. There was a poster pinned to a mural tree trunk. On it, foot soldiers with machine guns charged onto a battlefield. The sky of the poster depicted a jet airliner streaming by over the words *Fly Far, Far Eastern Airlines*. A black banner below invited tourism in bold white letters: THIS VACATION VISIT BEAUTIFUL...VIETNAM.

The Hammer Man set aside the guitar and leaned over to take a hookah hit, drawing the flame into a bubbling glass chamber that filled with swirling smoke. He exhaled a dense blue cloud that set Milo to coughing. The Enchanted Forest washed thin as a web in strong backlight. He touched parts of the mural that seemed to be moving and his hand went through the wall.

On the other side, he was blasted by a wave of heat. Beads of sweat prickled his skin. He was ducking under a chopper, with rotors raising dust from a dirt road as the door gunner fired quick bursts from an M-60.

Milo's shoulders sagged under the weight of a wounded man. Shadows grew thicker on the ridge followed by the arc of tracers aimed at him. His legs buckled meters from the deck. The wounded soldier on his shoulders rolled to the ground. Milo tried to get up, but couldn't. Rotors revved and Ghost Horse stood on its toes ready to lift off. The door gunner kept firing as the ship yawed hard right. Ghost tried to set it down easy, but the toe of a skid caught a log. The Huey pitched forward, its main rotors beating the ground. The broken blades still rotated as Ghost climbed out of the bullet-riddled hulk. Milo collapsed onto his belly. His eyes locked on the eyes of the wounded soldier, his head mummy-wrapped with bandages to stanch the flow of his head wound.

* * *

Milo entered another tunnel. This one flickered with torchlight. Each step stirred up cool air as he stepped onto rough flat stones. He found a burning torch and lifted it from its iron. He held the torch high. The walls were no longer concrete but constructions of logs and chinking of small sticks, mud and shell fragments. An impulse to run stabbed him in the heart. His bare feet slipped from stone slick with moss. He knelt down, scraping dirt from around a stone and found a small hole. He hadn't been walking on stones but half-buried human skulls.

The world *had* ended.

* * *

At the crossing of two tunnels, Milo discovered a locked door leading off to the right. Stacked-up sacks of rice blocked the other passage. The sacks were stamped with a hand-shake. He crawled through a gap and came out in a lighted warehouse. The warehouse was filled with American supplies. It was bigger than the PX in Da Nang. One whole section held food supplies big as a grocery store: sacks of rice and flour, restaurant-sized tins of instant mashed potatoes, Tang, peanut butter, cases of Sterno, canned peaches, green beans and stacked columns of Bumblebee Solid White in dented 12-ounce tins.

Another whole section was like a department store with neat rows of boots, fatigues, socks, t-shirts and boxer shorts. Milo found banks of refrigerators, toaster ovens, stereos, electric can-openers, hair-dryers, electric toothbrushes, disposable diapers, Corningware, cases of cigarette cartons, and an impressive supply of booze—cases of cognac and wine, Budweiser and Miller High Life.

And then there was the ordnance: racks of bombs and artillery shells etched with Chinese characters, wooden crates of M-79 grenade launchers and M-16s, mortars, machine guns, steel boxes of ammo, M-61 fragmentation grenades, Bouncing Bettys and Claymores.

Movement in the far corner of the aisle between digging tools and garden supplies made Milo crouch in stealth. A small fire sputtered there under a cooking pot. He inched forward. A man with his back to him played a slot machine, yanking the silver handle down and watching the colorful fruit turn. He wore a brown uniform and a netted helmet sprouting leaves. An AK-47 was strapped to his back. He took a drink of cognac and set the bottle down on top of a steel keg. An old woman squatted with the cooking pot stirring an Agent Orange porridge, her head cocked, puzzling over the plug on an electric coffeemaker. A mostly-naked ancient fellow with loose skin hammered on an unexploded bomb. Around him was a small stockpile of unsold lamps made out of bomb metal. Milo crept closer to the gambler. He could smell his sweat. The woman had no legs. Her torso had been set onto a furniture dolly so she could knuckle herself around. They'd broken up some wooden pallets to make a fire.

Milo's feet crunched in spilled Cheerios. The gambler wheeled around and pulled his AK-47 into a fighting posture, his face glowing eerily. Milo turned to run. The gambler circled the fire looking down the barrel. *"Dung Lai!"* he shouted. "Stop, G.I."

Milo didn't stop. He kicked over a tower of canned tuna as he stumbled toward another door. Here he found a small army of skinny villagers riding bicycle generators. They were generating electricity for their operating room. Splayed on an operating table was what remained of Geo. Throbbing lights powered by human muscle could not distract the NVA doctor who gripped a short hacksaw and began sawing Geo's leg. Intravenous tubes fashioned from rubber insulation stripped from electrical wire kept Geo alive through the amputation. Milo vomited onto a concrete floor slick with amputated limbs. He backed out. He had to go deeper.

He came to an arched doorway shimmering with strings of crystalline beads. Strange music compelled him to enter. It was an off-hours nightclub with a hardwood floor and a bamboo bar. A wall-sized mirror behind the bar reflected rows of colorful bottles and bright clean glasses. Wooden tables with candles in red glass flickered around a dance floor. The floor vibrated with Led Zeppelin's bass chugging through fog, swirling clouds like oil on water. Two Thai women in dragon-lady dresses sat on barstools. Their slender legs in nylons crossed at the knees. Straight obsidian hair flowed over their bare shoulders. Their shadowed eyes blinked over sad lips that bled onto powder-white faces.

A man in a swivel-chair swiveled around, his hips moving to the music. He wore dress greens. Smoke from a fat cigar billowed up into his wasted eyes; his hunger sucked the color from the cheeks of the Indochinese girls. The colonel's thick chest bore a rack of proud ribbons. He rolled a cigar between ungroomed fingers. His other hand clutched a glass of straight scotch. Even from where Milo stood, the stench made him gag. A toxic cloud of smoke hung in hazy half-light. The girls squirmed as the colonel scratched through his dull memory. He downed the rest of the drink and set the glass on the table. He nodded toward the girls, fumbling with his trousers.

The girls rotated on their barstools. "Numma one Joe," they repeated, eyes on the floor. They dismounted together, slipped off their dresses and approached in nothing but thongs. The colonel swayed, sopping and impotent on his throne. He slipped an arm around each girl's waist, resting a hand on their buttocks, caressing with all the warmth of a Wall Street banker. The girls leaned in until their bare hips touched each of the colonel's flushed cheeks. He reached up and curled the long black hair of the tallest girl around his hairy knuckles. "What's your name?" he demanded with a tug.

"Chu Len," the girl answered, averting her eyes.

He yanked Chu Len's hair but she would not go down easy. This did not make the colonel happy. "I do," the other girl volunteered. She kneeled in front of the colonel, one small hand cupping each knee as she stooped to his weak manhood. The colonel stroked the back of her head and pulled aside the curtain of black hair from her face to better watch her performance. He noticed the girl looking at his Rolex. "You like?" She nodded while working hard to raise his flag.

When the colonel loosened his grip on Chu Len, she rose up enough for him to force her nipple toward his mouth. As hard as the other girl tried, she could not resurrect the old soldier.

"Faster." He coaxed, gripping each side of the girl's head. "Faster."

It was no use.

"Jesus," he shouted, "not so fucking hard."

The hostess lifted her head with slack penis in hand. "No good, general."

The colonel backhanded her across the face. She fell onto her backside. He picked up the cigar and puffed it back to life.

Milo didn't even feel his body floating out through crystalline beads but he could hear her scream.

29.

Back in junior high, Nico and Jesse used to raid Mr. Morgan's cherry orchard. What was the boon of this incursion? Plump cherries. The challenge: old man Morgan who threatened to pepper their asses with rock salt. The boys fasted during main harvest, waiting to take a crack at Morgan's private reserve. Old man Morgan sat up on his porch with a shotgun on his lap. His yard lights were trained on the dark sweet cherries of the private reserve. Before he'd let those cherry raiders pluck even one, he'd prefer to watch them being snatched up by ravenous birds. One pre-dawn morning, Nico and Jesse hunkered in the ditch running along the property line. Their high-topped tennis shoes were squeaking wet when they popped up and raced for the trees. They couldn't bear the waste of those lovely cherubs engorged with sugar to the pecking order of crows. The boys were conservationists, preventing waste. They darted to the blue-ribbon cherry trees crouching low to the ground through tall grass and moved from tree to tree filling their pockets. Precious fruit stolen right from under Morgan's nose. Their shoes were heavy with mud, shirts caked with juice as they dived over the bank just as Morgan shattered the still morning air with a shotgun blast. He missed. With the rising sun, Nico and Jesse fell back with cherry on their breaths and a story to tell.

* * *

Think of the baby! Nico and Shelly worked Coco with the same message. She needed to change her life. *Think of the baby!* She deserved better. *Think of the baby!* Jesse was no good. *Think of the baby!* The abuse would only get worse.

Coco preferred to think about this at her mother's, not in The Castalia Lounge. First, she must stop off at home to pack some things. Shelly and Coco waited in the Cyclone while Josh and Nico wrestled around the unhinged door.

Later when the Cyclone pulled into the Walker driveway, the headlights swept a car parked on the shoulder, under a Dutch elm. Jericho was in his cruiser. Nico wasn't surprised because he had contacted the deputy sheriff. He felt responsible for Coco and wanted to make sure she got to her mother's okay. In spite of the whole pig blood incident and Sampson's untimely demise, Nico trusted Jericho more than anyone else in law enforcement.

The buckskin and appy waited under the yard light in the front corner of the lot, muzzles laid over the fence by the water trough. Nico didn't see the GTO. The Stinker trailer wasn't back by the barn either. They must have taken the Bomb to the station.

Coco unlocked the door.

"Where ya going?" Nico followed Coco out the back door.

"I need to feed and water the horses. I won't be here at feeding time. What if Jesse doesn't come home?"

"I'll do it," Nico offered. "You go pack."

Nico offered her a place to stay, but Coco didn't want her troubles to become Nico's. Lenny's commute from Horseshoe Bend into Meridian brought him right past the Walker home every day but he never once dropped by to see them. The Bird residence provided a good neutral setting because Lenny's long-standing animosity would keep Jesse away.

Nico unlatched the door to the tack room, a lean-to off the side of the barn. Coco's harsh whisper came from behind. "What's *he* doing here?"

"Who?" Nico stopped, half-turning.

Coco nodded toward Deputy Sinclair's brown and white cruiser.

"*Him*," she huffed. "What does he want?"

"It's okay," Nico assured her. "I called him."

"Why? Oh Jesus, Nico, you don't understand *anything*. I'm not in danger. I'm leaving because Jesse needs to decide if he wants to be married or not."

"I just thought it might be good to have someone watching your back."

"I have someone," she said.

Shelly appeared in the doorway holding a watering can. "Nico's just being cautious." Uncle Frosty must be climbing the walls. Nico didn't look forward to taking her home at first light.

Coco cringed when Nico touched her arm. "You want me to tell Jericho to leave?"

"Please." She went back into the house.

Jericho saw Nico coming and climbed out of the cruiser. He was leaning against the front fender, thumbs hooked in his pockets, when Nico reached him. Nico acknowledged him with a nod. "How's Junel?"

"They finally got her down," Jericho answered. "She'll be okay."

They got her down, Nico thought, like some insane woman who dived into the deep end because of another hero. Jericho could take a punch without losing his head. He would roll out of it and measure his distance before a face off. Jesse took every punch on the button and just re- fused to back-pedal. An easy knockout for somebody like Jericho. "Sorry, man. How are you doing?" Nico wondered. The deputy understood a vet's distrust of government after fighting in Vietnam and coming home to find the road was measured in more than miles. He might cut them some slack. "I have no idea how she got it."

"Not your fault," Jericho answered, staring ahead.

They all had to learn how to save themselves if they were ever going to save the world. Not even heavy dues paid in the Pleiku Campaign made Jericho's eyes water as they did last night outside The Enchanted Forest. He hadn't felt such fear since his green plunge, shaking in bamboo with a machete.

"Yeah." Nico swallowed hard. "I know."

Gazing up at the moon, full to the round with soft light, Jericho asked, "So where's Jesse?"

"Don't know, man. Coco came to pack for her mother's. I thought it best to have someone covering our asses."

"You think he'd really hurt her?"

Nico shrugged. "She says no. But I saw bruises."

"Accidents cause bruises. She hasn't made any reports." Jericho ran his tongue around inside his cheek. "I knew about them."

"Who?" Nico played dumb.

"Junel and Jesse. She told me."

"Why tell *me*?"

"Because of the way you look at his wife. Anything happen between you two?"

"Not since high school." Nico backed up to the cruiser's front fender and stood next to Jericho in semi-darkness. Nico trusted him, but didn't trust Lowman and Hightower not to tip him off about Willy. Would Jericho use Willy then to get revenge on Jesse? Why would the wife of a man like Jericho stalk a wild drunk like Jesse?

"She won't be chasing after him no more."

Nico couldn't read the deputy's face, but his body stiffened. He worried a little about Junel. "You're not looking for anything to happen, right?"

"Not unless he gets in the way."

"Maybe you should have sent somebody else," Nico said.

"You asked for me, remember?"

"Yeah well, Coco asked me to send you away. Now, I can't make you move, ya understand, but what if you were to park on 5 Mile Road, let's say? Out of sight. Out of mind."

In pre-dawn quiet, Nico opened a sack of oats and dumped two coffee tins into the black rubber grain feeder at the corner where the horses waited impatiently. A shadow buzzed the yard light. A bat. He watched it attack the light until Splash, the appy mare, stamped the ground. "Hold your horses. I'm coming." Nico broke open a bale of alfalfa and tossed it over the fence, dry seed belching dust on impact with the hard scrabble. Coco rode Splash for her dressage and barrel-racing. Bucky, the swayback gelding blinked his bubbling eyes as Nico hoisted a wedge of alfalfa over the fence. Bucky crunched a mouthful. "You're useless even as horsemeat," Nico said, patting him on the forehead.

Splash raised up from her oats and snorted as if offended. The shake of her head tossed a line of spume onto Nico's sweat-rank Stinker shirt. He rubbed the wet spot with a handful of alfalfa. "No editorial comments."

* * *

"Now what are you doing?" Nico asked Coco when he came into the living room and she had pulled out the Hoover vacuum cleaner. "We don't have time for that. Why aren't you packing?"

"I can't leave the house looking like this," Coco insisted, gesturing helplessly.

"Looks good to me." Nico's judgment carried little weight since he was fine with leaving dishes to stack up in the sink.

"I'm not leaving a mess," she said, turning on the vacuum and pushing it.

"Everybody leaves a mess, Coco!" he said, his tone cutting and totally unwarranted.

Coco started to cry. Shelly stepped in, hugging her. "It's okay, hon. I'll do that." She took the vacuum cleaner handle out of Coco's hand and glared at Nico.

Coco stomped down the hall and slammed the bedroom door. Shelly switched the vacuum on and pushed it toward Nico's feet aggressively until he followed Coco to the bedroom door.

"Let's just try to avoid a scene!" he shouted through the door.

"Instead you created one. Good job." Coco responded.

When he couldn't stand it any longer, he opened it. Coco threw a shirt in his face.

The bedroom was too frilly feminine for even his tastes. It had a walk-in closet full of women's clothes, hand-stitched bedspread, and a lavender dressing table that blended well with light blue carpet. He couldn't imagine Jesse living there. The only male presence one might deduce marred the left-side night table and big trunk at the foot of the bed. Nico couldn't tell where Jesse kept his clothes, but guessed they were mostly stuffed into drawers. A short stack of *Motor Trend* on the end table provided Jesse with his bedtime stories.

Coco tossed stuff by the handful into two open suitcases on the bed. Drawers stood open. She packed a cardboard box full of yearbooks, photo albums and keepsakes. She moved to the end of the bed and yanked the army blanket off the steam trunk. It was locked. She bashed it open with a geode bookend.

"What's in there?" Nico asked.

She squatted down in front of the chest and opened it up. "Vietnam."

Coco dropped an old bayonet on the floor, a flight suit and helmet. Nico dropped to his knees beside her and picked up the helmet. Across the front was the nickname: Ghost.

She handed back an issue of *Grunt*. The centerfold was a drawing of a nude Vietnamese girl. Long black hair covered her breasts. She sat naked on a peace symbol. In the background, fighter planes strafed a tangle of bodies, jungle and small weapons. The image reminded Nico of Chu Len. When he looked up again, Coco was holding a cigar box. The box was much like the one that belonged to Colonel Jefferson Hedges with photos of the Thai cabaret. Inside the box were papers and several medals: Purple Heart, Vietnam Service Medal, Bronze Star with "V" for valor.

Coco took the medals and headed across the hall to the bathroom. Nico dogged her, eyes popping as she dropped the medals into the toilet and flushed.

"What are you doing?" The ribbons pulled toward the drain, but the weight of the medals in a weak flush held fast to the bottom of the bowl.

"Oh, fuck it," she said, marching past him, back into the bedroom. Nico fished the medals out of the bowl and wiped them down with a towel. In the bedroom, Coco was tearing through open drawers tossing Jesse's clothes to the ground. Nico returned the medals to the cigar box and the cigar box to the war chest. In the paperwork under the medals he found the original commendation letter:

The President of the United States takes pleasure in presenting the Bronze Medal with "V" for Valor to Jesse Andrew Walker, Warrant Officer, U.S. Army, for conspicuous gallantry in action while engaged in military operations involving conflict with an armed hostile force on October 5, 1968, while serving with the First Cavalry (Airmobile Unit) in the Republic of Vietnam. On this date, Warrant Officer Walker distinguished himself with exceptionally valorous action when the Bell UH-1 Iroquois he commanded came under intense ground fire from a force of North Vietnamese Regulars. Forced to land the crippled craft, the steep ground at Mang Yang Pass near Route 19 in the Central Highlands caused the helicopter to roll. Warrant Officer Walker pulled wounded from the wreckage. With his door gunner pinned, his co-pilot dead, his life threatened by an enemy barrage, Warrant Officer Walker detached the M-60 machine gun from its pylon and laid down supporting fire. It was not until a MedEvac arrived to attend to the wounded that Warrant Officer Walker made any effort to save himself. With complete disregard for his own life, suffering a crushed arm and loss of blood, Warrant Officer Walker held off the ambush long enough for gun trucks from an 8th Transportation Group convoy to repel the attack, allowing the wounded to be evac-

*uated. Warrant Officer Walker's conspicuous gal-
lantry is in the highest tradition of military service
and reflects great credit upon himself, his unit and the
United States Army.*

Nico's memory flashed on the chopper barely clearing
the forest canopy, treetops scraping its belly as waves of heat
blasted through open doors. The door gunner was firing at
nothing and everything. *Blue leader, this is Blue Boy. We're
taking heavy fire, over.*

Under the official documents including Jesse's DD-214,
Nico found a black and white photograph of the UH-1 Iroquois. The photo was taken in June 1968 at Camp Radcliffe. Under the 1st Air Cav unit marking on the pilot's door
were the strange words: *Wanagi Tashunke.* Aft the pilot's
door, Jesse stood proudly in a flight suit, helmet under his
arm with the word *Ghost* in front. A stubby dark-skinned
soldier leaned against the frame of the slick's open bay, a
third crewmember sat on the deck, long legs dangling, and
a fourth crouched behind the .50 caliber. Ghost's crew. Jesse
had written nicknames from left to right: Stunted Horse,
Sonny, Undertaker and Ghost. Nico squinted and rubbed his
eyes. The handsome blonde in the door sitting on the deck
was Kon Barr. Nico's eyes burned with recognition. That
face, that bird-like nose, haunted Nico since the landmine.
Though he couldn't see it in the photograph, Nico knew
Sonny had a check-mark scar cutting from below the cheek-
bone to the hinge of the jaw.

Nico slipped into the bathroom, hands trembling as he
slapped cold water onto his face and studied his reflection.
He seemed to waver. He pushed the bangs off his forehead
and pressed a wet washrag against the head wound. The
words stitched on a 173rd Airborne Brigade bush commander's fatigue jacket he saw once at The Splendors entered his
mind. "To really live, you must be ready to die!"

"You okay?" Shelly called outside the bathroom door.
"Coco's ready now."

"Great. I'm coming." The wavering sensation disappeared. His cheek stiffened and his eyes shrunk into burnt raisins. The whole side of his face blistered in the mirror, his skin shrinking over blasted bone. He came out of the bathroom lost between worlds. As Kon Barr "Sonny" emerged more and more, Nico faltered, shrinking into the shallows of another dimension. He felt himself losing his grip.

In the living room, Coco held onto one of the suitcases. Shelly held onto the other, leaving the box of personal items and small portraits by her father. Nico bent over and lifted the box under his arm but before they could leave the phone rang.

"I'll get it," Nico said, heading Coco off, "just in case it's Jesse." He picked up the phone. "Hello?"

"Hello," a voice answered.

"Who are you calling?"

"Who are *you* calling?"

"I'm not calling anyone. You called me."

"No, you called *me*," the voice insisted.

"No, you called *me*."

"You sure you didn't call anyone?"

"Yes. Who is this?" Nico asked.

Mayday! Mayday! This is Blue 4. I say again. Mayday!

Nico hung up the phone and shrugged. "Wrong number."

* * *

The Cyclone's headlights eased softly out of the driveway and on to East Floating Feather Road. The clean outline of barren hills against a faint glow emerged from cloak of darkness. Jericho's cruiser no longer waited at the intersection. Maybe he'd been called off. Nico took a right on to the newly designated Highway 55, threading a narrow canyon. The car's eight cylinders purred in sync as Nico accelerated into the climb. He shouldn't have dragged Shelly along to Horseshoe Bend. He should have had Josh take her home, but he needed Josh to hold the fort at The Castalia. Light from the instrument panel clouded Coco's eyes, unmasking a tenderness captured in Vincent's timeless portrait.

The Cyclone muscled up the pass toward the 4200-foot summit, coming out on top in the pale light of pre-dawn. Going down was a twisting five-mile 1600-foot descent into Horseshoe Bend on the Payette River. Shelly was falling asleep in the backseat, her head resting on her arm, her elbow propped against the backdoor window. Nico glimpsed a Vietnamese girl with a smile, with black hair cascading over alabaster shoulders, her dark eyes fluttering open and finding him.

Out of nowhere, headlights appeared in the rear view. Before he recognized the car, he knew it was Jesse. He downshifted. The Cyclone leaped forward over the summit with a low growl. Shelly's head popped up. She turned in the backseat with one knee up on pleated vinyl, her arm hooked over the backseat. She shielded her eyes from the glaring headlights. "It's a GTO."

The summit road widened into a mountainous vista glittering at the crack of dawn. Nico's Cyclone couldn't outrun the GTO. He stomped on it and watched the tach shoot up as the engine wound tight. Nico put it in fourth and stepped on it. The GTO dropped off, then raced back up onto the Cyclone's bumper, horn honking, lights flashing.

They broke the summit and started their descent. Jesse made his move, pulling alongside the Cyclone in the other lane. His hook glommed onto the steering wheel, right hand gesturing for Nico to pull over. Instead, Nico sped up. He could hear a siren in the distance. If he held on long enough, maybe it was Jericho.

Morning light detonated the white interior of the GTO. Nico flipped a finger at Jesse. He wasn't letting him win this time. The panic in Coco's eyes ebbed into cautious resignation. "Just pull over, Nicky, so I can talk to him. He won't leave us alone until I do."

Nico knew where he'd come in on that picture. Coco would give in again and he would land in that place where Start and Finish were the same, right along with Jesse. He would win without either one of them going anywhere. So instead of pulling over, Nico jerked the wheel, turned into the front fender of the GTO. Jesse turned back into the Cyclone, his face pale with desperation. The two cars locked and squealed, wheel wells smoking where loose metal collapsed and burned rubber. Jesse disengaged by speeding up, pulling ahead. Nico stepped on it, trying to ride up the GTO's exhaust.

Both girls screamed. "Mayday! Mayday!"

The GTO swept in front, fishtailing. Nico saw too late the depression in the road that left an abrupt edge near the centerline, not far into the downhill grade. When the Cyclone hit the edge, the wheel jerked out of his hands. Nico lost control.

* * *

The mangled Cyclone rested upside down ten feet away from where Nico woke up, cloud of steam hissing from its cracked radiator. One headlight was broken, the other knocked awkward and burning in first light. Warm blood flowed off his forehead into his eyes. He couldn't feel his legs.

Shelly lay motionless, impaled on jagged steel, back arched, arms wide, eyes staring unfocused.

Nico wavered on the edge of consciousness as he rolled onto his side and pushed himself up. Jesse came running from the GTO. He threw himself to the ground, reaching back under the wreckage.

"Coco! Coco!" Jesse cried.

The high-pitched scream of monkeys pierced the green wall of rain forest. Kon Barr "Sonny" appeared through the rising steam carrying something in his arms. "Hang on, buddy."

"Help them," Nico sobbed.

Sonny gathered Nico into his long arms, tossing him over his shoulder. Nico was too numb and fighting the urge to fly out of his body. Jesse pulled Coco from under the heap. Sirens in the distance turned into angry bees, the *thunk* of an ax hacking the deck. Sonny stumbled, rolling Nico onto his back in the tall grass.

In the aft cabin of the medevac, Nico gazed up through a chink in the armor, into the blur of blades. Air pulsated, beating against his temple like a drum. Sonny lay beside him, blue-gray eyes fixed in shock, the front of his uniform ripped open, chest packed with compresses and still bleeding.

A round-shouldered medic in half-silhouette bent to the task, thumping Sonny hard in the chest with his fist, not once, not twice, but three times. He blew color back into the ashen face as if it were the breath of God.

Nico could barely understand what efforts were being made to save them. The medic's face was blurred through thick gauze wrapped around Nico's head. The chopper banked left and last light poured in through open doors. The medic's eyes were wide and unblinking, scared and somehow knowing. His owlish gaze penetrated the twilight. He took Nico's limp hand between his and searched for a pulse. "It's okay, soldier. You're heading home."

Good company for the long journey, Nico thought. He let go like a child learning to swim, trusting the water not to drown him, his weightless body riding on waves of heat like a raptor. He could see home. There. Just over the ridge.

The medic clipped the dog tags from around his neck, slipping them into the pocket of his fatigues. He searched Nico's pockets and found a picture.

30.

The tide was going out. The great river palpitated in rest-less sleep. Its body writhed under the bay-front dock, its boundless heart beating under the surface. Milo Simonson relaxed by a stack of crab pots. He whistled a Tex Ritter tune from "High Noon" as he watched a cormorant glide into a trough of waves. The bird dived in the shadows of the main span of the Astoria-Megler Bridge.

The 8th Street ferry was gone but souls timelessly traveled across a misted river to an inner world. Milo never found the right words to describe the calmness he felt when enemy fire ripped the cabin of *Wanagi Tashunke*. It was like standing on the promenade of the ferry, *M. R. Chessman*, gliding through morning mist.

Bumble Bee's foreman, Bill Brown, promised Milo a job when he was ready to work. He was ready to work. Because Milo worked the summers of '65 and '66, Brown felt obli-gated to offer him a job driving jitney. The disability might be enough for Milo to live on, after three months in V.A. rehab and another month recovering in Astoria, he needed to get back out there. Doctors warned against strenuous ac-tivity. The AK-47 bullet that ripped a near mortal wound in his chest diminished his lung power. The enemy stole his dream of playing trumpet professionally, so he took up the guitar and wrote some songs. Music hadn't finished with him yet.

For the last two months Milo walked downhill each day from his apartment past the vacant Astor Hotel, down to the abandoned ferry landing. He sat on the dock, watching the river run. There was no better salve for his wounds than the river. It made him think about the directionality of life. Not even backwaters of reflection suppressed the river's eventual outflow. At high tide when the river rolls backwards, a deep flow still followed gravity all the way to the sea. Milo sometimes could touch that flow with his mind with sun full upon the water. He could transport himself back to Vietnam in the twilight hours when his heart stopped.

Milo spent the day on the jitney picking up racks of canned tuna and delivering them to the warehouse. Mind-numbing work that paid well was just what Milo needed. He'd survived enough trauma to last a lifetime.

He'd wanted to major in music after high school but couldn't afford to go anywhere. Without a scholarship to the university, he hired on to work full time on the tuna line. He practiced trumpet but the high notes never came easy. Then he lost his student deferment. If he'd had Geo's foresight, he would have enlisted in the Coast Guard. If he'd known what the next two years would bring, he would have run off to Canada. Instead, the 23rd Infantry Division (Americal) was airlifted into Kham Duc days before the Special Forces base fell. In the chaos of evacuation, Milo was lucky to get out alive. Three C130s crashed, one filled with evacuees. Six choppers were shot down. The shell shock of that defeat must have impaired his judgment because he re-upped and requested a transfer to the First Cavalry. Four months later, he was crew chief on *Ghost Horse*, landing in hot LZs and saving lives.

Ghost was ship commander. He had friends in the black market. They accepted a mission to carry illicit cargo to a remote village off Route 19 east of Mang Yang Pass. Ghost shared his booty with the crew so they were all in on it. It made life in a war zone more bearable. The cargo included a whole pallet of canned tuna on skids—commercial solid-white albacore canned in Astoria, in the cannery where Milo once worked. The crew had only tasted tuna in casserole served with a P-38. Milo suspected the mission involved some serious payoffs. Milo and Undertaker, their door gunner, never asked too many questions.

Halfway to Kon Barr, Stunted Horse keyed the intercom. They were diverting the ship to medevac three wounded from a jeep accident at the Bridge 23 junction. *Ghost Horse* responded. They were the closest ship to the action. They didn't have a medic on the crew so when the ship set down Milo and the gunner jumped out to retrieve the wounded. Ghost kept the slick forward and light on its skids, ready for a running takeoff.

The jeep had hit a landmine. The soft glow of the instrument panel and the outline of the chopper were barely visible in waning light. The NVA had attacked Bridge 26 just a few days before so they were in the area. Even with route security forces and tank crews stationed at bridges and hills, the enemy hit the pipeline with impunity.

The action area was disarmingly quiet when they hit the ground running. Milo heard the steam hissing from the jeep's broken radiator. The landmine left the chassis a twisted, smoking pretzel. A quick assessment yielded three casualties: one American soldier and two Vietnamese girls dressed in fatigues. What was this crazy bastard doing this far outside the wire? he wondered. Sight-seeing? On a date with two Asian flowers? Jesus, the only date this guy had was with his maker.

Undertaker whispered, "Are we gonna recover all three?"

Milo kneeled and checked the soldier. He was still alive, breathing shallow. Both girls were dead. He pulled the soldier up to a sitting position, threw one arm over his shoulder and hefted him into a fireman's carry. "I got him."

Undertaker ran in a crouch back to the chopper, his loose uniform snapping under the rotors. The jeep driver was a small man, light to carry. Milo was on his toes when the NVA opened fire. Red tracers streamed from the tree line. Undertaker laid down cover fire. A bullet clipped him and spun him around. He took one round through the arm of his vest, into his chest. He crumpled to the ground. The wounded man rolled off his shoulder onto his back next to him, eyes open.

Milo couldn't recall how they'd gotten onto the deck of the ship, but he felt the chopper shudder as Ghost took off, nose down, skids scraping the red road. Before they came up and out of a turn, .51s ripped the co-pilot's station, along the side of the cabin, hitting the tail rotor. The tail whipped back and forth as Ghost tried to make a soft landing. The front of a skid caught on a shell-blasted stump and the Huey stood on its nose, dropped to its side, rotors beating the ground into fragments.

AK-47s concentrated fire on the riddled hulk. Cans of tuna exploded like targets, hit by ricochets, juice burping out of shredded tin cans rolling on the hot deck. The odor of white albacore permeated the sticky cabin. Undertaker pulled the M-60, climbed through the hatch and kept firing. Stunted Horse was gone. He bled out before Ghost could free his legs from tangled steel. Undertaker laid down cover fire as Ghost extracted the wounded driver and went back for Sunny, their crew chief. He had sustained a serious chest wound.

When Milo awoke with last light bursting through the open doors of a medevac, he saw the sweat-streaked face of a medic hammering his chest to get his heart started.

* * *

Bill Brown limped across the dock from the weighing room. "Hey, Milo," he called, clipboard in one hand, pulling off his Bumble Bee cap with the other, slicking back greasy hair. "How'd it go?"

"Never once forgot where I was," Milo said, arching his brow.

"Good," Brown smiled, "spend too much time in churches or bars and you tend to lose your way."

Eino Mattson, owner of the troller *Alma May*, followed Brown over and offered Milo his hand. He had a firm grip. "Welcome home, Milo."

"Thanks, Eino. It's good to be home."

Eino held out a blue cooler. "This here's for you."

"What's this?"

"Smoked sturgeon filets and a bag of salmon cheeks."

"No kidding? No canned tuna?"

"Solid White?"

"No, thanks." Milo accepted the cooler with a smile. "This will do fine."

* * *

In Pleiku when Milo's gurney rolled over the moonlit tarmac, he watched the sky as the specialists delivered his body. The medic pulled the Jeep driver's dog tags from his pocket and a photo fell out. It landed face-up where Milo could see it. Ghost's girl. Maybe he lost it during the crash. He blubbered that it belonged to Ghost. The medic said the photo was on the driver. It was the same picture Milo had seen dozens of times.

Ghost came to visit after he lost his arm. Milo asked to see his girl's picture once more. Ghost produced it.

"So you got it back?" Milo asked.

"What?"

"Your girl."

"Never lost her."

* * *

The pilot boat pulled alongside the three-story keel of a Norwegian freighter. The bar pilot on the boat spread his legs for balance. The waves made the boat rise and fall at the waterline. He hooked the ladder on the freighter and started to climb. A bar pilot's do-si-do with a sixty ton cargo ship bucking the outpouring of the great river struck Milo as nothing less than heroic. He knew men who had faced death in the heat of battle, but they were no more or less courageous than the bar pilot who daily danced over the Pacific Graveyard.

The tuna line shut down and Milo walked to the locker room through the live chatter of women filing over the boards in white smocks and headscarves. All day their feminine selves were kept wrapped up and muted in white. At quitting time they yanked off the gloves, headscarves and smocks and tossed them into a barrel, and all this color and vibrant feminine flowering erupted like a flock of pigeons.

One hung back, sitting on the edge of a pallet, waiting until the room cleared. She unwound the white headscarf and shook out thick red hair. Even from twenty feet away, Milo could smell a curious mix of tuna and Rose Milk.

The river defined life: its flow—sometimes easy, sometimes whipped into froth—into the sea inexorable and unobstructed. Yet the river never emptied. He'd fallen into this habit of thinking of life as a finite resource, an allotment of energy that must be conserved, measured out carefully. Yet the more he measured, the more exhausted he became. Often, he could barely muster enough strength to get out of bed, weighed down by suffering and loss, with a grudging obsession over what the war had taken. Vietnam was like the river. It would never empty until he learned to embrace moments like this, on the bayfront, watching the river flow.

He closed his eyes as the salt air filled his lungs. He imagined hitting high C and holding the note until his lungs burst. It was a weak C for sure but he hit it again and again. Until he could hold onto it forever.

Other Books by David Memmott

Lost Transmissions

Giving It Away

PrimeTime

Shadow Bones

The Larger Earth

House on Fire

ABOUT THE AUTHOR

David Memmott has published six books of poetry—most recently, *Lost Transmissions* (Serving House Books, 2012), an Eric Hoffer Award finalist. He is a Rhysling Award winner, Spur Award finalist, Fishtrap Fellow, Playa resident and recipient of three Fellowships for Publishing from Literary Arts, Inc. (Portland), for his work at Wordcraft of Oregon. He serves as a consulting editor for *Phantom Drift: A Journal of New Fabulism*. His digital art can be viewed on his website, www.davidmemmott.com.

redbat
books

For other titles available from redbat books, please visit:
www.redbatbooks.com

Also available through Ingram, Amazon.com,
Barnesandnoble.com, Powells.com and by special order
through your local bookstore.